REBEL'S RETRIBUTION

FATED LIVES SERIES BOOKS 1-4

KELLY MOORE

Edited by
KERRY GENOVA

Cover Designer
DARK WATER COVERS

TITLE

REBEL'S RETRIBUTION

KELLY MOORE

WARNING TO READERS

There are many trigger topics in this book related to human trafficking and PTSD.

DERRICK REBEL

FATED LIVES SERIES

Book One
Meet Derrick Rebel

Derrick Rebel was the Captain for the SEAL team The Gunners. He's a typical badass leader, but he's a broken man. The woman he loved betrayed him in the worst way possible at the cost of his team. It took him awhile but he finally got his act together, and now he's the leader of The Gunners again, but a different team with a different mission. His focus now is on US soil and keeping it's citizens safe. He found his heart again with Fallon Davis. He met her on their first mission and was unable to let her go. Rebel may be a hard ass when it comes to his job, but the way he loves will have you drooling.

CHAPTER 1

MEET REBEL AND EKKO

She wraps her firm leg around my hip and presses her core into my body, causing me to harden again despite a night of full-on sex. "Baby, you keep that up"—I look between my legs —"no pun intended, I'll never make the mission."

"God forbid you miss out on one mission." She unwinds her body from mine and throws the sheet off as she gets out of my bed. Her lean body and nice ass make for the perfect view.

"Come on, Ekko, and bring that fine ass back to bed."

"You know I hate when you call me that when we're not at work."

I fall back on the bed with a huff and rub my hand down my scruffy face. "Nina Pax, would you please crawl back into bed with me?" My team calls her Ekko because she's always in our ear over the coms, and when we disregard her orders, she repeats them over and over.

"I can't. I'm going to be late for my meeting with the commander," she says with a mouth full of toothpaste, waving her pink brush at me.

Groaning, I lift a leg up and hike myself out of bed, joining her in the bathroom. "You want me to skip out on a mission, but you're not willing to miss a meeting." I wrap my hands around her naked frame and press my teeth lightly into her shoulder.

"My life isn't on the line every time I go to work." She leans over and spits into the sink, pressing her ass into my dick. I place my hands on either side of her hips, then I smack her on the ass.

"Hey!" She laughs and turns in my arms. "You know how much I like your hands on me, but I really don't have time." She gives a quick kiss to my lips.

I reach for the shaving cream and lather it on my face. "When are you ever going to agree to marrying me?" I watch her reflection in the mirror as she dresses in her civilian black suit. She looks sexy as shit in it.

"We've talked about this. Neither one of our careers are good on marriages."

She's the handler for our SEAL Team Six Division, aka The Gunners. Everything about her is highly classified. She doesn't give much away, but I know her research of Afghanistan, and knowledge of tactical skills and weaponry, coupled with her negotiating skills, got her this job against some of the highest-ranking officers in the military. She even negotiated her way into staying a civilian rather than join the military. She wanted to be able to freelance her work to the highest bidder. She's brilliant and sexy. Killer combo.

I smooth the razor down my face as the shaving cream drips into the sink. "Why don't we both retire then?"

She sits on the small, rickety bench seat by the closet and slips on a pair of black shiny heels. "Neither one of us are ready for that. You love your job."

"I would give it up for you."

She gets up and stands beside me, looking at me in the mirror. "Derrick, I'm not ready to give any of this up. I have some things really starting to work for me." She winds her mocha-colored hair up into a bun.

I know when she calls me Derrick, she's serious. When we're in bed, she cries out my last name, Rebel. That's me, Captain Derrick Rebel. Leader of the SEAL Team Six Division. "I have no idea what that means. Everything you do turns out gold. You've gotten us out of more shit than any military leader I've had in the past."

"My lips are sealed." She smacks them together, spreading on her nude-colored lipstick.

"I know, highly classified, need to know only." I rinse off my face and towel dry before I grab her to me. "The only thing I need to know is that you love me." I kiss the tip of her nose.

"You know I do. Now please take your sexy ass back to bed and skip this mission. Let Captain Stark step in for you today. He'll be jonesing to go out on standby for you."

"Fat chance of that, and let him take all the glory? These are my men and the only way I'm not leading them is if I'm six feet under." Some emotion crosses her face, but I'm not sure what it is.

She squeezes her eyes closed and presses the palm of her hand against her temple. "Ahh...I really gotta go." She turns to leave, but I see her glance back in my direction. "I'll see you in the war room, Rebel." Her smile is gone, and her eyes look sad.

"You okay?"

"Yeah. Good luck on your mission today."

She cracks open the door and slinks out of my

barracks. She's only fooling herself thinking others don't know about us. My men called it the first time I laid eyes on her. She came into the camp's gym to work out in a pair of gray shorts and a white tank top. She had more muscles in her arms than some of the men.

She got on the pull-up bar, and I couldn't take my eyes off her. One of my men yelled out that he thought she could do more pull-ups than me. The challenge was real. She almost kicked my butt. I couldn't let her show me up. I pulled a bicep muscle rather than lose. I kept doing them despite the pain that was burning up my arm.

She was pretty pissed off, and my peace offering was a beer in the barrack's cantina. Her smart mouth and sexy lips had me hard the entire night, which led to me fucking her brains out. She was a tiger in bed, leaving scratches down my back. I think it was her way of paying me back for beating her in front of the men. I'd do it all over again to feel her nails dig into my skin from pure pleasure.

I open my closet door and take my fatigues off the hanger and pull out a white T-shirt from a drawer. I'm married to these clothes. I joined the Navy right out of high school. It was the only thing I ever wanted to do—to follow in my grandfather's footsteps. Now, at thirty-three, I wouldn't mind settling down and having a few kids running around. Even if I convinced Nina to marry me, she's made it pretty clear that she has no room in her life for children. It's not in the grand scheme of her life plan. She's very regimented and never flies by the seat of her pants.

Unlike me, I'm a hardcore rule breaker, and it drives Nina insane. My theory is, sometimes you have to break the rules to make things work. We've gotten in more knock-down, drag-out fights than I'd like to think about after a mission because I ignored Ekko in my ear. But damn, it was worth the make-up sex.

As I lace up my boots, a video pops up on my laptop with my older brother's face on it. "Hey, bro, you there?"

I slide into the chair in front of the small desk. "Hey, Sean. What's up? I only have a minute or so to talk."

"I wanted you to know I got the loan for the bar and you and the boys will have a place to celebrate when you come back home to Portland."

"Congrats, man. I'm happy for you. Did you pick a name for it?" I lean back on two legs of the chair.

"Sean's place." He's all smiles.

"Real original, man." I chuckle. How about Rebel's Bar."

"That would give you some claim to it, and you aren't getting your SEAL hands on it." He laughs. "You protect the country, I'll serve the beer."

"How are Mom and Dad?"

"Enjoying their retirement by traveling the world."

I glance at my black military watch. "I gotta go, man. Tell Mom and Dad I love them the next time you talk to them."

"Will do."

"Congrats again, Sean. Drink a couple for me."

Grabbing my gear and pulling on my hat, I run out the door and down the two steps to the dirty, hot ground of our platoon.

"Hey, Cap."

"Good morning, Barker." The lieutenant steps in pace with me. He's the oldest member in our team of eight.

"I hear we're going in dark on our mission to capture the leader of the MM20 group."

I pull my bag farther up on my shoulder. "Let's go find out."

CHAPTER 2
THE MISSION PLANS

My men are already gathered around a metal table in what we call the war room. Nina is huddled in the corner with the commander talking in hushed voices.

"Good morning, sir!"

"Good morning." I nod toward Theo, who is the youngest in our group. He's actually the youngest SEAL in any team at twenty years old. I thought for sure he had some rich or political parent who pulled strings to get him in, but it turns out, the boy has skills. I'd let him have my back any day.

"Mornin, Rebel."

Petty Officer Orie Severs hands me a cup of black coffee. "You look like shit, Severs. Did you have a late night with the hot little redhead who arrived here a few days ago?" Severs is a ladies' man and my best friend. We've been together since basic training.

"Wouldn't you like to know." His smile and the dark circles under his eyes give him away.

"Too much of a good thing might get you killed." I slap him on the shoulder.

We all take our seats as Commander Jeremy Lukas steps in front of the room.

"Captain Derrick Rebel."

"Petty Officer Orie Severs."

"Petty Officer Jon Barker."

"Petty Officer Ben Smyth."

"Petty Officer - Medic Josh Darcy."

"Petty Officer Theo Drake."

"Petty Officer Thomas Byrd."

"Petty Officer Graham Dutch."

He calls roll and nods at each of us.

"You've been our commander for over a year now, do you really need to do an official roll call? Just call us by our names, sir," Bryd says, resting his hands behind his head.

The commander laughs. "I want to make sure you remember what your real names are. You guys have so many nicknames I can't keep up." Nina hands him a folder, and he waves it in the air. "We finally have good intel on the notorious MM20 group. As you know, this group owns well-guarded poppy fields all over Afghanistan that are supporting their terrorist group with weapons and the ability to go in and out of countries undetected. They're single-handedly responsible for the last four terror attacks in the United States, killing over 8,000 men, women, and children. We have a location on where the terrorist cell has been operating out of, thanks to Ms. Pax." He turns toward Nina.

"Nice job, Ekko," Theo yells out. I cut my eyes at him, and he loses the smile he was wearing and clears his throat. "Sorry, Ms. Pax."

Nina picks up a rolled map and lays it out on the table. "My source tells me that they're hidden in this mountain." She points to an area opposite the poppy fields where we've been searching. "He has several smaller cells that guard the fields, but rumor is, he doesn't go anywhere near them. He has a house built into the side of the mountain. Guards protect it twenty-four seven and the desert area around him is covered in mines."

"Who's your source?" I ask.

Nina's brows draw together. "You know I can't reveal a source."

"How do you know you can trust him? Maybe he's a plant to get us up there." I lean back in my chair and cross my arms over my chest. "We've already lost one entire team this year based on bad intel. They were led into a trap and ambushed. I don't want the same for my men."

"And you think I do?" She taps her heel on the ground. It's her telltale sign that she's pissed off.

"I'm not saying that. I only want to make sure that this isn't the same source that had the other SEAL team killed."

As the commander and Nina chat quietly, Severs leans over close to my ear. "I don't think you'll be getting laid anytime soon."

I elbow him away from me. I love Nina, but I have to know her source is reliable so that I can keep my men safe. If that pisses her off, then so be it.

"This meeting is over for now. You men need to go get your gear gathered up and whatever supplies you need to take with you. You'll be leaving in the next two hours. You'll board a Blackhawk and be taken to an area west of his house and go the rest of the way on foot."

Metal chairs scrape across the floor as my men stand. "Captain Rebel. I need you to hang back." I nod and watch Nina gather her folders and head out the door, never making eye contact with me.

Once the last man is out the door, the

commander heads back over to the map. "This is by far one of the most dangerous missions you and your men will be on. I understand your reservations."

"I have no reservations about taking out the leader of this group. My doubt is our source, sir."

"We're going to have to trust Ms. Pax's ability to read people." He taps his finger on the map. "This area that you and your men will have to cover by foot is extremely dangerous. None of our men have ever been in this spot. I'll have a drone sent up to scout it out, but we'll be lucky if it's not shot down. Your mission is to try and bring in the leader alive." He clicks a button on a remote, and a face appears on the screen behind him. "His name is Abba Bari."

"Damn, he looks like a kid."

"His father has been training him since birth to be the leader of MM20." He clicks to another picture. "His father was killed last year by one of our teams. This is why the attacks have picked up in the US. This twenty-year-old is ruthless. Don't be fooled by his boyish looks. He's far worse than his father ever was. After you've gotten your gear together, I want you to bring your men back here and brief them on the mission and to memorize the face of Abba Bari."

"Yes, sir."

"If you can't bring him in alive, you've my permission to kill him, not just him, the whole lot of them."

"I'll have my men briefed within the hour, sir."

The sun is already beating down when I step back outside. I go back to my barracks and pack what I'll need, then head to the weapons room to stock my duffel bag. I tug on a bulletproof vest and snatch my helmet from a hook. Before I head out to gather my men, I want to find Nina.

"Knock, knock." I rap on her door, but she doesn't answer. It's unlocked, so I look inside. The high-heeled shoes she was wearing are toppled over on the floor, and her suit jacket is laying on her bed, but no sign of her.

I go to the gym thinking maybe she went to blow off some steam, but there are only a few men inside lifting iron. As I head over to the cantina, I see her standing between two tents talking on the phone. She has her hand covering her mouth, trying not to be heard.

When she sees me marching toward her, she hangs up and stuffs it in her pocket.

"What's going on here?" I ask a little too harshly.

"Nothing to concern you." She tries to walk by me, but I grab her elbow.

"Look, you can't be angry at me for wanting to protect my men."

"Do you really think I'd purposely put you in danger?"

"No, but I know how badly you want to capture Abba Bari, and I don't want your ego getting in the way by trusting the wrong person."

"My ego? You're the one that has an ego around here. Always disobeying orders. If anyone puts your men in danger, it's you."

"I've never lost one man. Wait, is this why you wanted me to bow out of this mission and let someone else take over? You don't like that I don't take orders from you?"

"No, that was not the reason, but maybe you should think about it!" She grits her teeth and scoots by me. I chase after her.

"I'm sorry if I embarrassed you in front of my men, if that's what's pissing you off, but I would've questioned anyone's intel after what happened to the last team. I don't want to send my men home in body bags."

"Are we done here, Captain Rebel, because I've a lot of things to do to prepare for while our team makes its way to Abba Bari's house."

"Don't be pissed, baby. I hate leaving on a mission with you angry at me."

"Then you should've thought about that before you started questioning me." She stops and glares at me.

"I wasn't questioning you. I was questioning how reliable your source is."

"It didn't sound that way to me." Her hands fly to her hips.

I wrap my hands through her arms and pull her to me. "Please don't be angry." I kiss her lips, but she doesn't soften toward me.

"I have a lot of work to do." She looks past me. I let her go, and she stomps off but turns around before she opens the war room door. "Goodbye, Derrick." Her words are cold and seem final. I scratch my head. I don't think I've ever seen her this mad before. Determined yes, but never mad enough to walk away from me.

CHAPTER 3

WHO'S LEADING

"Damn, he looks younger than me." Theo glances at the picture on the wall back in the war room.

"He's the same age as you and just as deadly." Theo can hit a target a mile away. "Study his face, sink it into your memory. If at all possible, we want to bring him home alive, but if we have to choose between him or us, make no mistake, we'll take him out."

Commander Lukas and Nina walk into the room. She stays in the back, and he walks up to where we're surrounding the map.

"This is where the Blackhawk will drop you. It will be dark, and you'll be on radio silence once you hit the ground. There will be no communication until you either have Bari captured or dead on the ground. Then you'll have to hike back down the jagged mountain to be picked up. None of our choppers can land in this area. They'll have to be further out to stay away from the minefields, so your mission doesn't stop until you're back to the pickup site."

I look up over at Nina; her eyes catch mine then she turns her head and juts her chin out.

Commander Lukas looks up at her, and she nods. "There's one other thing." He looks over at me. "Captain Stark will be leading your men. It has come to my attention that you haven't taken any time off that is required."

I glance over at Nina, and she looks away. "I haven't needed the time off, and we've all been putting in extra hours since the other SEAL team was killed, sir." It's everything I can do not to grit my teeth. Why the fuck is she doing this now?

"You know there's a specified amount of hours between missions that you need to take off, and from the report I received, you've never taken any of them."

"If Captain Rebel doesn't lead us, none of us are going on this mission," Barker growls.

"Yeah, what he said." Severs points to Barker and all the men start to grumble.

"If your men refuse to go, they'll be pulled from the team."

"Now, wait a minute, sir. I'm sure we can come to some agreement. You know how badly this team wants Bari. That SEAL team that he took out are our brothers. We've worked with them several times before."

"This isn't about what you want, Rebel. It's about you following rules."

I slam my fist on the table, and Nina jumps. "Everyone out. Now!" My men scramble.

Once the door is shut, I bend my head from side to side, causing it to crack, then I shrug my shoulders back, trying to calm my anger.

"Jeremy." I only call him that when he and I are shooting hoops. We're friends when he's not in the war room. "I don't know why Nina would try to have me pulled from this mission. Maybe she's afraid. You did say it was the most difficult one we've ever been on. But my men and I need this. Don't let her make this personal."

He pulls his hat off and rubs the back of his head. "I want you leading this team. I don't think there's another group of men that can pull this off."

"Then ignore the report. When I get back, I'll take all the time off that you want me to, but don't do this to me or my men. You know my men will not follow Stark."

He turns and points at me. "Your men are not supposed to have an option, Rebel, and you know it."

I raise my hands in surrender. "I do know that, sir, but you said yourself, you want me leading my men."

He paces the floor a few times before he says anything else. "All right, but you have to go back to the States when this is all over."

I pat him on the shoulder, "It's a deal, sir. My brother bought this bar, and I'd love to go have a few drinks with him."

"Rebel," his deep voice bounds as I open the door. "I'll deal with Ms. Pax and her report, you go calm your men down."

I nod and head out to find them, but I'm distracted wanting to go talk to Nina. More like wanting to strangle her for interfering. I'd like to think she has a better reason than she's worried about me. She knows the job. Every mission is risky.

The men are loading up their gear in a caravan of military jeeps that will be taking us to the Black-hawk. I see Nina leaning against the cantina wall. She has her dark sunglasses on, and her legs are crossed at the ankle. She has one finger tapping against her lips.

"You guys finish up here, I have something I need to handle."

Nina starts to walk away. "Wait!" I yell, and she stops. "Would you like to explain to me why you don't want me to go on this mission with my men?" I yank my sunglasses off my face.

"I'm afraid you won't come back from this one." She crosses her arms, and I see a tear roll down her face.

I close the distance between us. "Why? What makes this one different than any other one I've ever been on?" She bites at her bottom lip. "Is it because of the other team? Are you doubting your source now?"

"No. I just know how ruthless Bari is and if you get caught, he'll kill every one of you."

"And you think I'd let my men risk their lives and I step out of the way? Fuck that, Nina." I brace my arm on the wall behind her head. "I love you, baby, but don't think for one minute that you'll take this away from me. This is what I do." I place a quick kiss to the side of her face and head back to my men.

I look back to see her hightail it to her barracks.

"That's one pissed-off woman," Severs says, laughing.

"She'll get over it." I march past him, picking up my duffel bag.

"Well, if she doesn't, my hot little redhead has a friend." He slaps me on the back.

"Shut the fuck up, man." I get in the front seat with the driver, and he climbs in the back seat with Theo.

My mind is racing on Nina instead of on the mission, which isn't good. I need to focus, so no one gets killed except for our enemy. I just can't figure out why she'd pull that shit at the last minute. She was in my bed all night and never mentioned her report. There was never even a moment between us making love that she talked about anything serious, much less having me pulled off this mission.

I close my eyes behind my dark glasses, and all I can see are her tits in my hands as she rode me. Her hair was covering her face, but I could see her biting her bottom lip as she moved up and down, her hands planted on my chest. The feel of her fingernails embedded in my skin has always been such a turn on to me. I rub my hand across my chest to try to bring back that feeling.

"Sir, we should be there in an hour," the driver's

voice brings me back. I shift in my seat to rearrange my dick, so it's not tenting in my pants.

I pull out my phone and study the face of Bari and the plan for the next hour. My phone never goes with me, so it will stay with the driver. If the enemy ever got their hands on it, they'd see pictures of my family and Nina. I never risk bringing them along. The terrorists' arms are far-reaching, and I'd die before I'd put my family in harm's way.

The sun is high and hot when we finally make it to the camouflage tents hidden in the desert. We're greeted by soldiers that specialize in recon missions. The Blackhawk pilots are a special breed that I've great respect for.

"Gentlemen." I shake their hands one by one. "Is your man ready to fly us in?"

Lieutenant Bush looks at his watch. Fifteen hundred and the blades will be spinning." He makes a twirling motion with his index finger.

I turn to my men. "Go get hydrated and eat something, then meet back here in fifteen minutes."

CHAPTER 4

THE MISSION BEGINS

As promised the blades are rotating as the last man finds his seat and straps into it. The sun has just tucked in for the night, and the cool desert air flows through the Blackhawk. These men that I'm leading are the best at what they do, and I trust each and every one of them with my life and I'd give mine for every single one of them.

There are very few lights on the ground, and the pilot is flying blind. Every now and then the bird jostles to go around one of the mountains. Resting my head back, I close my eyes to find my focus. I don't need any distractions to get in the way of my job.

"Sir, we'll be landing in the next fifteen minutes," the pilot yells over his shoulder.

I don't have to ask these men if they're ready. They know their jobs and the risks involved. "When we get close to the ground, make sure to stay low when you land. Keep your head down and locked and loaded, ready for anything. Drake, you hang with me. We'll be out front. Severs, you divide the rest of the team and split them on our wings. You stay in the back with Barker." I keep Theo with me so he can scout out front and take out any necessary targets.

"It's going to take us some time to make it to Bari's house on foot. Get your jackets on and make sure to drink plenty of water. I don't need you getting dehydrated on me. I'll protect you, but I'm not carrying your sorry asses across the desert because you tried to be a tough guy."

"Remember, our mission is to bring Bari in alive unless we can't. None of you are to go in alone. Always have your backup partner."

"Sir, I'm bringing this bird as close as I can to the ground."

One by one, each man jumps with his gear to the ground. They roll and stay low, making it into the ridge of a mountain. The darkness helps hide us, but we don't know what's waiting for us, so better safe than sorry. Each man puts on his night goggles and gets their weapons ready.

Eight men strong, we take off in the direction of Bari's house. There are areas we have to crawl on our hands and knees to get under sheets of barbed wire that've been laid out to keep out their enemies. Strands of clothing and flesh hang from the barbs where others have tried to make it through.

When we all make it out, Dutch pulls out his bomb-detecting equipment and starts running it back in forth in the sand. We follow one step at a time in his path. He finds several buried in the sand and changes our direction. We have to move due east before we can start moving north.

"This is a designed path to keep people out. Keep your eyes open for Bari's men." It feels like lambs being led to the slaughter.

Drake suddenly drops to the ground, aiming his rifle in front of him. We all follow suit and drop to the ground. I crawl up next to him. "What do you see?"

"There, in the hole in the side of the mountain, there are two men on lookout."

"Can you take them both out?"

"Does a monkey eat bananas?" He laughs

quietly. Reaching in his side pocket, he pulls out his silencer and places it on the end of his rifle. Then he takes aim, dropping one and then the other right behind him.

Without a word, we get up, and Dutch continues his search for bombs until we make it to where our path is all hard rock.

"Shit," Byrd says under his breath. "There are wooden spikes stuck between the crevices of the rocks." He's holding pressure to his thigh.

"How bad is it?"

"It ripped through my skin pretty good."

Darcy, being our medic, removes his goggles and pulls out a small flashlight from his pack and examines it. "He could really use some stitches."

"Clean it up and slap some Steri-Strips on it," Byrd says.

Darcy takes out his first aid kit and rinses out the wound, then pulls the skin together and applies the strips to hold it together. "Done."

"We need to keep moving, keep away from the spikes, and look for other booby traps. Drake, you scout out ahead of us. Stop when you get to the ridge."

"Yes, sir." He takes off up the side of the mountain.

We keep moving due north. It's a slow pace to keep from any further injuries. In several of the areas, the spikes only have about six inches between them on either side. We have to hold our gear up in the air and move sideways through them, tearing holes in our fatigues.

It's taken us over an hour to move approximately one mile. When we finally make it to the gap, I see a light shining off the side of the mountain. It's flashing in short bursts.

"It's Drake," Barker says. "He's using Morse code. He says there's a group of armed men ahead of us. He says to stay put."

"We'll wait for him to come down here before we make any more moves. Cop a squat and hydrate while we wait." I put my pack down and pull out my canteen of water.

Drake makes it down to us in no time. He moves swiftly but quietly. "Sir, once you cross the next section, there's a camp full of armed men sitting between us and Bari's house. There are too many of them for us to take out."

"Then we'll go to plan B." I pull a map of the area out of my bag.

"I don't remember there being a plan B." Dutch takes off his helmet and scratches his head.

"There's always a plan B with Rebel." Severs laughs.

"We'll set up camp here for a few hours. Just before dawn, we're going to change our route and come in on the other side of them." I point our path on the map.

"But, sir, his house is built inside that mountain. If we go around it, we won't be able to get inside," Drake adds.

"Then we better hope that Bari has an escape exit out the back of this mountain. In my experience, there's never just one way in and one way out."

"So why don't we keep moving. The plan was to take him in the dark," Bryd questions.

"Because there's a good chance we won't find the other entrance in the dark. I'm sure it's very well camouflaged." I look at my watch. "You have two hours to get some shut-eye. I'll keep watch here, and Drake can keep an eye out from his perch on the mountain."

"Yes, sir." Drake takes off into the dark.

Severs takes a seat in the dirt next to me. "I sure hope we get this bastard."

"Me too, but more than that, I hope we all make it back alive."

"You made the right call having us sit here and

wait. I never like doing a mission in the dark, especially when we're dealing with someone as ruthless as Bari."

"Get some rest."

He nods and leans back, shutting his eyes.

CHAPTER 5

ALL HELL BREAKS LOOSE

I shake Severs's leg. "It's time. Get the men moving," I order as I stand and brush the sand from my knees. My legs are sore from being on them all night, and the numerous times they got scraped on either a jagged rock or one of the wooden spikes.

Drake must have set an alarm because he shows up right on time. "Listen up. We're going to follow Drake up this mountain and over the other side. Then we're going to make our way behind Bari's mountain. He may have more of his men guarding the backside too. I want dead silence as we move. Keep your eyes open at every angle. Don't shoot your weapons unless it's necessary. Drake, that doesn't include you. You keep your silencer on, and if you have a clear shot, take it. Now let's move."

Most of our climb is vertical. I don't know how Theo did this in the dark and didn't tumble down the side of the mountain. "Climb up a few feet and tie some rope off. We'll have to go up a section at a time. How in the hell did you make it up here not once but twice in the dark?"

"I'm like a cat, sir. I can climb anything." He skates up like it's nothing while the rest of us pull our weight up the rope, one by one. Then, we move to the next section, repeating the process of tying off the rope until we've made it to the top. Orange and pink are slathered across the sky tucked in between dark gray rain clouds.

"Great, that's all we need in this shit."

"I fucking hate getting rained on," Barker grumbles and pulls his helmet lower. "I'm getting way too old for this shit. I'm thinking retirement on some island that never gets rain."

"You'd miss the action too much," I say as we start making our way back down the other side of the mountain. I stop on the ledge and look out to see which would be the best area and the fastest to get down on. "There are smooth areas over there. I bet we could sit on our asses and slide down. Tie all our gear together, and we'll pull it down behind us."

The men start looping together our gear. Once we reach the softer area, the first man down takes the rope with him. The next one sits and grabs one of the bags to help it move down. One by one, we each make our way to the bottom and gear back up.

Drake was the first man down and has been on the lookout with his binoculars. "Any sight of Bari's men?"

"No, but if there's a back way in, I'm sure they are out there."

"Keep moving. Scout out the area before we get there and keep your head low."

He nods and takes off in a trot.

"We need to make it across this open area as fast and as quietly as we can. Keep your eyes peeled for traps but keep moving."

The team follows close behind me, all with their rifles out and ready. We've made it halfway across when I see Drake waving for us to run. We make it to him in time to hide behind some rocks as a caravan drives through the pass. They're moving slowly and are filled with armed men in the back, leading away from Bari's house.

"Do you think they spotted us?" Barker ducks his head lower.

"No, but they're looking for something. Otherwise, they'd be moving quicker."

A few of the trucks stop, and several men pile out, keeping their weapons drawn. "We've got to get the fuck out of here. If they see our footprints, we're done for. Get your bags and crawl to the other side."

As soon as we start to move, the rain lets down, making some of the rocks we're crawling over slick.

A weapon dislodges in the air from the pass, signaling that they've found something. We crawl faster until we make it to the back of the mountain that Barı's house is in.

"I'm betting that's a way in, sir." Drake points to where two men are standing guard. "I can take them both out."

"You need to do it in a hurry, son. Those men behind us will catch up with us soon." I turn toward my team. "Severs, you and the rest of the team, stay behind and hold them off as long as possible. Drake and I are going into Bari's house. If we capture him, we'll have leverage to stop his men."

"And if you don't?" Severs asks, already knowing the answer.

"Then we're all dead because someone tipped them off that we're here."

Drake takes out both men guarding the back, and we take off in a full run to where they're dead on the ground. One is shot directly between the eyes, the other in the temple. "Good shot. Neither one of them knew what hit them."

"Help me push this rock out of the way." Severs is grunting trying to move it with all his might.

Gunshots ring out from where my men are held up. I lean into the rock, and we push it far enough out of the way to get inside. I can see a light coming from the other end of the tunnel and voices shouting out. We both move close to the slick walls and make our way to the light. As someone goes out the front door and leaves Bari alone, we both rush into the room, aiming our weapons at him.

"Don't move and don't utter a sound or I will kill you."

He raises his hands in the air. My stomach wretches at the thought of killing this man who looks no older than fifteen. I know without a doubt that it's Bari, but he looks so young. "Move to the tunnel." I cock my head in the direction without lowering my gun.

His white clothes glow in the tunnel as he moves slowly toward where we came in.

"How did you get inside my house?" he asks in broken English.

"Shut up and keep moving." Drake nudges him with the tip of his rifle.

He stumbles but catches himself on the rock wall. "My men will kill you."

"Not if we use you as a shield, and if they kill you, then our job is done here."

"This place is surrounded by my men. You'll never make it out of here alive."

"Never underestimate us. We made it this far."

We make it back to the rock, and I look outside. There's smoke coming from the area I left my team. Shots are still being fired, but I can't tell who's firing them.

"I had the other team that was sent here tortured. You, my brother, are going to have the same fate."

I lose my cool and deck him. "I'm not your fucking brother. If I had my way, I'd kill you with my bare hands." My fingers are wrapped around his throat. He gasps for air when I loosen my grip. I grab him by the shoulder and take off running toward my men. Drake is picking off men as we move.

When we make it to them, the first thing I see is

Bryd lying in the sand with vacant eyes and blood pooling on the earth around him. Barker has a bullet in the thigh and Severs is popping up from behind a rock, still taking out Bari's men.

Dutch, Darcy, and Smyth are partially hidden behind a layer of smoke. Smyth is screaming out in agony. A hot round of mortar struck him, and his foot is lying on the ground next to him. Darcy is removing his belt and tying off Smyth's leg.

"Help him up!" I yell at Dutch. "We have to get moving," Smyth screams out as he hoists him up. We back out of the area and head due east. Severs stays in the back and Drake is out in front. I have a firm grip on Bari, shoving him along.

We're within a mile of our pickup spot when a loud noise has me covering my ears. In that split second, that I let go of Bari; he takes off running. I take off after him but am blinded by a flash of light and then I'm on the ground surrounded by black smoke. I can't see as blood pours into my eye, but I can hear the cries of my men, then gunshots. Sand sticks to the blood running from me, making it harder to see. I hold the side of my head as pain sears through it. I manage to get to my knees and then to my feet. I shuffle my way through the dark cloud of smoke and the sand beneath me. I stop when I nearly trip over something. I reach down, hoping like hell it's my rifle, but instead I feel the shoelaces of a boot.

I get to my knees and make my way up the body. Darcy is missing half his face and a few feet from him, Smyth lies dead with his eyes and mouth wide open.

"I told you, you'd never get out of here alive," Bari's broken English cuts through the smoke. I feel for a weapon in the sand. As soon as I feel the metal in my hand, a boot connects with my face, knocking me backward.

CHAPTER 6

THE TRAITOR

Drip, drip, drip. Muddy blood drips onto my leg. I try to move, but my hands are tied behind me and ropes bind my legs to a chair. My right eye is so swollen I can't open it.

My head is yanked up from behind, and I'm face to face with the young, ruthless leader of MM20. He has one of our military guns in his hand. I hear a noise to the left of me, and I see Drake sitting on the ground, leaning against a wall. His right arm is missing, and he barely looks alive.

"I see you're still with us, Captain Derrick Rebel." He spits in my face. "So unfortunate for you and your friend."

I yank at my binds and feel them loosen. Whoever was behind me lets go of my head, and I hear them walk away. "Let him go." My voice cracks it's so dry. "Where are the rest of my men?"

"You're in no position to be asking me questions, but this one, I will enjoy answering. They're all dead, just like the other team that was sent here. When will you Americans learn that you can't stop me? The more you try to fight me, the more innocent people in your country will die."

"You're a sick little fuck!" I get my fingers free of the rope and start trying to unwind it from my wrist without him noticing it.

He has the laugh of a young boy. "You have no idea how powerful I am."

"Even the powerful fall. We took your father out, and you'll be next."

Anger runs through his body. He balls his fist up to strike me but stops. "You're a dead man, but because of your words, I will make it slow and painful." He motions for one of his men to come over. He's yielding a blood-stained sword. He has grenades on either side of this thick black belt.

"I made it this far, I deserve to know who tipped you off that we were coming." This time, I spit blood out at his feet.

He rubs his boot in it and then squats down in

front of me. "You do deserve to know because it will cause you much pain."

Then it hits me. "Wait, how did you know my name was Derrick?" My military patch only has Rebel on it. I hear footsteps come up behind me again, but this time they come and stand in front of me. I look up to see someone with a black mask covering the lower part of their face. Those eyes I'd recognize anywhere.

"Ekko." I swallow her name.

She reaches up and pulls down the mask. "I tried to convince you not to come on this mission, but you're one stubborn SEAL."

"You're responsible for the death of my men? They trusted you. I fucking trusted you! Why would you do this?"

"They were the highest bidder. Bari realizes my worth. He knows my knowledge will make him more powerful and richer than any other person on this earth."

"Money! This is all about money for you!"

"It's always been about money."

How did I not see any of this? She's been in my bed for months and never once did I suspect she was this evil. "Let Drake go. Kill me but let him go."

She kneels down in front of me. "I'd rather you

watch him die than kill you." She runs her hand down the left side of my cheek. "I cared enough about you to try to get you out of this mission. Why couldn't you have obeyed orders? I'm going to miss fucking you. Better yet"—she stands—"maybe I'll keep you around and fuck you anytime I want."

The rope falls to the ground, and I reach up and grab the grenade off his belt. I pull the pin and topple my chair over to cover Drake's body. In slow motion, I hear the grenade roll across the floor, feet scattering, and voices yelling to run.

The loud explosion echoes through the room. I tuck my head in as debris flies through the room. Something falls on top of me, and smoke painfully fills my lungs.

I wake up, and for a moment, forget where I am. I can't move. My legs are still bound to the chair, and something heavy is lying on me. Drake's body is wedged in between me and the floor. The curvature of the way I landed on him is the only thing that's keeping me from crushing him. I push up with all my strength and roll off whatever is lying on me.

"Drake, are you alive?" I feel for a pulse. It's faint, but it's still there. I move off him and then realize what fell on me was Bari's body. I don't have to feel for a pulse. He's got a gaping wound in his neck where all his blood drained out of him.

I quickly untie my legs, and when I go to stand, I slip back to the floor in Bari's pool of blood. Raking my hands down my body that's covered in blood, I feel for any injuries, thinking some of the blood is mine. The only cut I feel is the one on my face, keeping my eye from opening.

I make it to my feet and look around the room. There's no sign of Ekko. Bari's man that had the grenade in his belt is scattered around the room. My first instinct is to go after Ekko, but I need to get Drake out of here. I pull him up to a sitting position, then I lean down and put him over my right shoulder. I use the wall for leverage so I don't slip in the blood again. Stepping over wood and chunks of rock from the walls, I make my way out the door that leads to the tunnel. It's eerily quiet.

The light is almost blinding when I make it outside. I have no weapons on me and hope like hell none of Bari's men are out here. I take off in a full run with Drake bouncing on my shoulder. He lets out grunts every time my shoulder digs into him. I run until we're back at the explosion site. I lay Drake down on the ground and start looking for the medical kit. I find Darcy's bag and dig out dressings and apply them to where Drake's arm used to be. He moans loudly and opens his eyes.

"You're going to be okay. I'm going to get you out of here." My bag lies a few feet from me. I pull out my canteen and hold Drake's head up as I give him sips of water."

"Are they..." He swallows. "Are they all dead?"

I hang my head and tears flood my sight in my left eye. "Yes," I sob.

He raises his left hand and places it on my shoulder then passes out again. I pick him up and start walking in the blistering sun to where the Blackhawk should be waiting for us.

I round the top of the last hill and go to my knees when I see the chopper and men waiting with rifles. Placing Drake on the ground, he thuds like a mannequin, and I wave my arms in the air. As they run toward me, I fall face down in the desert sand.

They pick us both up and drag us to the Blackhawk. The last thing I remember is telling them where the bodies of my men are. "They need to be brought home."

CHAPTER 7

IN THE HOSPITAL

"Your hair smells so damn good, woman." I hold it to my nose as her head leans on my chest and her fingers toy with my nipple. "It smells like sunshine and coconuts."

She rolls off me. "Close, mango and kiwi."

I move with her and pin her underneath me and inhale her scent. "Then mango and kiwi smell like sunshine." I trail my lips across her collarbone, and she wiggles underneath me, making my dick hard again.

"We could shower together, and I could bathe you in my fruity-smelling shampoo, and then I could take my time licking the scent off you." She hisses as I draw a taut nipple into my warm mouth and then twirl it between my teeth.

"I think that's what I'll do to you." I move lower on the bed and settle between her long, firm legs.

She places her hands on either side of my face and forces me to look up at her. "I love you, Derrick."

"Ah...where the fuck am I?" Sweat is pouring over my body as I spring up in the middle of a hard cot.

"You're at a medical base in Germany," a man in a stark white uniform answers me.

I run my hand down my face and feel the bandage covering my right eye. "How long have I been here?"

"You were brought in three days ago. You were pretty beat up and dehydrated." He sits on the empty cot across from me. "Do you remember what happened?"

I close my eyes, and it all plays out behind my eyelids. Ekko, Bari, my men...Theo. "Where is he?" I stand and rip out the IV that's in my arm.

"Whoa there, Captain Rebel. You need to move slowly and try to get your strength back."

I wobble and sit back down. "Who are you?"

"Dr. Sabal. I've been in charge of your case since you got here. I took care of your wounds. Unfortunately, you're going to have a nasty scar." He points to my face.

"I could give a fuck. Where's Theo?" I stand again, but this time bracing myself on the way up.

"Petty Officer Drake is in our critical care unit recovering from his injuries."

I let out a huff of relief. "He survived. I want to see him."

"I'm afraid you'll have to wait. There're some pretty high-level officers here to see you. They want your story."

"Well, you tell them they can't have my fucking story until I've seen Theo."

A door opens, and Commander Jeremy Lukas marches in my direction with two men dressed in full military garb almost in step with him. I don't bother for them to make it all the way to me. I meet them halfway.

"Jeremy..." He cuts his eyes to the men behind him. "Commander Lukas, I know you have questions for me, but it's important that I see Petty Officer Drake."

He takes a deep breath in, and I think he's going to deny my request. Instead, he turns on his heels and address the two men behind him. From their rankings, I know they're high enough up that they report back to our government. "Sirs, we've waited three days, another thirty minutes is not going to change anything." They look back and forth at one another and then nod in agreement.

"Thank you, sir."

"I'll take him to the ICU." Dr. Sabal takes me by the elbow and escorts me to the elevator, where we go up two floors.

The fluorescent lights make my good eye water, and I blink to clear it. We stop at a glass door. I see Theo hooked up to all kinds of machines, and the right side of his body is wrapped in white gauze. A nurse is in with him trying to get him to eat. He sees my reflection in the glass and glances over at me, then lays his head back, and I see his tears roll down his cheek.

A sudden anger and hatred roll over me. I lost all my men, and the one that did survive lost his arm. I squash my emotions and walk in and stand beside his bed. "I'm so sorry, Theo."

He raises his head off the pillow, and his light brown eyes pierce me. "I'm alive because of you."

I pull up a padded wooden chair and sit next to him. "You lost your arm because of me."

"How do you think any of this was your fault."

Leaning forward, I rest my elbows on my knees and my head on my fists. "Nina." Her name gets caught in my throat.

"You're not responsible for the actions of our handler. She's the one that killed our team. She set us all up."

Her betrayal of me is one thing, but to have my men taken out like they were nothing is another. She may have had second thoughts about killing me, trying to get me to not go on the mission, but she never intended for any of the team to survive.

"Please tell me that they caught her?" He sobs louder.

"No, they did not," Commander Lukas says from the doorway. "I was hoping that there was something the two of you could tell us that might give us a clue as to where she went. As of right now, she's a ghost."

"She didn't tell me anything while she was trying to kill me, sir. I do know that we got Bari and that's who she was working for, so she's probably on the run trying to find a new place of employment." I seethe.

"You're confirming that Bari is dead."

"A grenade took him out. Nina was in the same room when it went off, but there was no sign of her when the dust cleared the room."

"She has made it to the top of our most wanted list for war crimes. It's imperative that you tell us everything that happened."

I nod. "What's going to happen to Theo?"

"He'll be shipped back to the States and fitted for a state-of-the-art prosthetic."

"Will I be able to get back on a SEAL team, sir?"

I lean on the bed next to him, knowing the answer. "I'm afraid not, son. Your war days are over."

Theo rests his head back, and his broken body starts to shake. I wrap my arm around him and cry for him. He had such a bright future ahead of him, and that bitch stole it out from under him. "I swear to you, I'll find her, and when I do...I'll have no problem killing her." I whisper the last part next to his ear.

The nurse gets a sedative and gives it to him. I stay with him until his body finally relaxes and he drifts off to sleep. I stand and hike up my pants. "I'm ready, sir. The sooner we get this over with, the sooner I can get back to my post."

"You're not going back, Derrick."

I pull him outside Theo's room. "What're you talking about?"

"One of those men out there is the commander of US Special Forces Division. He's been reviewing everything that Ms. Pax was doing. He found the report that she sent saying that you needed to be removed from the mission because you hadn't taken any time off."

"So?"

"So, he thinks that the stress and fatigue you were under, that somehow you missed what she was up to."

"You've got to be fucking kidding me? Did you or anyone else that dealt with her see any signs?" I'm yelling.

"Lower your voice, Captain."

"What else did they find besides a report on me?" My voice is lower, but my teeth are clenched together so hard my jaw aches.

"They were able to hack into her computer. All her files were encrypted, so they're still working on it. What I can tell you is that it looks like she had been planning this for months. She had the first team taken out because they tripped onto Bari. Your team was planned because she analyzed that the Gunners were the only team actually capable of taking Bari out of power. She knew if she took out your men, you'd go in a tailspin and be powerless. Since you weren't willing to step out of the way, she'd have you removed."

My stomach wretches. I run over to a garbage can behind the nurses' station and pick it up, losing nothing but bodily fluids. I haven't eaten in days, and the dry heaves are racking through my gut. When I put the can down, I stumble backward against a wall, leaning over trying to catch my breath. One of the nurses tries to help me, and I swat her away with my hand.

"Please, just leave me alone." When I stand straight, there's nothing left inside me but hate. Hate for the woman I wanted to marry. The woman that killed my brothers in arms. Now all I want is to see the life go out of her eyes.

I SPEND the next week going over and over every detail of my personal and professional life with Nina Pax. There were no signs of her betraying us. She was very meticulous in her plan. I really believed she loved me and I'm not sure I'll ever trust myself with a woman again. I'll be suspicious from the very beginning.

Today is the day my team is being flown home to be put to rest. All of them received gold stars and purple hearts for their act of bravery. Theo is being released from the hospital today to be there when the plane arrives. The Navy has had all the spouses flown in to receive their loved ones. Nina's betrayal is hard to deal with, but this will be by far the worst day of my life. I don't have any idea as to how I'm going to get through it.

I dress in my military uniform and grab my hat. As I go to grab the handle of the front door, someone knocks. I open it thinking it will be Commander Lukas picking me up to take me to the airstrip. When I open the door, I go to my knees. My father, mother, and brother Sean try to catch me. All the angry tears I've been holding back come crashing out.

"Hey, man. It's okay." Sean is on the ground with me. My dad's hand is on my shoulder, and my mom is crying beside him. God, I fucking hurt, and the big badass SEAL in me is gone. I'm just a man that needs the support of his family

CHAPTER 8
PAIN AND GUILT CAN RUIN A MAN

The day was brutal, seeing the faces of families I've seen a million times in photos. I know them, I know their children. I know how much each and every one of them sacrificed for their husbands due to the job they loved. I also know the crushing heartache they feel right now. I feel it tenfold for every coffin that's laid out in front of me with a flag folded over it.

The more I watch the faces of the families, the more anger builds inside me and hatred for myself for being so damn blind. I was their leader, and I led them to their deaths all because I trusted the wrong person. I should be in one of those coffins, not any of them.

"Hey, Cap." Theo takes the seat behind me. "I know what you're thinking. I feel it too."

I turn to look at him, and he's by himself. "Where's your family?"

"My mom just got remarried and is on her honeymoon."

I stand, grab a chair from his row and set it beside us and point to it. "Today you're my brother by all sense of the term." He gets up and takes the seat between Sean and me. We sit shoulder to shoulder, listening to the service until it's my turn to speak.

I look down at the small podium and wonder if I'll find the right words to ease the pain on the faces of the men and women who trusted me with these men. I brace my hands on either side and watch as my own tears land on the wood top. I blink back the tears to be strong for all of them.

"I had the honor of serving with these men. They were some of the bravest men in the military. They were my brothers, my best friends." My voice cracks. "I loved each and every one of them and would've given my life for them. They followed me into the most hellacious bowels of the earth without question. And...I was responsible for them, yet they lost their lives...and here I stand."

"They followed you because you were a good

leader and they knew you had their backs." Theo stands and moves next to me. "I know this because I felt the same way. We knew the risk. They knew the risk." He sweeps his hand out toward the caskets. "We fought anyway. Each of us had our own reasons as to why we chose to fight. The best thing that happened was when the eight of us got paired together with you in charge. I remember the first day we all met. On the outside, I was a cocky young kid. On the inside, I was terrified. The experience all of you had over me made me look like I should still be in diapers. But you gave me a fair chance. You had read my records and told me not to doubt that I belonged in the team. I watched you grow every one of these men's skills, and you equally learned from them. That's a leader. You're not responsible for these men not making it back alive. It was a choice they made with every mission they took. You're not responsible for me losing my arm. If not for you, I'd be in one of those draped coffins today. You protected me with your life and almost lost yours bringing me home." He pats me on the shoulder and then returns to his seat by my brother.

It takes me a moment to regain my composure. Clearing my throat, I continue. "I'm sorry for the loss of these brave soldiers. They sacrificed so that our world could be a safer place for our families. I'm honored to have been part of that with them."

After the ceremonies are over, I mingle with the families, listening to them tell their stories, many of them mentioning how much their husbands respected me and would've followed me anywhere. Their words clench in my gut. They followed all right, right to their deaths. My jaw hurts from clenching it so hard to not yell out the pain I'm feeling inside. All I want to do right now his head back to my platoon and go after Ekko. I want her to pay for her betrayal.

As the hours pass, I'm finally left alone with my family and Theo. Sean has worked it out that Theo will come and stay with him while he's recovering and going to physical therapy. Mom and Dad board a plane back home, and Sean hangs behind to travel back with Theo.

"I think we could all use a drink," Sean says, slapping his hand on the back of my shoulder.

"That's the best thing I've heard all day." I could use a little drowning in my sorrows.

One drink led to another and then another. Sean and Theo ended up carrying me back to my room. "Get some sleep, man."

"Derrick, baby. Wake up. You were having a bad

dream." Her hands run through my hair, toying with the ends. "You have a meeting with Commander Lukas in thirty minutes."

I peek one eye open and watch her drop her robe as she walks into the bathroom and turns on the shower. It was all a dream. My men are fine. I knew Nina loved me and wouldn't betray me. My head throbs feeling guilty that I dreamed such terrible things about her.

Rolling out of bed, I stretch the soreness from my body and head to the shower to join her.

"Mmm..." she moans as I wrap my arms around her wet body and kiss the top of her shoulder.

"Good morning."

"You were restless last night. You kept yelling out in your sleep." She turns in my arms and lathers up my chest with her hands. "Anything you want to talk about?"

"Only something I want to forget." I splay my hands on her ass and press my hardening cock against her middle.

"I'd love to oblige you"—she looks down between us—"but I have a meeting I have to get to."

I lean down and kiss the nape of her neck. "I think we should both skip our meetings this morning."

"Don't be silly. I'm meeting Abba Bari."

I bolt up out of bed with a ringing in my ears and a throbbing headache. "Fuck me!" I lie back down still dressed in my uniform from yesterday, minus the jacket. A wave of nausea hits me as a cold sweat builds on my skin. I rush to the bathroom, emptying the contents of last night's drinking fest. I flush the toilet and sit on the cold tile floor, resting against the wall with my hands in my hair.

"There had to be some fucking clue that I missed. She couldn't have been that good to cover every move." I bounce the back of my head off the wall several times trying to remember anything she said or did that I missed.

"Derrick, are you in there?" I hear Sean's voice as he's beating on my door.

I get up off the floor and head to the front door. "Hey, man," I say as I open it for him.

"Our flight leaves in an hour." He pushes through the door.

"I'm not coming with you. I need to get back to my platoon."

The door opens as I try to shut it. "I thought you might say that." Commander Lukas stands in the doorway. "You're going home with your brother."

"Sir, I need to help find Nina. She needs to pay for her crimes."

"I agree, she does, but you won't be the one looking for her. Your mission is done. You'll go home, take a long-needed break and then will be reevaluated as to whether or not you're fit to come back."

"Fit to come back!" My temper rages and I ball my fist, punching it into the wall. "What the fuck? That bitch betrays us all, leads my men to slaughter and you're questioning whether or not I'm fit for duty!"

Commander takes his hat off. "Derrick, you know this isn't up to me, but you've suffered a tragic loss, and you need time to recover."

"I don't want time. The more time that passes, she'll get further and further from our grasps!"

"This isn't about Nina. It's about you dealing with all of this mess...and learning to be a civilian again." Sean steps up beside me.

"What the hell are you talking about? A civilian? I'm a SEAL. That's all I know."

"You're being placed on inactive duty."

My mind is spinning along with my body. In a fury, I topple over the small dining room table and then rush at the couch, shoving it up against the sliding glass doors.

"Derrick, calm down, man. I'm sure all this is only temporary," Sean says, shoving me up against a wall. I ball my fist up, and he takes a step back, raising his hands in the air.

"He's right, Derrick. Go home, get your life in order, get the required therapy for any soldier who's suffered a tragic loss like you, then I'll go to bat for you, but not until then."

CHAPTER 9

THE LONG ROAD HOME

We land in Portland in the wee hours of the morning. It's a sight for sore eyes. I haven't been back here but once since I became a SEAL.

Sean hails a cab, and the three of us hulking men fill the back seat. We drop off Theo at the medical rehab base, and we head downtown. The cab stops in front of a remodeled concrete building with architectural decor covering the front. A flashing neon sign says "Sean's Place" in the front window.

"Wow. I was expecting a dive. This place looks nice."

"Don't get too excited. The inside is nothing fancy."

"I thought we're going to your apartment?"

"We are." He points up. "Upstairs apartment. You can help me clean out the small one next to mine, so Theo has a place to live once he's released." He digs the keys from his pants pocket and opens the door, then throws them on the counter.

"My apartment is upstairs on the right. Make yourself at home and get some rest."

"What about you?"

"The bar has been closed long enough. I need it up and running today."

"Why don't I help you?" I look around the dark-colored walls with thin strips of light highlighting them. The bar stools are old, but the bar top itself looks new. "Did you build this?"

"Yep. The old man and I hand made it."

Its slick wood covered on the sides with corru-gated metal. "Nice work."

"Look, go get some rest. Tomorrow you can work on the apartment." He starts pulling glasses from underneath the bar and setting them out.

"I'm thinking tomorrow I'll need to be looking for a job." I sit at the bar.

"A job can wait. Besides, you can always work here. Lukas said you need to check in with the medical facility here so you can start your therapy classes right away."

I stand. "I'll get right on that. Maybe you're right. I'll go get some rest."

He laughs. "For some reason, I don't believe you."

The old wooden stairs creak as my boots land on them. The apartment door is unlocked when I turn the knob. It has a fresh coat of paint and new wood floors, but the kitchen needs to be updated. I walk through the hall and see which room is Sean's and lay my bag in the other one. I fall back on the bed and stare up at the drop ceiling. "This is my fucking life now."

I try to shut my eyes, but every time I do, I see the faces of my men and their families at their caskets, leaning over them crying. "He's got to have some liquor in here." I roll off the bed and rummage through the cabinets until I find a bottle of whiskey. "I think you and I are going to become good friends." I don't even bother pouring a glass. Removing the cap, I tip the bottle up to my lips and guzzle down several swallows before I stop.

Taking the bottle with me, I sit on the couch and dig the remote out of the cushions of the denim couch. I mindlessly flick through the channels until I find an old war movie. I used to love to sit and watch these with my brother when we were teenagers. I thought we'd join the military together, but he decided it wasn't the life he wanted. For me, it wasn't a want; it was a need. It was part of me before I even knew it. There has never been anything else for me. Now look at me. I'm sitting in an apartment in the middle of Portland. I'd much rather be in the desert sands of Afghanistan sweating my balls off than listening to cars go by on the busy streets.

This is not my life. "Goddamn you, Nina!" I scream and set the whiskey on the table.

Two years later...

"Hey, Derrick. Check out my arm." Theo raises and lowers it and moves his robotic fingers. "This is so cool."

"Yeah, cool." I down another beer.

"Commander Lukas signed the recommendation that I could be put back on active duty teaching young new cadets on the firing range."

"Good for you, man. Far stretch from being a SEAL." I reach over the bar and grab another bottle of beer.

"He asked about you."

"Who?"

"Commander Lukas."

"Ah, and what did you tell him?"

"I told him you're still being a dick." He laughs and gets his own beer.

"Let me guess." I turn on my barstool to face him. "He wanted to know if I'd skipped out on any of my therapy lessons?"

"Skipped out would be stretching it. You actually have to go to one to skip out on one." He uses finger quotes with his new hand. "See, isn't that cool."

"Tell him to reinstate me, and I'll go to all the therapy sessions he wants me to."

"That's not how it works, and you know it. Why are you being so damn stubborn?"

I slam my empty beer bottle on the bar. "It's a fucking waste of my time. She's long gone by now. Like he said two years ago, a ghost."

"When are you going to move on? None of us saw through her."

"Move on. Six of my men are dead because I was blind to a woman and she just disappears!"

"All I'm saying is, if you'd go to the classes and quit wallowing in your own self-pity, you might get your job back. Instead, you enjoy not sleeping, walking around the city at night, drinking your days away. As far as I can tell"—he gets up—"you're not the man I'd follow into battle. You've let that bottle take all your good senses. Rather than fight back, you've completely given up."

The barstool slams to the floor as I move toward Theo. Sean comes out of nowhere and seizes me from behind.

"You ungrateful little shit!"

"Derrick, that's enough." Sean is holding me back.

Theo laughs. "Ungrateful would've been me sulking for the past two years because I lost my arm. Instead, I've done the work, and I sleep at night. That's more than I can say for you."

I lunge toward him again.

"Theo, I think you need to leave," Sean tells him. "Not that I don't agree with you one hundred percent, but I don't need a bar fight in here tearing this place up."

I shrug out of his hold. "Get the fuck out of here!"

Theo raises his mechanical hand and shows me the middle finger. "You think you're the only person that's ever been betrayed or shit happens to? I picked up my first gun at sixteen years old and started practice shooting every day." He pauses as his lip quivers. "My old man used to beat the shit out of my mom routinely. I'd come home to find her laying in a pool of blood more times than I could remember. So, I practiced and practiced my shooting skills, and that's how I'm as good a sniper as I am today."

"Where's your father now?" I ask.

"Six feet under, and my mom is remarried and happy." He turns on his boot heel and heads upstairs.

I reach over the bar and pour myself a whiskey. "Fuck!"

"I take it you didn't know any of that." Sean wipes the countertop with a towel. "Don't you think you've had enough to drink today?"

I raise my glass and gulp the amber liquid down.

"Yeah, that's what I thought. Theo was right. You aren't the man I'd follow. You're headed down a path you can't come back from."

"Maybe I don't want to come back."

"That's too bad because I miss my brother. The badass one."

"He doesn't exist anymore." I spin the empty glass on the bar.

"Well, you better fucking find him because I don't want to have to bury you in the ground. Now get out of here and go to therapy or get a fucking job. Do something." He storms off up the stairs, and I hear him knock on Theo's door.

CHAPTER 10
MY FATE BEGINS

I wake up two days later, filthy and sleeping under a bridge. My mouth feels like cotton balls, and I already want a drink. I climb out the gutter and brush the mud off my torn jeans. I step over a homeless man with his dog curled up next to him. I've no idea how the hell I ended up here and not at my apartment. I don't even remember the last place I came from.

Stepping up onto the road, I make my way into the heart of the city. A sign on a building has me stopping. It's the place I've found myself outside of many times, but never went in. For some reason, today I decide to take the first step. I open the door, and I'm greeted by a young woman with a headset on. The sparsely decorated waiting room is empty.

"Do you have an appointment?" the young girl asks.

"No...I...never mind." I turn to walk out, and a tall woman with dark glasses comes out of a room.

"Can I help you?" She hands the young girl a file.

"I'm supposed to meet with someone."

"Your name?" She sticks out her hand. "I'm Dr. Lauryn Ruth. I know, ha-ha funny. Not that Dr. Ruth." Her sense of humor puts me at ease.

"I'm Derrick Rebel."

She stands tall. "I know who you are, Captain Rebel."

"Don't call me that." I shove my hands deep into the pockets of my dirty jeans.

"I've gotten a call every week for two years from Commander Lukas asking me if you've shown up yet. I guess this week I get to give him a different answer." She opens the door to her office. "Please come in Cap...Mr. Rebel."

"I should leave." I angle toward the door.

"I wouldn't think a man like you would scare off easily."

"I'm not afraid."

"Then what's it going to hurt?"

I step around her and walk into her warmly decorated office.

"Please, have a seat. But not on the couch. I reserve that for the patients that are afraid of me." She laughs. "Since you don't like to be called by your military title anymore, what should I call you?" She takes a seat behind her desk and folds her hands together on top of it.

"Derrick."

"Your commander tells me you were the best SEAL in the Navy."

"If I were the best, six of my men wouldn't be dead and the woman I loved wouldn't have betrayed me," I snarl.

She leans back in her chair. "Cut to the chase why don't we. Your men are dead because of the job they chose to uphold. They died serving this country and were killed by our enemies, not by you."

"I led them there." I bite the inside of my cheek so hard I taste blood.

"And they willingly followed on the mission that the commander gave them. Why don't you blame him, if you have to blame someone? You followed orders, and so did they."

"It's not that simple."

"Why isn't it? If I took my family to a crowded

football game and some lunatic set off a bomb killing them, would that make it my fault?"

"It's not the same." I clench my jaw.

"Why not? I led them there." Her hands drop to her lap.

"This was a mistake." I stand.

"Because of the woman you trusted?"

I stop with my hand on the knob. "Because I was too blind to see what she was up to."

"And you're going to waste your life and everything you've worked for because the woman you loved covered her tracks so well that no one else saw it either?"

I turn toward her in anger. "Look, Dr. Ruth, all I wanted to do was go back to my platoon and do my job. Be the SEAL I was trained to be and bring her back to justice for her crimes."

"I understand that, but you needed to grieve not get your revenge."

"That's where you're wrong, lady." I open the door.

"Derrick, I wish you'd let me help you."

"I'm too fucking far gone for anyone's help!" I slam the door behind me.

"It's a little too early for you to be in here today," my brother says loudly while tapping his watch from behind the bar.

"Fuck you, Sean." I sit in my usual spot at the end of the bar.

"I can see you're in your usual suck-ass mood." He sloshes a glass of draft beer across the concrete countertop. "You look like shit, man. Do you ever sleep or bathe? You smell like dog shit."

"Well, when you pass out with the dogs," I mumble and tip the cold beer to my lips, guzzling it down. I wipe the back of my hand against my mouth and feel the scruff of my face as it scratches against my skin. "I'll take another."

"You were here until two in the morning, and it's not noon yet, man."

"You're still here." I slide him my glass.

"I kinda own the place." He chuckles and pulls the lever down and fills my glass, then walks over to me and places it in front of me. "Are you trying to drink yourself to death?"

"Does it really matter?"

He picks up the glass of beer and throws it on the ground behind the bar. Glass shatters and beer splatters onto the countertop.

"What the hell, man?" My jaw clenches.

"It fucking matters to me! Why won't you go to therapy? You won't talk about it so no one can help you." He grabs a towel and wipes off the bar. "You used to be bigger than life. Someone I was proud of. What happened to that Navy SEAL? Where did he go? All I see now is an empty shell of a man that ain't worth a damn."

My barstool scrapes across the floor as I push off it. He grabs me by my shirt collar and pulls me against the bar. "You don't get to just walk out of here. Say something. Say anything. Cuss me out, just act alive!"

For a split second, I want to rear back and punch him in the jaw or throw a glass and shatter the mirror behind him. I want the pent-up rage let loose. My chest heaves hard as I struggle to regain control. His gaze bores into me, pleading for me to let it go. I can't...that would mean I deserve to live.

"Let go of me, brother."

Tears stream down his rugged face as his fists loosens their grip. "Derrick, please man, let me help you."

"I don't want your help." I storm out the bar door. I'm a dick, and I know it, but that's all I deserve to be. Straightening my shirt, I debate going back inside. The neon sign of the bar flashing Sean's Place distracts me, taking me back to flashes in the dark of the night with bombs going off around me. Squeezing my eyes tight, I make them disappear before my head starts to throb and my heart races out of control. "I need a damn drink."

I walk down a few blocks to the liquor store. Portland is full of them, and they don't give me shit about how bad I look or how much I drink. They only want my money. I buy a large bottle of whiskey and head back to my small apartment on the top floor of an abandoned building. At least that's how it appears. I bought the place not long after I got out of the Navy. I restored the top floor, but not the rest of the brick building. It gave me a distraction. Windows are broken out on every floor, and I posted signs that say condemned on the wooden fence that surrounds it.

The old caged elevator still works, and I prefer it over the broken-down stairs. I open the metal door into a world I thought I could survive in. The entire fifth floor is one open area with expensive leather furniture, artwork from another century, a sixty-inch television that never comes on, and top-of-the-line appliances filling the open room. My Harley Davidson sits untouched in the far corner near my walled-off bedroom. A half wall closes it off from the rest of the room. It's funny; I spend more time waking up in ditches or park benches than I do at this place.

Pulling out a round ball of ice from the freezer, I fill a short, square glass with it, pouring the whiskey to the top and carrying the bottle with me. The soft leather of the couch doesn't even creak when I sit on it. Resting my glass on the stained wood planked coffee table, I bend down and take off my black lace-up boots and prop my feet up on the table.

"Alexa, turn on some classic rock," I say before I take a swig of my drink. Her lights flash and she responds, playing my favorite station. "Turn up the volume." I rest my head back and soak in the sound of the music. The one thing I hate is the silence, which is funny coming from a man who only wants to be left alone.

I shut my eyes and the guilt of how I treated my brother weighs on me. He doesn't deserve it. At thirty-eight, he's three years older than me and in a hell of a lot better shape. Mentally, anyway. Physically, I could still kick his ass. He's always played the big brother role and protected me. Not once has he ever let on to our parents how bad of shape I'm in. Our dad was born and bred military, and he would kick my ass.

I guzzle down my whiskey and don't even bother pouring another one. I tip the bottle up and drink until I can't stand the burn any longer. Getting up off the couch with the bottle firmly in my grip, I make my way to the shower. It's barely covered by a white curtain on one side of the open shower. There's a large granite top sink with dark wood cabinets that cover one side of the wall. A rectangular mirror hangs over it. I reach over, turning on the shower that sprays out of four different heads from above. Before the heat of the shower frosts the mirror, I catch a glimpse of my face. It's the face of a man much older and wiser than he should be. First, I rub the scruff, then the raised scar that runs over my right eyebrow, down my temple to the side of my jaw. It's a constant reminder of what happened, and I have to look away.

Ripping my shirt off, sending buttons flying, the tattoos of men's names down my left arm brings on a stabbing pain. It's a pain I want to remember. Each of them was my brothers in arms, and I wish I was with them. I should be with them. I have no idea how I survived. I wad up my filthy clothes and throw them in the garbage instead of the hamper. My brother's right; I smell like dog shit.

I tip the bottle up one more time and get under the spray of the shower with the whiskey still to my lips. As the liquor eases my pain, the room starts to get out of focus and I sway, stumbling to the tiled floor of the shower. I sit bare naked in the middle, watching the swirling water go down the drain. Even in my liquored-up state, I relate it to my life going down the drain with it.

Sean was right. I was bigger than life and as fierce and cocky as they came. My missions wouldn't allow anything else or I'd be killed. "Nina...Nina." I repeat her name several times out loud just to hear it again. The name I used to love to say now leaves a bitter taste in my mouth.

Her long, lean legs would wrap around my waist, and the world that existed for me would disappear. All the war and bloodshed gone. Her body did that for me. Her betrayal shattered me.

My hand slips on the wet bottle as I bring it back to my mouth. It hits the floor, spilling out its contents. It rolls, and I lean to get it and end up flat on my stomach with my cheek pressed against the tile. My dark, wet hair that is now too long falls in my eyes, but I don't bother pushing it away. I turn over, and the hot water beats down in the middle of my chest, and I let out an animalistic cry of pain. "Ahhh-hh!" Tears mingle in with the flowing water as I continue to yell out. "Ahhhh! Why the fuck am I still here!" I stumble as I get up but catch myself before I fall. Dripping wet, I walk over to the nightstand by my bed and pull out my pistol. I sit on the edge of the navy-blue sheets that cover my bed and place the pistol in my mouth like I've done so many times before. My body convulses with the need to pull the trigger, but something always stops me.

I fall back onto the bed, soaking the sheets. My body is raked with emotions I can't seem to control. I curl up in a ball like a small child and cry until there's nothing left.

CHAPTER 11

MAKING AMENDS

I've been sober for two damn days, and I really need a drink. Instead, I find myself back at Dr. Ruth's office.

"I didn't think I'd see you again." She welcomes me back inside. "I told your commander I thought you were a lost cause."

"I'm not saying I'm not, but I need to find a way to quit being such a dick."

"Well, that I can't fix." She laughs.

"Then how about you help me not want to put a gun to my head every day."

Her smile falls, and her face fills with empathy. "I'd love to help you with that if you'd let me."

"I'm not sure I know how to let someone help me. I've always been in control and a leader."

"There's always a first time for everything, but I want you to gain your control back. There's nothing wrong with being in control or being a leader. You've been wounded and haven't taken the time to heal."

I rub the scar that runs down my face.

"I'm not talking physical wounds, Derrick. They're easier to heal from. The body does the work. But the emotional trauma you've experienced takes time. Our brains have to do the healing and, in your case, your heart, and that's a beast that may never heal until you let someone in again."

"Fat chance of that." I sit on the edge of the couch.

To my surprise, she joins me. "So you tell me, Derrick, what's your goal in therapy."

I sit further back and drape my arm over the back of the couch and rest an ankle on a knee. "I've already told you the goal, to not want to put a bullet in my head."

"I'm talking long-term."

"I haven't even thought in long-term goals."

"Do you want to be a SEAL again?"

"I am a SEAL. That's all I've ever been."

"Somehow I don't doubt that. I can picture you as a little boy running around playing army." She laughs then leans forward to look at me. "What about Nina?"

I inhale sharply and knot my hands in my lap. "I want to see her pay for her crimes."

"That has to be hard for you?"

"What do you mean?"

"The file I have on you says that you asked her to marry you. Do you still love her?"

"I fucking hate her...but I love the woman I thought she was. How will I ever trust anyone again? I never second-guessed myself or my gut until that day."

"You may never trust again, but I hope you will over time. Every woman you meet can't be held accountable for the sins of one. Have you had sex since Nina?"

I squirm in my seat. "What does that have to do with it?"

"You're a big, strong, handsome man with needs. I want to know if you've trusted yourself to be intimate with another person?"

My hand goes to my scar again. "I'm damaged goods. This ugly mug can't pick up women like I used to."

She gets up and sits in her desk chair. "Funny, I didn't even notice your scar until you pointed it out.

If it bothers you that much, you could have plastic surgery."

"No," I respond sharply.

"Ah, I see."

My brows crease together. "You see what?"

"It's your punishment for *her* and your men."

I stand. "My punishment is living every day knowing my men are dead."

"The purpose of therapy is to work through your emotions. I'm okay if you want to get angry, yell, or hit my punching bag over there in the corner, but what I'm not okay with is you walking out. If you want to be the man you were before, you have to stay and walk through the pain."

I sit. "I don't know if I want to be that man anymore." I brush my hand through my hair that has grown out. "Being in charge of someone else's life and safety is not a job I want anymore."

"But you just said you wanted to be a SEAL again."

"No, I said I am a SEAL, and that's all I've ever known."

She clicks a pen several times. "Today was a good start. I want to see you every day for the first two weeks, and then we'll see how you progress. Can I pencil you in, Derrick?"

I stand again. "You tell me when, and I'll be here."

I DON'T KNOW why I finally gave in and got help. Maybe I had hit rock bottom and knew it. I hated what I was doing to Sean and how badly I had treated Theo. They didn't deserve it. My sessions with Dr. Ruth over the last month have started to help. I'm sleeping at night, in my own bed, not a ditch. The nightmares aren't as bad thanks to the medication she put me on. I hate taking it, but it does help.

I've written letters to the families of the men I lost. It was part of my therapy session and learning to let go. My life is by no means back to normal, but I've quit pulling out my pistol every night.

I haven't seen Sean since I started therapy and my goal for today is to make amends with him and Theo. It's early evening, and I know there will only be one or two people in the bar. His place doesn't get crowded until ten in the evening.

"Hey, Sean," I say, coming through the door. The last time I was here, I think I told him to fuck off, so I'm sure his nose is still out of joint.

Theo comes down the stairs. When he sees me, he turns to walk away.

"Theo, Sean, can we talk?"

"Not if you're going to be a dick again," Theo snarls.

"Or tell me to go fuck myself." Sean crosses his arms over his chest.

"Quite the opposite." I pull out a barstool for Theo to sit. "I'm sorry, to both of you. I wanted you to know that I've been going to therapy, and I haven't had a drink in over a month. I know it's not much, but it's a start."

Both of them lose their defensive mode. "That's great, man. I'm glad to hear it." Theo puts his hand on my shoulder.

"Does that mean you're going to be my badass brother again?" Sean chuckles.

"Given time, maybe. I hope to be that man you can be proud of again."

"I'll toast to that." Sean fills three glasses with water. "This will have to do." He hands me and Theo one. We clink our glasses together. "Here's to getting my brother back," Sean cheers.

"Me too," Theo says and grabs me into a hug. "I've missed you, man."

"I've got a long way to go, but I know I can count on the two of you giving me grief if I go off track."

Theo releases me and clinks his glass with mine. "You know it, brother."

"Theo, I'm sorry for not knowing your story. It was my job as your leader to know my men, and I had no idea about your family."

"It's all right. Don't beat yourself up. I hadn't been under your command as long as the other men, and it was about the time you started seeing Ekko."

"So, you're saying he was too preoccupied with a woman to get to know your story," Sean adds.

"Thanks for clarifying that." I glare at Sean. "All I can say is that I'm sorry and I'll never let a woman cloud my brain again."

"I don't think that's what she was clouding," Sean says and they both laugh.

I hear the bar door open behind me, and Theo's gaze is glued to whoever walked inside. The clicking of heels comes toward us in a rush.

"Please I need help," a frantic, out-of-breath woman's voice says, and I turn around. "Someone is following me."

FALLON DAVIS

FATED LIVES SERIES

Book Two
Meet Fallon Davis

Fallon Davis is an innocent woman who gets thrown into a world of crime. All she ever wanted was to save her sister, but in doing so, she became the hunted. Rebel took her case on for his first mission. No matter how much of an ass he was to her to keep her at arms length, in the end, he couldn't resist falling in love with her. Fallon is sweet, sexy, a successful business woman, and likes her independence, which may prove to get in the way of the alpha male SEAL that's in love with her.

CHAPTER 1

MEET FALLON AND JOSIE

"Fallon, your sister is on the phone." My social media assistant, Sharon, peeks her head through the door.

"Tell her I'll have to call her back. Unless it's important, then put her through." I click over to my client who is in the middle of her exercise routine. I'm an online trainer slash consultant to individuals and families throughout the United States.

"Ten more reps, Mrs. Hampton, then go onto the shoulder routine." She's in her fifties, and thanks to my routine for her and the diet I designed specifically for her, she looks damn good. She's lost forty pounds and turned her body into muscle. She wasn't too overweight to begin with, but she had no muscle tone at all.

"I'm sorry, Fallon, but it sounds important. I think she's crying." Sharon is apologetic.

"Mrs. Hampton, you keep going with the routine and send me the list of foods you ate this week. I'll check in with you via email." I quickly hang up and switch my Bluetooth connection to my sister.

"Josie, what's wrong?"

"He left me." Sobs are almost vibrating my headset.

"What happened?"

"He said he didn't want to deal with a sick girl that he didn't have time for it in his career."

"He's a doctor for god sake! He deals with sick people all the time."

"I know!" She cries louder.

"Oh, Josie. I'm so sorry. Where are you?"

"I'm in my car two blocks away from my apartment."

"I'll meet you there." I run down the stairs of my office and onto the streets of Portland. My second-floor office sits above an old used bookstore. I could work from home, but I wanted to be able to get out of my apartment during the day. I opened the doors of Fitness and Health for Life by Fallon the day I graduated from Oregon State University at age twenty-two. Four years later, I've built up a good-sized clientele. My first purchase after I reached my savings goal was an all blacked out Audi A4 Sportster that I keep in a garage below my apartment, only four blocks from my work. I don't drive it to work or around town, but I love to take it to the coast on the weekends or when I visit my sister in Vancouver, which is just on the other side of the state line in Washington.

I slow my pace when the crosswalk has the orange hand flashing with two seconds to spare. Traffic is busy this time of day, and there are pedestrians by the herd. As I wait for the light to change, I see a good-looking man outside a building, hanging a neon sign. It's lit up saying "Sean's Place." It's a cute, newly renovated bar. I'd love to peer inside, but the light turns, and if I don't move with the crowd, I'm afraid I'll be trampled on.

"Mental note: Go back to the cute guy's bar." My long mocha-brown hair blows in the air when a gust of wind blows between the buildings. I always wear a band on my wrist, so I pull it into a pony as I make my way to my apartment building.

Beep. My car door unlocks as soon as I slide my hand between the handle and the door. The radio blares classic rock music, and I smile thinking about the last disaster of a date I went on. The guy was so unimaginative and boring, and I needed a little rock-and-roll in my life on the drive home.

My car drives so smoothly in and out of traffic, I find it hard to go the speed limit. My phone rings through the Bluetooth and Josie's name appears.

"I'm on my way, I promise."

"I can't believe Scott dumped me. I don't think I can handle going through a breakup on top of everything else. It's just too much."

"Hey, don't talk like that. Us Davis sisters can handle anything."

She cries harder.

"Do you want me to stop by Dr. Asshole's house and run him over with my car?" I love the zooming sound the engine makes when I kick it in gear to pass another vehicle.

"You love that car." She lets out a small laugh.

"I love my sister more. Besides, I have insurance on it."

"No, but please be careful driving. I know how heavy of a foot you have."

"I'll be careful and be there shortly." I push the disconnect button and redial Sharon. "Hey, will you let my clients know that I will be out of the office the rest of the day and they can email me with any questions. Oh, and send out the pending emails on my desktop."

"How about your schedule for tomorrow?"

"Don't change anything. I'll be there after I hit the gym in the morning. Why don't you take the rest of the day off after you contact my list of clients today."

"Will do. See you tomorrow."

My car flies easily over the Interstate Bridge that runs from Portland to Vancouver. I don't slow my speed until I'm at my sister's apartment. She lives on the ground level of a quadplex. As I roll into her driveway, the front door opens, and the girl looks a mess. Her black curly hair that is normally put together is all over the place, and her silver-blue eyes are bloodshot. Her olive skin looks paler than normal.

"Hey, Sis." I pull her into a hug. "You look terrible."

"Thanks." She gives a crooked smile.

"Please tell me you've been taking your medication."

"I have, but I think I need to have the dosage adjusted. I can barely keep anything down these days."

"He didn't break up with you because he doesn't

have time for you. You look like shit!" I laugh and take her hand, dragging her into the house. "When's the last time you brushed your hair?" I plug my nose. "Or took a shower?"

"It's not that bad."

"Yes, it is." I point to her bathroom. "Go get a shower and I'll order us some pizza, and we can cry on the couch all night."

Josie started feeling sick shortly after our parents died in a freak boating accident a year ago. She's in medical school and has been struggling to keep up. Scott is a third-year intern at the hospital she has clinicals at. She fell hard and fast for him. When she started showing symptoms of kidney failure, Scott quickly diagnosed her and got her into to see a specialist. She was feeling better initially, but lately, she seems to have gotten worse.

The two of us were adopted at about the same time from two different families. I don't ever remember a time without her in my life. I didn't even realize we were different until we started school together. I never saw her skin color. I only saw her, and I loved her. She's strikingly beautiful with black locks of curls and see-through silver-blue eyes. Her dark olive brown skin glows with her beauty. I didn't understand why kids teased her because I was envious of how pretty she was and proud to call her my sister. She was the beauty; I was the brains. I was tall and lanky with braces and wiry mocha hair that I didn't learn to tame until I discovered hair products and a straightener. Even with the braces, I still have a small gap between my front teeth. My mom always told me it made me look like Lauren Bacall. Of course, I had no idea who she was, so I checked her out online. After that, I felt better about myself because she was a raving beauty in her day.

I grew into my skinny body and filled out a full C cup. I'm still lean, but I've worked hard to build muscle, and I have nice biceps if I say so myself. I've had to work out in defense of my love for food. Mom always said it was because I was starved my first year of life until she got her hands on me, then I never quit eating.

"I hope you ordered a ham and pineapple pizza." Josie has her wet hair wrapped in a towel on her head.

"I ordered one for you and a meat lovers for me." I sit on her soft yellow couch and draw one leg underneath me.

"I don't know how you stay so thin with all the crap you eat." She joins me on the couch.

"Uh...I work out every day."

"Yeah, and you eat like a horse."

"And you don't eat enough." I rub my hand down her arm, and a tear rolls down her cheek.

"I get why Scott broke things off with me," she sniffs.

"Because he's a twat waffle?"

"No, because I went to see my specialist a few days ago."

"So."

"I need to have my right kidney removed."

"Why am I just now hearing about this?"

"I was hoping if I didn't tell anyone, it wouldn't be true. He said if I don't it could kill me."

"What about your other kidney?"

"It's okay for now, but he said it could take a serious hit once the other one is gone."

"Then what?"

"I'd need to go on dialysis until I could get a transplant."

"Oh, sweetie. I'm so sorry, but I'll be here for you every step of the way, and if you need one of my kidneys, it's yours."

"It's not that simple. You have to be a match."

"I'll get tested, so we know."

"You hate needles."

"Yes...yes I do, but I love you more."

"I was thinking..." She draws her lip between her teeth and bites it. It's a nervous habit.

"Spit it out." I laugh.

"I know Mom and Dad were our real parents, but maybe it's time I find out who my biological parents were and my history."

"You can have some DNA testing done. A few days ago I was reading an article on all the things they can find through DNA testing now, including organ matches. There's a new company that was advertising in Portland."

"Do you remember the name of it?"

"geNetics.com was the website."

Her lip starts to quiver. "Now you see why Scott didn't want me to weigh him down."

"He's an ass. We'll figure all this out and get you feeling better."

"I quit school today."

"You did what?"

"I've missed too many days and fell behind. My professor said that if I drop out rather than fail out that maybe when things settle down, I could pick up where I left off."

"How about for now, we concentrate on getting you better and eating pizza. You go dry your hair, I'll get the door."

CHAPTER 2

SOCIAL MEDIA

"Your new client is trying to connect with you." Sharon lays a stack of folders on my desk.

"I didn't know I had a new client today." I tap my pen on my glass top desk.

"He requested your services early this morning. You had an opening, so I fit him into your schedule. His name is Craig Palmer, and he's an accountant."

I click on the link. "Mr. Palmer, good morning. What can I do for you?"

"Ms. Davis, I got your name from an associate of mine whose wife you've done wonders for."

"Which client might that be?"

"Teresa Tessler."

Teresa was a house wife for years, bored with her

life and overweight. I connected with her when she joined a yoga class that I was teaching. She lost over a hundred pounds, and it rejuvenated her marriage. "Ah, Teresa is a hard worker. Tell me a little about yourself."

"I want to go on a date with a woman I met a few weeks ago."

"I'm not a dating service." I laugh. "I'm afraid you have the wrong idea."

"No...I'm sorry. I'm not explaining myself very well. Probably why I have a hard time getting a date."

I lean back in my chair. I'm curious now. "Go on."

"I'm awkward and a little overweight. She's beautiful and thin."

"And you think she won't like you for you?"

"Yeah, that's the idea."

"In my profession, I've learned that you have to like yourself first." I don't have dating advice for him; I haven't been on a date in years.

"That's where you come in. If I could lose some weight, I'd feel better about myself."

"You know women want a man for who he is on the inside, not what's on the outside."

"Well, it helps if the outside package isn't soft

and mushy like an overstuffed marshmallow." He laughs.

"I'm betting you're underestimating your attraction. You seem to have a good sense of humor. Women love a man that makes them laugh."

"So, you won't help me?" He sounds so defeated.

"If you're looking to lose weight, exercise daily, and eat healthy, I'll gladly help you, but getting this woman to fall for you is not something I can help you with. I do know that if you feel better about yourself, you'll gain more confidence."

"That's something I do need, and I'd love to get rid of my spare couple of tires around the middle. Sign me up."

"I'm going to put you back through to my assistant, and she can set everything up for you. She'll be sending you a schedule and paperwork for you to fill out so that I get to know you and what type of things you like."

"Thank you, Ms. Davis."

"I look forward to working with you." I disconnect my Bluetooth connection.

I lean back in my chair, allowing it to spin a little in place. I'd love to go on a date, see a movie, maybe have a nice romantic dinner with someone. Josie claims I'm too closed off and a workaholic, which she's right on both accounts. She says men flirt with me all the time and that I'm too blind to see it. I'd rather spend more time on the punching bag at the gym than dating.

I reconnect my Bluetooth and scroll to Josie's number. "Hey, how are you feeling?"

"Better. My doctor changed some of my meds around, and I have a little more energy today. He's scheduled my surgery two weeks from now. I really need you to be there with me."

"Of course I'll be there. You don't even have to ask."

"Thanks, Sis. I'll text Sharon to put it in your schedule."

"The Rio theater has a special showing of old war movies tonight. Do you think you are up to it?" Josie and I have seen almost every military movie that was ever made. We both love a soldier in uniform, and our dad used to tell us stories of his days in the army.

"What no date again?" She giggles.

"Who needs a date, I have you."

"Yeah, I'd love to go, but only if we can hit the cafe across the street when the movie's out. They've the best lattes."

"Great. I'll be home after I hit the gym for a couple hours."

"Later."

I finish up work, lock up and head straight for the gym a few blocks down. It's always packed this time of night. I watch as couples workout together, women are taking Pilates, and businessmen are coming in after work and changing out of their suits. The hardcore weight lifters are groaning and sweating, not paying attention to anyone around them. The men that are here for women to gawk at them are walking around flexing in the nearest mirror and watching their reflections in the mirror to see who is eyeing them. Then they take off to flirt with whichever woman was admiring them.

None of these personalities match up with mine. I want someone strong, loyal, charmingly funny, and a man that knows who he is and what he wants. Not someone who has to lull a woman in by how he looks. I need a man that's not intimated by someone like me. Someone who is independent, has a good career and is trustworthy to a fault.

"Did you sit in a pile of sugar?" A somewhat cute young guy stands behind me in the mirror.

I pull one earphone out of my ear. "Excuse me?"

"Did you sit in a pile of sugar?"

I crane my neck to look behind me to see if I have something white on my butt. "No."

"'Cause you have a pretty sweet ass." He laughs at his own corny joke.

I set the dumbbells back in the rack and grab my towel off the bench I was using. "That's funny. Why don't you go use that line on someone your own age." I throw my towel over my shoulder and head toward the steam room. I can't help but laugh to myself. A young girl his age might find him quite charming, but that line would not have worked on even a younger me. I look over my shoulder before I open the door to the steam room and see Mister Jokester already hitting on some young girls who are giggling at him, and he's all smiles. He looks over at me and gives me a thumbs-up.

CHAPTER 3

DATE NIGHT WITH MY SISTER

The old movie theater is sparsely filled when we walk in and find a seat near the back.

"I'm really glad we're doing this. I've been feeling a little cooped up and needed to get out of the apartment."

"I'm glad you're up to it," I mumble with a mouth full of popcorn.

"You really do need to find a date. Oh, how about him? He's kind of cute." She points to a guy dressed in fatigues sitting at the end of our row.

"Isn't that Brent Dagwood?" I lean in and whisper to her.

"Who's Brent?" she says loudly, and he looks our direction.

"Shhh. We went to high school with him. He enlisted in the military and left the day after graduation."

"God, I don't know, that was four years ago, and it's really dark in here." She squints to try to see him. "The movie is about to start. No more talking," she hushes me and snatches the popcorn out of my hands.

Halfway through the movie, I hear Brent swearing. I look over, and he's rubbing his hand back and forth over his forehead. He stands like he's going to leave, does a complete circle in place, and sits back down. Then stills.

A few minutes later, I hear him say something again. This time he's leaning forward with his elbows on his knees, and he's rocking his body back and forth.

"Do you think there's something wrong with him?" I whisper to Josie and point at Brent.

She swats my finger away. "He's probably really into the movie."

I try to focus on the screen, but him rocking back and forth is distracting. He finally stops and storms out of the movie. Something about him was making me tense, and now that he's gone, I can sit back and enjoy the show.

"That was really good, don't you think?" Josie is making her way out of the aisle to the steps, and she wobbles off-balance, catching herself on a theater seat.

"You okay?" I grab onto her arm.

"I got up too quickly, that's all."

"Maybe we should call it a night and go home."

"No. We're going across the street to the cafe like you promised." She starts walking again, using the chair backs this time for balance.

When we reach the steps, I wrap my arm in hers, and we walk down together and across the street to the café, which is buzzing with people. We find a small, round metal table in the front window and order our lattes.

"How is work going?" Josie sips from her cup.

"Great. I took on another new client today. I was thinking about expanding my market into Europe. What would you say to a trip over there to work on some marketing?"

"I think you should totally do it, but I don't think it's a good time for me to be away from my doctors right now."

"I'm not going to Europe without you, so I'll wait until you're feeling better."

"You're always so optimistic." She places her

mug on the table and rests back in her chair. "You know my condition is only going to get worse, right?" Her big eyes look burdened with worry.

I reach over and place my hand over hers. "You know I'll always be here for you. Whatever you need, just ask."

"There may come a time that I need a kidney." She looks up from her long lashes.

"And if I can give that to you, I will or campaign to find you a donor."

"Thanks, Fallon. I'm so glad we're sisters. I don't know what I'd do without you in my life," she sniffs.

"Good thing you'll never have to find out." I sit back and sip my latte.

We spend the next hour eating Danishes and drinking more coffee. Neither one of us will be able to sleep tonight with the caffeine overload. "What do you say we take a walk down to this new bar I saw opening?"

Josie looks at the time on her cell phone. "It's getting kinda late. Do you think it's safe to walk there?"

"It's only a couple blocks over, and we have to walk right by it to get to my apartment."

"I don't know. I should call a cab to come get me."

"Don't be silly. You can crash at my place tonight, and I'll drive you home in the morning. Come on, you can have a glass of water and watch me drink a margarita. Please. The owner was really hot. You could totally embarrass me."

"Count me in." She gets up from her chair and pulls me by the hand out the door. "What's this place called."

"I saw it when I was walking to work the other day, and the hot guy was hanging a neon sign that said Sean's Place."

"Well, I hope this Sean guy is ready for the two of us." She laughs as we cross the street.

The sidewalks are brightly lit except for one section that the city has been working on for months. It encompasses an entire block, and there is a dark alleyway between two buildings. I pass by it during the day, but I never feel uncomfortable in daylight, but tonight I have an uneasy feeling.

"How about we cross over to the other side of the road, and we'll cut back over," I say, drawing Josie closer into my side.

"I don't know. I'm feeling kind of tired. I'm not sure how much further out of the way I can walk."

I look ahead into the dark area. "Okay but stay close and walk as fast as you can."

CHAPTER 4
OUR NIGHTMARE BEGINS

We step off the sidewalk and cross over into the darkness.

"What are you two ladies doing out here after curfew?" A deep, angry voice comes out of the darkness.

We're both startled and stop in our tracks when the guy from the theater jumps out in front of us. He's dressed in full fatigues, and his hat sits low on his face. His hand is resting on a gun that is lodged between his belt and his pants.

We start backing away. "Stop, where you are," he barks and pulls his gun out. "Are you two carrying a bomb for the enemy?" He cracks his neck to the side.

"No, we're headed home," Josie says.

"Aren't you Brent Dagwood," I ask, raising my

hands in the air and taking one step in front of Josie, pushing her behind me with my hand.

He angles his gun sideways at me. "How do you know my name?"

"We went to high school together. You were in my history class and sat two seats behind me."

He blinks a few times. "Liar!" he yells. "I went to school in America!"

"Brent, we're in Portland, Oregon." I push Josie further behind me.

Sweat begins to pour off him. "Don't try to confuse me. You two aren't supposed to be out in the streets this time of night. There's a martial law forbidding it." He steps closer. "So you must be up to something." Even in the dark, I can see that his eyes are fully dilated. I don't know whether he's high on something or completely delusional.

"Is he on something?" Josie whispers from behind me.

"I think it's more than that," I say quietly.

"Shut the fuck up! What are you two whispering about?" He shoves me, and I bump into Josie, causing her to stumble backward landing on the road.

"Please, we're headed home. We didn't mean to break any curfew," I play into him and help Josie to her feet.

He steps up close to me and places his gun under my chin. His gaze roams my body. "I should take what I want from you right here."

"Take what you want from me but let her go." My heart races from fear. I have to get Josie out of here.

"No!" Josie screams, causing him to take a step back.

"Make her shut up." He presses his other hand to his temple.

I stretch one hand out to him, and the other is on Josie. "She'll be quiet, just let her go."

He waves her off with the pistol. I glare at her, hoping she won't say another word but go get help. Tears stream down her olive skin as fear takes over and she starts to tremble.

"What the hell is wrong with her?" He waves the gun around. "Get the fuck out of here before I change my mind!"

"She's sick and needs to go home." I start to walk with her, and he stops us in front of an old building that has one large window left intact.

"I didn't say you could leave." He pushes the gun into my back, and I raise my hands.

"She needs help. She's not going to make it by herself."

"That's her problem. You should've thought about that before you started roaming the streets of Afghanistan at night after curfew."

"What's he talking about?" Josie whispers. I take her hand and place it on the brick wall of the old building.

"Use the wall for balance and make your way home."

"I'm not leaving you."

"Yes, you are. Now go."

She keeps looking back at me every few steps.

"You're lucky I let her live," Brent says from behind me.

I slowly turn around to face him. "Thank you for letting her go."

"You're going to pay the price for both of you. I know how you ladies work. You sneak into our compounds and place bombs in our barracks. Are you the one that killed my brothers?" The gun aims sideways again.

"Brent, you're confused. Let me get you some help. You're not at war anymore. You're here in Port-land. I saw you at the movie theater tonight." That must be what triggered his PTSD. I take a step closer. "Please, let me take you to the hospital.

He shakes his head back and forth a few times. "No! No hospital! All they want to do is poison me!"

"Okay, then what can I do to help you?"

"Get on your fucking knees!" His hand tightens around the gun, and his eyes widen.

I bend down one leg at a time until my knees are on the pavement. I know if I don't do something, he's going to kill me. I spread my arms open wide. "You said you thought we were carrying bombs. You can check me and see that I don't have anything."

"You're trying to trick me again!" He shakes the gun at me but takes a few steps closer. "You killed my best friend in his sleep!"

"No, it wasn't me, I swear." My insides start to tremble because he's not backing down. "Brent, you know me. Think hard."

He closes his eyes tight and, for a moment, I think that I have a chance to escape, but he reopens them. "Fallon?"

"Yes, it's me, Fallon." I slowly raise up. "You're safe here. You're home."

He closes his eyes again, and when he opens them, the fleeting moment of recognition is gone. "Liar!" he yells and raises his gun with both hands on it. I rush toward him and grab his arms, pushing them upward and him toward the glass window. A shot fires into the air, causing pain to sear my eardrum. I continue to push him backward with all my might, and the gun goes off again, shattering the glass around us. We both fall into the opening of the building where the glass window stood.

In slow motion, I see his head crack on the concrete floor, and the gun goes flying across it. I land on my side and the glass from the window rains down on me and around me. I raise my arms to protect my head and feel the stabbing of the glass breaking my skin. I fold my legs up to my body as small as I can.

I keep my eyes open to watch for Brent's next move, but he lies unconscious next to me as shards of glass continue to rain down.

When it finally stops, I lie in shock, unable to move and terrified if I do, it will jar him, and the nightmare will start all over again.

Out of my periphery, I see Josie rushing through the opening, and I see her lips moving, but I can't hear her words. She bends down and unfolds my body. She says something again, then I feel the weight of her small body pressing down on my arm and warmth surrounds me. I feel blood pooling underneath me ,and a wave of nausea hits me right before darkness surrounds me.

CHAPTER 5

I'M ALIVE

The sound of something dinging wakes me up. I'm lying in a hospital bed, and my body feels sore. I lift my head to see Josie sleeping in a chair next to the bed. An IV is dripping into one arm, and the other arm is wrapped in white gauze. There are nicks and cuts all over my hands. I try to raise my head higher, and it's weighted down with a bandage covering my left ear.

Then fear rushes in, and I hear a monitor alarm as I try to get up to get away from Brent. "Fallon, it's okay. You're in the hospital." Josie is on her feet by my side.

"Where is he?" My eyes feel as large as saucers.

"He's in the hospital, but he's locked to a bed. He can't hurt you anymore."

I try to slow my breathing down and rest my head back on the pillow. "I don't remember anything after the gun went off. Did I get shot?" I lift my bandaged arm in the air.

"No, the bullet shattered the window of the building and a piece sliced through your brachial artery. I got to you as quick as I could, and blood was already everywhere." Her eyes start to water. "I held pressure with all my might. I had already called 9-1-1 when you sent me down the block. I knew they were coming, but I nearly died when I saw you fighting him for the gun. And, when you went through the window with him, I thought you were dead." Her voice trembles.

"You should've kept away. He could've shot you."

"If she would not have come in when she did, you would be dead," a woman in a white coat says as she enters the room carrying a chart. "I'm Dr. Kearney, and you are one lucky lady. The glass severed your artery, but thanks to your sister's quick action, she kept you from bleeding out, and we were able to stitch you up."

"What's wrong with my ear? Why does everything sound muffled?"

"The gunshot that close to your ear, damaged your eardrum."

"Will it go back to normal?"

"I'm sorry, but you'll more than likely have some permanent hearing loss in that ear."

My sister starts to cry. "It's okay, Josie. I'm alive thanks to you." I grab her hand, and she sits next to me.

"When can I go home, Doc?"

"We'll get you up and moving today and discharge you tomorrow morning. You're going to need some therapy on that arm and some antibiotics for a week. The wound should heal fine, but you're going to have a good-sized scar. We had to cut pretty deep and long to reattach the artery. You were given a couple units of blood, and your hemoglobin is at a normal level now."

"Thanks, Doc."

She places her hand on Josie's shoulder. "She's the one you need to thank."

I nod, and she walks out.

"You don't have to thank me. If it wasn't for you convincing him to let me go, I might be dead."

"You're not dead, and we're both safe now." She cries on my shoulder, and the word "safe" rolls around in my head. I remember saying those words to Brent. As terrified as I was, I think about what he must've gone through in the war to get him to such a bad place. It's not his fault, and I hope he can get the help that he needs, but I don't know that I'll ever be the same. I have a new perspective on war and how it affects the soldiers. I've no interest in ever watching a movie about war again.

***

OVER THE NEXT SEVERAL WEEKS, I spend time in therapy every day to get the strength back in my right arm. The wound is now healed, but a pink scar runs from under my armpit down to the inside of my elbow. My ear hasn't healed as well. I hear faint sounds but nothing I can make out if I cover my right ear.

Josie has been camping out at my apartment since her surgery. It only took her a few days to get back on her feet, but I think she's afraid to leave me alone. We've been taking care of each other, but I'm worried about her growing fatigue. My tiredness comes from the nightmares that plague me every night. It's like my mind is on rerun from that night.

Hers may come from the same place, but I think it's something more. I wish she would make a follow-up with her doctors. She insists she's okay, and I want to believe her.

We both had to file a police report, and we were assigned to a caseworker that keeps us up to date on Brent. Josie was angry at me initially when I decided not to file charges against him. His options were bleak, and they wanted to lock him away. I felt it was more important that he gets the help he needs rather than being locked behind bars and forgotten about. He served this country and went through God knows what over there. He doesn't deserve to have his country turn its back on him for something that's out of his control. He needs help, not to be held prisoner. I felt it would only make his PTSD worse and he might try to harm himself or someone else if he didn't get treatment.

He's in a mental health facility run by the state that specializes in PTSD in soldiers. I know he's where he needs to be, and at some point, I'd like to go visit him to make sure he's getting better. I think it would help ease my nightmares, but I don't dare tell Josie my plan.

It's early, and I have a client that likes to meet online at six in the morning, so I drag out my laptop at home and make a pot of coffee. When I walk down the hallway, I hear a retching noise coming from Josie's room.

"Hey, Sis, you okay?" I say, rapping lightly on her door as I open it.

Retching continues to come from her bathroom. I walk in, and her black curly hair is pulled to one side, and she's on her knees leaning over the toilet. I grab a washcloth from the linen closet and run it under cold water. Then I sit on the tile floor next to her and wash her face, trying to soothe her.

"How long have you been in here?"

"Most of the night?"

"Can I get you anything?"

"I have some Zofran in my nightstand, but I haven't been able to get off the floor to get it."

I get up and open the drawer of her nightstand and pull out the foil packet of pills labeled for nausea. I pop one out and head back to her, filling a small glass of water before I sit back down next to her.

"Here," I say, and she opens her mouth, letting it dissolve under her tongue.

"You should carry your phone with you at all times so you can call me for help." I brush a stray strand of hair from her cheek.

"I got up to go to the bathroom, and it hit me out of nowhere. It's been wave after wave for hours."

"Take a couple sips." I hand her the glass. "I think we should call the doctor and take you in to see him."

She sips the water and retches again. I lift her off the floor and help her get dressed. I don't even bother calling for an appointment; we just load up in the car and head straight to the office.

After the doctor checks her out, he assures her after she's been given some IV fluids and rehydrated, she'll feel much better.

CHAPTER 6

TRIP TO EUROPE

"Don't worry about me. You've barely left your apartment in the last month since the attack. This trip will be good for you, and I'm feeling much better since the doctor adjusted my medications." Josie hugs me. "Now, go get on that plane to Europe."

"I don't know, Josie. I feel like the timing is all wrong." I reluctantly take my luggage from the trunk.

"Don't be silly. You only think that because of me. Who wouldn't want a month of exploring Europe?"

"Then come with me." I wrap a finger in one of her curls.

"You know I can't. My doctor doesn't want me traveling yet. If I tag along, you won't meet some handsome man to fall in love with." She drapes her arm around my shoulder and walks me to the airport doors.

"I'm not going there to find a man to fall in love with. I'm going to be working and taking some classes. I still have my clients here that I'll need to check in with every day."

"Please promise me you'll try to have a little fun." She holds her finger out for me to pinky swear.

"I'll try, if I survive the plane ride." I hate flying, and I have to practice my mantra. *The plane will not crash into a fiery ball and fall and plummet to the earth. I'll be safe and kiss the ground when I land.*

"Please don't start with the fiery ball shit." She laughs. "Did you bring some Xanax?"

I nod and hug her. "You call me if anything changes. I'll get on the next flight home." I have to admit, she looks healthier than she has in a while.

"Nothing is going to happen. I love you, Sis."

"I love you, too." I drag my luggage behind me.

"Don't forget to send me hot pics of that sexy man you're going to meet!" She yells loud enough that people turn around and stare at me. Ugh, I swear sometimes I could kill her myself.

I make my way through security just in time to board my international flight. It's a huge plane with three rows of seating. The row in the middle has four chairs, and the outside ones have three.

I look at my ticket to find my seat and make my way toward the back of the plane. The row I'm in is empty so far. I stow my luggage and take my window seat and buckle in. I take out my Nook and open my book on sign language. Me losing part of my hearing got me interested in learning the language, and I plan on adding hearing-impaired clients to my list.

I watch as passengers pile in and find their spots. Taking out my headphones, I connect with my Bluetooth to start my lesson to distract me. I close my eyes and try to find a peaceful spot in my mind to not think about the plane rolling off down the runway.

The seat jostles next to me, and I look up to see a young man dressed in fatigues settling in on the outside seat. He's very cute in a young boy sort of way. I'd guess him to be no more than eighteen years old.

He sees me watching him, and his face lights up. "First time on a plane," he says. He sounds excited.

"Not mine, but I still don't like to fly." I pull one earphone out of my ear.

"I can't wait until this bird takes flight."

The intercom goes off, and the flight attendants start their speech on safety. Sure, I'm going to do all that if this plane goes down. The only thing I'm going to do if the plane starts plummeting at a million miles an hour is kiss my ass goodbye. I place my earphone back in and concentrate on my lesson, keeping my hazel eyes closed as the airplane starts its slow roll to jockey for takeoff.

The plane moves faster down the runway, and I have a death grip on the armrest. I'm thankful no one is sitting in the middle, so I have somewhere to grasp. I open my eyes when I feel a hand cover mine. I look over at the soldier, and he's smiling and rubbing his thumb over the top of my hand.

"This is awesome," I hear him say loudly.

I can't help but smile at his enthusiasm, and for some reason, it calms me a bit. When the plane finally levels out, the soldier leans over and pulls my earphone out. I turn my head so I can hear him.

"Do you mind if I look out the window?"

"Not at all." I pull the blind up, and he unbuckles, taking the seat next to me.

He's leaning over me, so I decide I should probably introduce myself since he has no sense of personal space. "I'm Fallon." I stick out my hand.

"Theo." He smiles and grips my hand. He has these sandy-colored eyes that I bet the young girls swoon over. They match his short hair, which looks like its recently been shaved.

"How long have you been in the military?"

He smiles and sits upright in his chair. "Eight weeks of boot camp and two years of military school. I'm on my way to my first assignment."

"You look so young."

"I was sixteen when I enrolled in school."

"Is it something you've always wanted to do?"

His bright eyes turn sad, and he loses his smile. "No, but my life will be better for it."

I sense he doesn't want to give any more details. "What are you going to be doing in the military?"

"I've trained to be a sniper for a Navy SEAL team." His smile is plastered back on his handsome face.

"That's awful ambitious. Good for you. I'm sure your parents are very proud."

And that quick, his smile fades again, and he toys with the hat he's been holding in his hands. "My mom is. My dad passed a couple of years ago." His voice drops off after mentioning his father.

"I'm sorry," I say and peer out the window for the first time.

"Are you going on vacation by yourself." His words have me facing him again.

"No. I'm going on business, but I'm hoping for a little sightseeing while I'm there."

"Have you ever been to Europe before?"

"No."

"Well, then you have to take time and explore. I have one day before I have to catch another plane and report to duty. I've never been anywhere before. What do you say to us exploring it together?"

"I'd say I'm a little too old for you." I laugh.

He frowns. "You're too old to be my friend?"

He has such an innocence about him. "I'm sorry, you're right." I pull a map out of my bag. "I marked a few things on here I'd like to see if I found time. Do any of these look interesting to you?"

He takes the map into his lap and studies it. "We could take the train to the Château de Versailles—the home of King Louis XIV."

I take out my planner and look at the times I have classes set up. "I think we could make that work."

"Great! It's a date then...I mean a non-date...not like a guy-girl date. Just friends." He chuckles.

I'm so glad Theo is the one that sat next to me on the plane. We watched movies together and laughed for hours. He made the long plane ride pleasantly bearable. He has the innocence of youth, but I can tell there is deep-seated pain that lies beneath the surface. Something that in the quiet moments, eats at him. I can relate to that feeling. In the darkness of the night, I still see the face of my attacker. He stole some of my innocence of youth, and it makes me curious as to who stole some of Theo's.

CHAPTER 7

MY SHORT TIME WITH THEO

"This place is so exquisite. It says here in the brochure that the floor of The Royal Opera of Versailles can be raised to seat 1200 people." I'm in complete awe as I look around the opera room. "I wonder how old this wood is? It's still shiny and polished looking."

"It says here, the late 1700s, and did you know it was built as a celebration of the marriage of the dauphin—the future Louis XVI to Marie Antoinette," he adds.

"Wouldn't it be great to see an opera here?"

"Not my thing, Hazel."

I stop running my hand down the wood walls. "Hazel?"

"You have the most beautiful hazel-colored eyes." He points at them.

"Are you flirting with me?" I ask, laughing and continue to explore.

"No, just stating the obvious." He chuckles. "I thought women loved a man in uniform."

"They do, but I prefer mine to be a tad bit older."

"You know in a few years when I'm twenty-five..."

"I'll be almost forty." I walk by and punch him in the shoulder. "You're like a kid brother I never had."

"One day you're going to regret not taking me seriously." He laughs "When I work out every day and get bulging muscles and can grow a beard, you'll be sorry." He flexes his bicep.

"Let's go see the Hall of Mirrors while we're here." I take his hand, and he follows me. I'm betting in a few years he will be even more charming than he is now.

WE SPENT the rest of our day exploring inside the palace and then took the train back to see the Eiffel Tower.

"Hazel, come here. Let's get a selfie with the

tower in the background," Theo yells.

I'm standing under the tower getting a picture looking up, and Theo is down by the railing looking up getting a picture. I snap the shot I wanted and head over to him.

"I may never see you again, so I want a picture of the two of us."

I join him in the frame of his phone. "The one that got away," I tease him.

He holds his hand over his heart. "The one that broke my heart." He snaps the shot as I turn to look at him.

"Hey, redo. I wasn't looking."

He holds the phone up again, and he pecks me on the cheek and snaps the picture. I can't help but laugh at him. "You're impossible. Now be still and take a serious one."

He pouts out his lower lip. "Okay, Hazel. I'll be serious." He wraps an arm around my shoulder and leans into my side, then presses the button.

"Are you happy now?" He shows me the picture, and I snatch the phone from him. I quickly send all three shots to my phone.

I hand it back to him. "Thank you for today, Theo. I had a lot of fun."

"The day's not over yet. Let's go walk down by

the water."

"I don't know. It's getting late, and I don't like to be out after dark in strange places. Besides, I really need to check into my hotel room. Where are you staying?"

"I don't know. Park bench." He shrugs.

"You didn't make reservations?"

"I was planning on sleeping at the airport until my flight out tomorrow."

"Come on, you can stay with me."

He raises his eyebrows.

"On the couch...fully clothed." I laugh and take his hand.

We check in, and I unpack while Theo orders us something to eat. We spend almost the entire night talking. Several times he grew quiet if the topic of his family came up, so I made sure to steer away from it.

I wake up the next morning to find a note on the coffee table next to the couch where he slept.

Thanks for hanging out with me, Hazel. I'll always cherish the time I spent with you and your kindness to a stranger. I hope your business goes well while you're here. And, your sister was right, try to have a little fun. You can skip meeting the hot man because I've already stolen your heart, you just don't know it yet.

In all seriousness, thank you, Hazel. I will never forget you.

Your handsome and charming soldier - Theo

I'M KIND OF sad that he left without saying goodbye this morning. In some small way, Theo has touched my life, and I too will never forget him. I grab my phone and look at the pictures of the two of us. There is a phone number attached to them. I only hesitate for a moment before I call him.

"Hello."

"Hey, it's me Hazel."

"I knew you'd chase after me." He laughs.

"You left without saying goodbye."

"I didn't want to wake you, and I didn't want to miss my plane."

"Thank you, Theo. Stay out of harm's way and good luck becoming a SEAL. You're going to do great. Don't lose your sweetness. Ladies love that and the uniform."

"You never know, our paths may cross again one day."

"They just may. Bye, Theo."

"Bye, Hazel."

CHAPTER 8

TWO YEARS LATER

"I know how much you hate needles." Josie is squeezing my hand.

"I do." I focus on my breathing as the young male phlebotomist inserts the needle into my vein.

"Thank you for doing this," she says, sadly.

I open my eyes and look at her square in the face. "I want to do this for you." Her health has deteriorated, and she's been on dialysis now for a month. Her doctor was hoping for some improvement with it, but her numbers are looking worse every week, and he placed her on a transplant list. I've been dealing with the stress of her illness by working out like crazy. The punching bag gets most of my worries.

She gave up her apartment in Vancouver and moved in with me permanently. After my blood is drawn, I'm taking her to the coast to soak in its beauty. Cannon Beach is one of her favorite places to chill, and it's only an hour and a half away from here. Not too far, but far enough to get her out of the city and close enough to get back if anything happens to her.

She researched geNetics.com and decided to use them not only for the blood mapping, but to find out her family history. It has a vast database and has become one of the largest research testing companies in the world in the past two years. They guarantee being able to find a donor for her. My hope is that I'm a match and we can get the process done quickly.

"How's it going with your new clients?" Her voice breaks my thoughts.

"My deaf students?"

"Yeah. How many do you have now?"

"Three, and I have them in a group class online. I'm loving it, and so are they."

"It's such a good thing you are doing for them."

"Believe me when I tell you I've gained so much more from them. None of them let their disabilities interfere with their lives. They're such a blessing to me."

"I enrolled in a class to learn sign language. You've inspired me to help out. As soon as all of this is over, I'd like to teach the hearing-impaired."

"That's awesome. You'll be taking those classes in no time."

"All done, miss," the young man says as he applies a bandage.

"Nice job, Sis," I say, knowing she was distracting me.

"Let's get out of here." She grabs her walker. She started using it a few weeks ago when she became so weak she was stumbling all over the place.

"I'm looking forward to the ocean air on my skin, at least in between my dialysis days."

"We'll make the most of it. I've downloaded some of your favorite books to read while you try to relax."

Almost as soon as we get settled into the car for the drive, she drifts off to sleep. I hate seeing her so frail, and every day when I wake up, I go to her room to make sure she's still with me. God, I hope I'm a match so that I can help her.

T WO WEEKS LATER...

"Josie, a there is a letter from geNetics.com." I rush through her bedroom door to see she's still asleep at noontime. "Hey, you okay?" I brush the hair from her eyes that look sunken.

"Yeah, I just don't seem to have any energy." She slowly sits up and rubs her dry lips together.

"Here's the letter you've been waiting for." I hand it to her.

She looks at the mailing label then flips it over to open it but stops. "I can't. You do it." She hands it back to me.

I put my finger in between the flap and open it carefully as to not tear the letter inside.

Dear Miss Josie Davis,

Thank you for using geNetics.com. All of your blood work has come back along with your sister's, Fallon Davis. Unfortunately, your adopted sister is not a match for you. We did, however, locate a client in Europe that is a perfect match. We'll be in touch with our client to determine health and willingness to donate a kidney. All information is confidential, and no information will be released until the client has been processed and agreed to the medical arrangements. This part takes time, and you'll hear back from us in a couple of weeks.

Also, as part of our service, by your blood work,

we've determined your DNA is from an Irish and South African background. If you wish, we can take it one step further and run your DNA through our program to see if we have a match to identify your parents and any siblings you may have. There is an extra fee for this if you decide this is something you want to pursue. Please give us a call so that we can discuss the costs in detail.

We'll be in touch soon,

N.P. Parrot

"THIS IS GREAT NEWS." I look up, and she has tears streaming down her face.

"I've never thought about having any other brothers and sisters before," she sobs.

"Oh, sweetie. I know it's a lot to take in, and you don't have to decide right now. Let's concentrate on the positive. They have a match. I'm sorry it's not me. I'd do anything to help you." I wipe the tears from her face with my hands.

"I know you would, and I love you for that. I couldn't ask for a better sister, but I'm glad you don't have to go through surgery and give up so much for me. You've already given up your apartment and all

your free time. You have no social life because
of me."

"I had no social life before you." I laugh and hug
her to me.

"When this is all over with, you need to find you
a man."

"One day, maybe. Now dry your eyes and go get
in the shower, you stink," I tease. "I've got a few
errands to run." I throw her sheet back and help her
out of bed. I wrap my arm in hers, and she takes a
few steps then I feel the weight of her body go limp.

"Josie!" She falls back against the bed, and her
eyes roll back. I snatch up her cell phone that's
charging on her nightstand and call 9-1-1.

I try to wake her, but her eyes don't open. Her
skin is pale and clammy. I feel for a pulse in her neck,
and it feels thready. "Josie, please wake up! You can't
give up," I cry.

A few minutes later, I can hear the ambulance
siren coming toward us. I rush down to the bottom
floor and wave them down. "Over here!"

The rest is a whirlwind. They have her on a
gurney and hooked to monitors, carrying her down
the stairwell. "Will she be okay?" I ask as I climb into
the back of the ambulance with her.

The paramedics places a mask on her face to

give her some oxygen. They started an IV in the apartment, and there is a bag of fluids he's hanging to a hook above her. "We've got her stabilized for now," he says as he continues to work on her.

After what seemed like hours, but was only a short period of time, Josie is in the ICU surrounded by nurses and her doctor.

"How is she?"

"Fallon, Josie's kidney failed, and her other organs are shutting down. We need to intubate her for support and start her dialysis right away."

"The company she was working with found her a kidney." I have the letter clutched in my hand. "She has to make it a couple more weeks," I sob.

"I'll check this out and look into our national database. This should move her to the top of the list. Our only drawback is that her blood type is rare. I'll get ahold of this company and see if I can speed up the process."

I HAVEN'T LEFT her bedside in three days. They've kept her sedated to help her body rest. Her doctor hasn't been able to locate a match in their database, and he hasn't gotten a response back from geNetics.com

"Your sister is stable, and we are doing everything we can to keep her that way. Go home, get some rest. I'll call you if anything changes."

I reluctantly agree. "I'll be back, Josie." I kiss her forehead.

I think I've gotten only three hours sleep in the last three days. Exhaustion has finally taken over, and I'm on autopilot as I take the elevator down to the ground floor. I'm aware that there are a few people in the elevator with me, but I'm so lost in my fatigue, I couldn't even say anything about them.

I catch a cab home and head straight for a long, hot shower. My brain tells me to hurry up so that I can get back to the hospital, but my body wins out. I throw on a nightshirt over my wet head and climb into bed.

I'm startled awake by a sound, or maybe it was a dream. My bedroom is dark. I must have slept the entire day. I reach over to turn on a lamp. I don't see anything or hear another sound. I quietly open my bedside drawer where I keep a loaded pistol, just in case I wasn't dreaming. Padding barefoot on the carpet, I open my bedroom door to nothing but a small light coming from a burner that melts a fragrance in the apartment. Keeping a firm grip on the pistol, I slowly walk through the open area of the living room. Switching on the light, I don't see anything.

"It must have been a dream." I lower my pistol and place it on the kitchen counter and start a pot of coffee, but not before I've checked out Josie's room. Everything is in its place, except for her. I trot back to my bedroom to grab my cell phone to call the hospital to check on her. As I walk around the apartment, talking to her nurse, I see a drawer to a small filing cabinet slightly open. I don't remember getting into it, but maybe Josie did, looking for information for her DNA testing. I open it further to investigate but don't see anything out of the ordinary.

"She's still stable, no changes?" I ask the nurse as I continue to look around. She tells me she's the same and will call if I need to come back tonight.

I've slept the day away and can't just sit around this apartment. I get dressed and decide to go to the office and check my emails. Sharon has been handling everything for me, but I want to personally respond to each email. Besides, it will help me get my mind off Josie.

I finish my coffee and place the pistol back in my drawer. I put on a pair of yoga pants and lavender hoodie and my running shoes. A jog to my office will do me a lot of good.

I take off in the direction I've been a million times before. The street lights are on, and the sidewalks are scarce of people. I run a few blocks; I get an uneasy feeling like the night Josie and I were attacked. Stopping dead in my tracks, I look around, and I see a shadow duck in between two small houses. A dog barks for a moment and then stops.

I wish right now I had brought my pistol, but I grip my keychain with mace attached to it. I pick up my pace and keep looking back. I can't shake the feeling that someone is following me.

My hand shakes as I unlock the door to the building and make my way upstairs to my office. I flip on the light and lock the door behind me. I'm panting, out of breath from running so fast. I keep a small fridge with healthy snacks and water behind my desk. As I take out a bottle of water to guzzle down, I see the light beeping on my recorder, indicating a message. I push play, and all I hear is the soft sound of someone breathing slowly. It's then I notice that my computer is on. I always turn it off, and I haven't been here in days. I snap up the phone and call Sharon.

"Hey, Fallon. Is your sister okay?" She sounds like she was sleeping.

"She's stable. Listen, I came to the office to answer some emails. Have you been on my computer?"

"No. I never touch your computer."

"Huh."

"Why?"

"It's on, and I always turn it off."

"You've been so distracted lately, maybe you just forgot to log out."

"I guess you're right." But it doesn't feel right. "Okay. I'm sorry I woke you. I'm going to work for a couple of hours and then swing back by the hospital."

"All of your clients have been informed of a family emergency, and they send their best."

"Thanks for handling things for me. I'll talk to you tomorrow."

I'm trying not to be paranoid, but something is really off. Nothing else is out of place. I get the feeling that someone else has been in my space. I fly through my emails and turn off my computer, watching it until the apple on the back goes dark, so that I know it is completely shut down.

I lock both doors behind me and start walking

back toward my house. I want to grab a few things and take my car instead of a cab back to the hospital. The streets have their usual homeless walking around, a few couples walking arm and arm and a man stumbling out of a bar. I'm watching every movement around me. There is a man standing in the shadows across the street. I swear he's watching me and moving when I move. Taking off in a slow run, I see him pick up his pace and cross over to my side of the road. The moment he pulls a mask over his face and I see him remove something out from under his belt, I take off in a full run and go into the first place that I see open. The neon sign flashes "Sean's Place" and the moon glints off the pane window.

My heart thumps hard as I fling open the door. Three men are sitting at the bar. One pair of familiar eyes flashes to mine.

"Please, I need help," I say breathlessly, "someone is following me."

THEO DRAKE

FATED LIVES SERIES

Book Three

Meet Theo Drake

Petty Officer Theo Drake is a young man who was dealt a bad hand in life, but turned it around when he joined the Navy and became a SEAL. He was the sniper for The Gunners lead by Captain Derrick Rebel. He's the only surviving member of the team other than Rebel. He didn't come out in one piece. He lost his right arm, but he never let it slow him down. Theo was a carefree, fun loving guy until he met Fiona and lost her. Now, he's angry and his only focus is on finding her.

CHAPTER 1
THE BASTARD

"Damn bastard! I'm going to kill him!" I can feel my nails biting into my palms.

"No!" my mom pleads as she gets off the floor. She slips in a pool of her own blood before she's able to get to her feet. "If you kill him, you'll go to prison," she cries as her body trembles.

"And if I don't, you'll be dead!" I wheel around to face her. My eyes tear up seeing the beating that my dad gave her because his dinner wasn't as warm as he would like it. I ran late from wrestling practice and found my mom on the floor. His stench of alcohol still floating in the air even though he's gone.

"I'm not going to let him do this to you anymore. The bastard only beats you because you're weaker than him." I barrel toward my bedroom and jerk open my closet door, throwing things out of the way until I have what I want grasped in my hands.

"What are you going to do?" she cries as she follows me.

I remove the Colt .45 from the box. I saved money for over a year and had one of my friend's college buddies buy it for me. We live out in the mountains of Oregon, and nobody cares if we practice shooting in the woods. I've ridden my four-wheeler out every weekend deep into the woods and practiced aiming at a target. I've gotten damn good at shooting from a distance.

I stick the gun in the back of my jeans and roll up my sleeves. "First thing I'm going to do is take you to the hospital." I place my fingers on her chin to turn it sideways. "It looks like you need some stitches on your forehead."

"You know I can't go to the hospital. They'll ask me all kinds of questions." Her chin dips down.

"So, quit protecting him!" My nostrils flare, and spittle flies from my mouth. I unclench my hands to try to calm my rage. It's not at her, and she doesn't deserve my anger.

"You don't understand. He said if I ever told anyone, he'd take you away and I'd never see you again." She grabs at my arm, trying to stop me from leaving.

"When he's dead, you won't ever have to worry about it again." I lower my voice and wipe a tear from her face.

"Theo, please. Don't do this. You are only sixteen years old. You shouldn't have to deal with any of this."

"And you shouldn't be beaten by your husband," I scream at her back in full rage mode and jerk away from her.

"I'm begging you, please don't go after him." Her pleading slows me down.

I stand facing the front door, not wanting to look at her and then punch the door so damn hard I hear a crack in my knuckles. I blow out air, trying to block the pain searing up my arm. Turning to face her. "This won't ever stop until one of us puts an end to it."

"I'll find a way to stop him." She splays her hand on my cheek. "Let me see your hand." She holds out her shaking hand, and I place mine in hers. "It's already swelling. I think you may have broken something."

"I'll go get it looked at if you go with me to be checked out."

She nods. "I'll tell them we were in an accident."

"They didn't believe your story last time. What makes you think this time will be any different?"

"Because this time, you're injured too." She grabs her purse and keys. "Get rid of your gun, Theo."

I pull it out from the back of my pants and look at it. "I swear, if he touches you again, I will kill him." Walking away from her, I head to my room and put the gun back in the box and on the top shelf of my closet and join her in the car.

THE ER WAIT IS LONG, and by the time I get seen, my hand is swollen, and I can't move my fingers. They put us both in the same room, and the questions start right away.

"I was riding on the back of Theo's four-wheeler, and we wrecked." Mom's gaze pleads with me to back her up.

"A deer ran out in front of me, and I swerved then overcorrected. We hit a ditch and went flying off."

"These knuckles look like they took a direct hit to something." The doctor holds them up to look at them. "I'll order an X-ray, but I'm sure they're broken." He turns to my mom. "We'll get this cut above your eye cleaned and stitched, but I need to examine the rest of you."

"I'm okay," she says, tugging the bottom of her shirt down.

"Mom, let him check out your ribs, you hit pretty hard."

"Mrs. Drake, this is your third visit here in the last two months with various cuts and bruises covering your body. Last time your shoulder was dislocated," he says as he examines her, and she winces. "This time it appears you have some broken ribs."

"I'm accident prone." She looks over at me as the doctor turns to face me.

I should tell him the truth. I hate fucking protecting the bastard, but if the police arrest him and then let him go, I'm afraid of what he'll do to her. I meant what I said—I will kill him so that he'll never hurt her again. "She does fall down a lot." I can't look him in the eyes and lie for her.

I know he doesn't believe us, but with neither one of us budging, there isn't much he can do about it. I'm taken to X-ray as Mom is being stitched up. It confirms it's broken, and I end up with a cast that runs from the tips of my fingers to my elbow. My wrestling coach won't be too pleased, but I'm more concerned that I won't be able to target practice for a while.

When we get home, my father has returned and is passed out on the couch. The bastard's knuckles are still bloody from where he struck my mom in the face with his fist. I want to yank him off the couch and beat the shit out of him, but instead, I take her by the arm and walk her to the bedroom.

"He wasn't always like this, you know," she says in a whisper.

"What changed him?" I remember when I was younger, he was a good father. He taught me how to swim, fish, and ride a bike, just like any other dad. He was sweet and gentle with my mom.

She drags me into her bedroom and shuts the door. "When your brother died, he blamed himself, and he's never been the same."

I was only four when my eight-year-old brother was killed. I don't remember a lot about him but the stories that were told around town. He and my dad had gone camping up in the mountains, and it started raining, causing mudslides. They loaded up in my dad's truck and headed down the mountain. A tree had fallen over and was blocking the road. Rather than my brother staying in the truck, he got out, and my dad had him stay off to the side while he moved the tree.

A truck was coming from the other direction. He was moving too fast and swerved to miss the tree, but instead, ran over my brother. My dad tried to save him, but he died in his arms on the mountain. The man that hit him was my dad's best friend. When the rain started, he was headed up the mountain to see if they needed help. Mom told me that neither one of them were ever the same. I'm not sure what happened to Dad's friend, but I lost my dad that day, along with my brother.

"That's when he started drinking." She sits on the edge of the bed.

"Is that when he started beating you too?"

"No, that came later. The drinking made him mean, and our marriage fell apart. I tried to leave him one day. You were at summer camp. He came home early and saw that I'd packed a suitcase and he went mad. He had already lost everything, he wasn't losing the rest of his family."

"So, he beat you?"

She nods. "I felt sorry for him. I missed our boy too. He grew paranoid after that about me taking you away. Then every little thing I did was wrong."

"He needs help." I sit beside her and drape my arm over her shoulder.

"He's a proud man and will never ask for help."

I let out a big sigh. "He's never laid a hand on me."

"He's not angry with you."

"Fuck, Mom. This is messed up." I stand.

"Watch your mouth, Theo." She points a finger at me.

"None of this justifies what he's done to you."

"I keep hoping one day he'll realize, and I'll have my sweet husband back."

"That man you remember is gone, Mom. One of these days he's not going to stop until he kills you. Please, let's get out of here. We can go to Grandpa's house and call the police."

"I'm tired, Theo. We'll stay here tonight and pack in the morning after he's gone to work."

I kiss the top of her head. "Okay. Get some sleep, but we're getting out of here tomorrow."

CHAPTER 2
I TAKE AIM

Morning comes way too early when I hear my dad's raised voice. In one move, with only my boxers on, I jump out of bed and grab my gun. When I scramble into the living room, my dad's fist is drawn back in a striking motion.

"Don't do it." I cock the gun, and his head turns in my direction. He raises both his hands. "You need to leave and never come back." My teeth are clenched together, and I can feel the veins in my neck straining against my skin.

"Where did you get a gun?" His face looks ashen as he takes a step toward me.

"Get your shit and leave. Now!" I roar and wave the gun at him. My hand starts shaking, wanting him to walk away so I don't have to kill him. I'm not used to shooting left-handed, and I'm not sure how good my aim will be.

He stops in his tracks and hesitates as he stares at the barrel of my gun. When he finally moves, it's toward the door. He takes his jacket from the coat rack and glances back over his shoulder at my mother before he storms out the door.

"Pack your bags. We're getting out of here." I lower my gun and help my mom off the floor.

Her body is trembling as tears stream down her face as she runs to her room.

Walking over to the window, I see my father peel out of the driveway as the dust lifts in the air. The only other vehicle we own is in the barn on the other side of our ten-acre farm.

While Mom is in her room, I rush to mine and stuff a few things in my duffel bag and get dressed. I throw it over my shoulder and head to check on my mom. "Stay in here until I get back. Lock the door behind me. I'm going to the barn to get the pickup truck." I shut her door and wait to hear the click of the lock before I take off, out the back door. Running full speed on the dirt road that leads to the barn, I pull the keys from the hook and jump in.

Grrrrrr, grrrrrr. "Come on, damn it! Not today."

Grrrrrrr. I push on the pedal again. Grrrrrrr. "Shit!" I bang my fists on the steering wheel. The door swings open as I jump out and pop open the hood. The battery cables are corroded, thick with gray dust all over them. I take them off and find a wire brush in a toolbox on the shelf.

The flakes brush off as I scrub the connectors and the cables. I quickly refasten them and tighten both to make sure there is a good connection. Jumping back behind the wheel I turn the key again. Grrrrrrr, grrrrrr.

"Why does this beast never work when I need it to?" The gas needle is stuck on half full, and I have no idea when fuel was put in it last. The red gas can under the cabinet sloshes as I pick it up and pour it into the tank. I throw the can to the side and jump back in. Grrrrrr.

"Start already!" I beat my forehead on the steering wheel. I jump back out. With my head buried in the engine, I pull each spark plug one at a time. Two of them look bad. I don't have time for this. I'll have to call us a cab.

As I'm heading out the barn door, I see my dad's rifle that lays against the wall. I remember seeing a box of shotgun shells in one of the cabinets. I find the box and stick the shells in my pocket and fist the rifle in my hand. Looking toward the house, I see my dad's car parked sideways in the driveway.

I take off in a full run. I can hear my mother's screams. Her bedroom window is open, and I can see my dad striking her. I'm not going to make it there before he beats her to death. I squat down and yank hard on my cast, but only the cotton stuffing comes out. I reach in my pocket and pull out the shells and load it into the rifle. I get down low and rest the rifle in the dirt and balance it on my cast.

I see my dad pick up the lamp to strike her with it, and that's when I take my shot. One single shot and his body jerks, and he disappears from eyesight. Crawling out of the red dirt, I run as fast as I can to the house.

My dad's body is on the floor with blood pooling around his head. My mom sits beside him all bloodied and rocking back and forth. There's a single shot to his left temple, and his eyes are fixed open.

"Is he dead?" my mom cries.

I feel for a pulse, but there is none. I can feel mine beating outside my chest. "Give me your hand." I reach mine out. "We have to get out of here."

"No. We need to call the police and tell them

what happened. If we don't, you'll be on the run for the rest of your life."

She's right. It's either run or face the consequences. It was self-defense for my mother. He would've killed her this time. I reach over to the land-line and call 9-1-1.

"There's been a shooting." I want to scream, *I killed the bastard* into the phone.

"What's your address?" the operator asks. "Are you safe at this time?"

"Yes, but send an ambulance, my mother's been injured." I step over my dad's lifeless body and sit on the floor next to my mother. She cries, and I watch the dark red blood as it seeps into the carpet. I cradle her in my arms like a small child as she cries.

Neither one of us moves as the sirens come up the driveway. The front door creaks open. "Police, anybody here?"

"In here," I yell, and two officers walk in holding up their guns.

"Are you two okay?"

"He's dead," my mom says in a monotone voice.

He reaches down and feels for a pulse. "What happened?"

"I killed him."

The police officer calls for backup on his walkie-talkie. "We have a body, call in the coroner." His radio hisses with voices.

"You need to stand up, son."

I don't put up a fight. Mom stands with me, and we step over the body. As soon as I'm next to him, he starts reading me my rights and cuffs me with my hands behind my back.

"He was protecting me!" Mom yells.

"We still have to take him until the situation has been investigated. He's admitted to killing him, and with a homicide investigation, he has to be taken into custody."

"It's okay, Mom. Call an attorney and have them meet me down there. She needs to be examined," I tell the cop.

"I'll make sure she gets to the hospital," the officer responds.

The ambulance pulls off the property with my mother, and I'm thrown in the back of a smelly police car. When we arrive at the station, I'm taken to a room with a single table and two chairs. One wall has a mirror that I'm sure someone is standing behind, watching me.

After a long night of interrogation, I'm placed in a holding cell. I'm told I'll be in here until further investigation.

The next day, I'm assigned an attorney that looks to be my age, but I know he's not. He's tall and skinny in a freshly pressed suit and just out of law school. He looks eager, but nervous when a detective comes into the same room they had me in last night.

"I want to take the boy out to the crime scene." His deep voice is commanding, and my attorney simply nods.

We drive back out to the house, and when I see the spot that my father's blood stains the carpet, the reality of what I've done sinks in and I collapse to my knees with my hands cuffed behind my back.

The detective bends down and unlocks them, then helps me off the floor. "Come on, son. I want you to show me exactly where you were when you shot your father."

His kindness surprises me. I've seen lots of shows where the cops were assholes, but he's not. I lead him outside, and we walk through the grass out into the pasture until I'm about where I think I stood. Keeping my eyes to the ground, I search for the shotgun shell.

"I think I was in this area somewhere. There should be shell casings."

The deputy looks at me, then turns his head to

look at the house. "Are you sure? That's a pretty good distance."

"Pretty sure." I kick at the dirt, looking for it. My attorney stands quietly with his briefcase clutched in his hand; the detective starts looking a few feet behind me. When I don't find it where I am, I walk out a little further and see the casing.

"Here. I shot him from here." I point to the ground.

"You're telling me that you got one single shot to the head from this distance?" He walks over and picks up the casing.

I nod.

"Where did a boy your age learn how to shoot?"

"I taught myself." I shrug.

He stands and leans close to me. "You've been planning this for a while, haven't you, son?"

I nod again.

"I saw your mom's medical file, and I can't say that I blame you, but she never reported the bastard."

I stay quiet. My attorney is on his cell phone, not paying any attention.

"Did he ever hit you?"

"No, only her."

He takes a deep breath in and blows it out. "If

she would've reported the abuse, you'd walk away a free man."

"It was self-defense for my mom. He would've killed her this time."

He places his hand firmly on my shoulder. "I have no doubt from the looks of things, but unfortunately you're in deep shit."

"I don't care. I'd do it again if it meant saving her life."

"I might have an out for you. At least a way not to go to prison. I'll work on it, but for now, you'll be arrested for the murder of your father."

"Can I see my mom before you haul me off?"

"I'll have to cuff you again."

I hold out my hands and let him clasp the metal around my wrists. "Why are you being so nice to me?"

"Because if I would've seen my mother beaten the way you have, I can't say that I wouldn't have done the same thing at your age." We walk past my attorney who is still on the phone. "I would suggest we get you better representation." His thumb gestures over his shoulder.

We all climb back in the detective's car and head for the hospital as promised. Mom is in the ICU recovering. The doctor told me they had to rush her into the operating room last night to repair her internal injuries. She has a few more stitches in her head and a broken wrist, but she'll recover.

"Theo!" She tries to sit up in her hospital bed when she sees me.

"I'm okay, Mom." The detective unlatches my handcuffs.

"I'll be right outside the door," he warns.

I sit on the side of her bed, and she cries on my shoulder. "The doctor says you're going to be okay."

"What's going to happen to you?"

"I don't know yet, but whatever it is, I'll be fine, and you'll be safe."

CHAPTER 3

MY LIFE BEGINS AT EIGHTEEN

"It's all set up. You'll take the bus to Texas and an officer will escort you to military school." Detective Michaels leads me to the side of the bus to stow my bag.

The past month, he has fought for me every step of the way. He went to the judge himself and pleaded my case. He told him I wasn't a killer and that I had fiercely protective instincts, not to mention I had good aim and thought I'd serve a better purpose in the military than in jail.

The judge agreed to all charges being dropped if I was sent to military school for two years, but if I left or failed, I'd be sent to prison.

Two years later, I can say that it's the best thing that's ever happened to me. My shooting skills were so good, they enlisted me into a private training course geared for snipers. I became so skilled, I was asked if I'd be interested in joining a SEAL Team. My response was, "Hell yeah."

My mom has written me almost daily. She was lost at first without me around, but I encouraged her to sell the property and find a place to start over. She went back to school and took culinary classes, and that's where she met Cliff. She's sent me pictures of the two of them, and she's never looked happier or more beautiful. Faded scars are the only thing that remains from her time with my dad. She planned her wedding hoping that I could come, but it was written in the judge's order that I was not allowed to leave until I graduated.

That day is today. At eighteen years old, I finally get to start my life. I've made it through security at the airport and headed to gate eighteen. I've never flown in an airplane before much less been to Europe. I have a one-day layover in France, and I'm going to take advantage of it and explore as much as I can.

Almost every seat at the gate is taken. Several men, when they saw me in uniform, offered me their seat and thanked me for my service to the country. When they announce over the intercom for special boarding of military, elderly, and people with small children, I stay in my seat. I don't want any special treatment. I like to people watch, and I'm in a good place to do that.

My gaze follows a young brunette woman with the most beautiful hazel eyes I've ever seen. She doesn't notice me, but I can't take my eyes off her. I watch her until she's disappeared inside the plane. I grab my duffel and get in line.

"Row 24, seat C," I read my ticket. The flight attendant smiles and welcomes me on board. I make my way to the back of the plane, and there she is, Hazel. She's in the window seat in row 24. I place my bag in the overhead compartment and sit. Her eyes were closed until I jostled the seat. She has a shy, sweet smile on her beautiful face.

"My first time on a plane," I tell her, and then she tells me that she doesn't like flying. I'll distract her.

"Do you mind if I look out the window?"

She pulls up the window shade, and I slide over.

I purposely lean over her, and she sticks out her hand. "I'm Fallon."

"Theo." I smile, and my first thought is to kiss the back of her hand, but I'm guessing that would be pretty corny.

"How long have you been in the military?"

I smile and sit upright in my chair. "Eight weeks of boot camp and two years of military school. I'm on my way to my first assignment."

"You look so young."

"I was sixteen when I enrolled in school."

"Is it something you've always wanted to do?"

A pit builds in my stomach. I never had a chance to decide what I wanted to do with my life like normal people. "No, but my life will be better for it."

She looks at me like she senses something in me. "What are you going to be doing in the military?"

"I've trained to be a sniper for a Navy SEAL team." I feel a smile plaster on my face. This beautiful girl is really talking to me.

"That's awful ambitious. Good for you. I'm sure your parents are very proud."

And that quick, my smile fades, and I toy with the hat I've been holding in my hands. "My mom is. My dad passed a couple of years ago." I can hear my own voice drop off after mentioning my father. This is not a subject I want to broach.

"I'm sorry," she says, and peers out the window for the first time.

"Are you going on vacation by yourself." My words have her facing me again.

"No. I'm going on business, but I'm hoping for a little sightseeing while I'm there."

"Have you ever been to Europe before?"

"No."

"Well, then you have to take time and explore. I have one day before I catch another plane and report to duty. I've never been anywhere before. What do you say to us exploring it together?"

"I'd say I'm a little too old for you." She laughs.

I scowl. "You're too old to be my friend?"

She looks at me like I'm an innocent young kid. I may be sexually inexperienced, but I've lived far too much for my age.

"I'm sorry. You're right." She takes a map out of her bag. "I marked a few things on here I'd like to see if I found time. Do any of these look interesting to you?"

I take the map into my lap and study it. "We could take the train to the Château de Versailles—the home of King Louis XIV."

She pulls out her planner and looks at the times. "I think we could make that work."

"Great! It's a date then...I mean a non-date...not like a guy/girl date. Just friends." I chuckle. I'd love to have a date with her, but she probably thinks she's too old for me.

"This place is so exquisite. It says here in the brochure that the floor of The Royal Opera of Versailles can be raised to seat 1200 people." She looks around the opera room. "I wonder how old this wood is? It's still shiny and polished looking."

"It says here, the late 1700s, and did you know it was built as a celebration of the marriage of the dauphin—the future Louis XVI to Marie Antoinette," I tell her. I'd like to impress her, but I don't think reading if off a brochure will do it.

"Wouldn't it be great to see an opera here?"

"Not my thing, Hazel."

She stops running her hand down the wood walls. "Hazel?"

"You have the most beautiful hazel-colored eyes." I point to them.

"Are you flirting with me?" she asks, laughing and continues to explore.

"No, just stating the obvious." I chuckle. "I thought women loved a man in uniform and all my lines would work on you."

"They do, but I prefer mine to be a tad bit older."

"You know in a few years when I'm twenty-five..."

"I'll be almost forty." I walk by and punch him in the shoulder. "You're like a kid brother I never had."

"One day you're going to regret not taking me seriously." I laugh to hide my disappointment. "When I work out every day and get bulging muscles and can grow a beard, you'll be sorry." I flex my biceps.

"Let's go see the Hall of Mirrors while we're here." She takes my hand, and I follow her like a puppy in love.

WE SPENT the rest of our day exploring inside the palace and then took the train back to see the Eiffel Tower.

"Hazel, come here. Let's get a selfie with the tower in the background," I yell to her.

She's standing under the tower getting a picture looking up, and I'm down by the railing looking up, getting a picture. She snaps a shot and heads over to me.

"I may never see you again, so I want a picture of the two of us."

She joins me in the frame of my phone. "The one that got away," she teases me.

I hold my hand over my heart. "The one that broke my heart." I snap the shot as she turns to look at me.

"Hey, redo. I wasn't looking."

I hold the phone up again, and I peck her on the cheek and snap the picture again.

She laughs at my antics. "You're impossible. Now be still and take a serious one."

I pout out my lower lip. "Okay, Hazel. I'll be serious." I wrap an arm around her shoulder and lean into her side, then press the button.

"Are you happy now?" I show her the picture, and she snatches the phone from me. She sends the pictures to her phone.

She hands it back to me. "Thank you for today, Theo. I had a lot of fun."

"The day's not over yet. Let's go walk down by the water."

"I don't know. It's getting late, and I don't like to be out after dark in strange places. Besides, I really need to check into my hotel room. Where are you staying?"

"I don't know. Park bench." I shrug.

"You didn't make reservations?"

"I was planning on sleeping at the airport until my flight out tomorrow."

"Come on, you can stay with me."

I raise my eyebrows. A man can dream.

"On the couch...fully clothed." She laughs and takes my hand.

The feel of a woman's skin on mine is something I've never felt before, and I like the way her hand fits in mine. I wonder what her lips would taste like?

We check in, and she unpacks while I order us something to eat. We spend almost the entire night talking. Every time she would ask me about my family, I'd grow quiet. She seemed to take the hint and changed the subject.

When I wake up early to my alarm on my phone, there is not a peep coming from Hazel's room. I quietly open the door, and she's sound asleep with a small snore passing her lips. I've never in my life thought about what sexy is on a woman, but she would be my definition. Her long, lean, defined body has me hard as a rock as I stare at her. Too bad I have to leave. I'm sure given another day or two, I could make her fall in love with me.

I close the door behind me and find a notepad on the coffee table. For my own good, I should leave before she wakes up.

I put pen to paper and write.

Thanks for hanging out with me, Hazel. I'll

always cherish the time I spent with you and your kindness to a stranger. I hope your business goes well while you're here. And, your sister was right, try to have a little fun. You can skip meeting the hot man because I've already stolen your heart, you just don't know it yet.

In all seriousness, thank you, Hazel. I'll never forget you.

Your handsome and charming soldier - Theo

I meant what I wrote. I'll never forget her, but my life belongs to the military. I grab my duffel and take the elevator down to the foyer of the hotel, and the concierge calls a cab for me.

Just before I arrive at the airport, my phone rings and I almost don't answer it because I don't recognize the number.

"Hello."

"Hey, it's me Hazel."

"I knew you'd chase after me." I laugh.

"You left without saying goodbye."

"I didn't want to wake you, and I didn't want to miss my plane."

"Thank you, Theo. Stay out of harm's way and good luck becoming a SEAL. You're going to do great. Don't lose your sweetness. Ladies love that... and the uniform."

"You never know, our paths may cross again one day."

"They just may. Bye, Theo."

"Bye, Hazel." I really hope to run into her again one day.

CHAPTER 4
MEETING THE BADASS LEADER

"I'd like you to meet your new lead sniper, Petty Officer Theo Drake," Commander Lukas introduces me to the SEAL team leader, Captain Rebel. I stand tall and salute him, and all he does is eye me up and down.

"He's just a kid," he snarls and steps up close to me. "Your daddy pull some strings to get you here?"

"No, sir." I don't change my stance.

"What am I supposed to do, change his diaper when the enemy shoots at him?" He turns to face the commander, and he has his arms outstretched.

"Why don't you give the man a chance and see what he's capable of?" Commander Lukas stands strong with his hands on his hips.

"He's not a man, he's just a boy!" He flings a

hand around to point at me. "I asked for the best sniper in the military, and you send me some snot-nosed kid who's still riding on training wheels."

"He is the best." The commander crosses his arms over his chest.

"Why? Because his daddy wrote some big fat check to get him here?"

"Petty Officer Drake, go to the arsenal room and pick your weapon of choice. Meet me and Captain Rebel at the shooting range in fifteen minutes."

"Sir, yes, sir." I salute him and head out to find my weapon. I'm not mad at Captain Rebel. He's right. I am just a kid, but I have mad skills, and that's what I need to prove to him.

I find the shittiest piece of crap rifle I can find among the many weapons. If I can hit a target with this thing, he'll really be impressed. I gear up and meet them at the sniper range. They are standing off to one side, having what looks like a heated argument, and I'm sure my name is being thrown out there. I refuse to let him intimate me, even though he has a reputation for spitting out new recruits. The Gunner SEAL Team is one of the hardest teams to be a part of.

I secure the rifle around my shoulder and walk up next to them.

"Look, he can't even pick out a decent rifle. How do you expect me to work with him?" He points to my weapon and the commander laughs.

"I think he's trying to prove a point. This kid graduated with the highest levels I've ever seen in my career. I'm sure he knows his weapons."

"We'll see about that," Captain Rebel spits out. "Up on the mountain, there is a range target. If you can hit it from here with that piece of shit, you can join my team."

The commander steps close to him. "Derrick, you've never tested any of the other snipers that far out. That rifle he's totting can't be aimed that far."

"That's not my problem that he picked it out. And, if he's as good as you say he is, this distance shouldn't be a problem, should it, Petty Officer Drake." He squares his shoulders at me.

"Not a problem at all, sir." I take my rifle off my shoulder and make a few adjustments to the scope. Hopping down in the dirt hole, I brush off a mound of piled dirt until it's level. I rest the rifle on it and look through the scope, scanning the area for the target. It's a good clip out, and for the first time, I'm having doubts as to whether it was a good idea to be a smart-ass and pick this piece of shit. The target is further out than I've ever shot with my ideal weapon.

I crack my neck from side to side as sweat starts to bead down my face. I can feel the dampness building under my fatigues. I blow out a few deep breaths and get in position. My father's face flashes before my eyes, and I dig in my elbows to set for a better aim.

Just as I'm about to pull the trigger, a few men crowd around Captain Rebel. Their voices are quiet, but I can still hear their comments.

"Are you taunting the new kid?" One of them laughs.

"I got twenty bucks says he hits the mark," another one says and pulls out his wallet.

"I'll take that bet," yet another man says, and they're all handing cash to Captain Rebel.

"I'll tell you what, let's make this interesting for those that bet against him. If he misses the target, I'll give you each an extra week off to spend with your families. If he hits it, you're going to take turns cleaning his weapons after practice every day for a month."

"I'll take that deal. So, will I," a couple of them say. "Hell, I'll even wash his feet every day if he hits that target." I look up to see the name Byrd on his patch.

I concentrate on ignoring the rest of their

comments and focus on the small target marked with an X. My finger rests on the trigger as I adjust slightly in my scope. I watch the wind's direction, and I adjust again. Taking aim, I hold my shoulders in tight and lock my gaze. In one swift movement, without any hesitation, I squeeze the trigger. The sound carries in the distance. I pull up and lean back in the ditch, not even looking to see if I hit my mark.

"Severs, go see if he even grazed it." Captain Rebel chuckles.

Severs takes off in a run toward the target. I climb out of the ditch and brush off my clothes, then stand a few feet away from the men.

"I can't wait to get that extra week with my family," one of them says and pulls off his hat.

I stand and wait quietly for Severs to make his way back. He gives nothing away as he trots back up with the target behind his back.

"Well?" Captain Rebel says, holding out his hand.

"Not only did he hit the target, the bullet went right through the middle of the X." He hands him the metal target.

He looks at it and then looks at me. Several of them moan, and the commander laughs as he starts counting the cash.

Captain Rebel hands me the target. "Where did you learn to shoot like that?"

I shrug. "Someone pissed me off once, and I started practicing."

He steps back and salutes me. "Welcome to the Gunner SEAL Team, Petty Officer Drake."

I right my rifle on my shoulder and stand at attention, saluting him.

"I told you the boy was good." Commander Lukas slaps him on the shoulder as he walks by him.

"Come on, kid. I'll teach you how to fit into this motley crew." He plants his hand on my back, and I follow him into a tent that's a makeshift bar.

"I don't drink, sir," I say, but take the barstool beside him.

He laughs. "You will."

The rest of the men join us, and one by one, they shake my hand, introducing themselves. I sip on my Coke and listen to their stories as they razz one another.

Captain Rebel tells me each one of their skills and what part they play in the Gunners. They all seem to have a bond with one another like none I'd ever seen.

Whistles fill the bar when Commander Lukas walks in with a beautiful woman with long sexy legs sticking out from her blue fitted skirt. Her mocha-colored hair hangs around her shoulders and face. Captain Rebel stands to greet them.

"This is your new handler for the team," the commander says.

The woman sticks out her hand. "Nina Pax."

"Captain Rebel," he says and pushes me off the barstool with his shoulder. "Join us." He smiles, and all the men surround her.

CHAPTER 5

THE MISSION

Two years later...

As promised, the blades are rotating as the last man finds his seat and straps into it. The sun has just tucked in for the night, and the cool desert air flows through the Blackhawk.

There are very few lights on the ground, and the pilot is flying blind. Every now and then the bird jostles to go around one of the mountains.

"Sir, we will be landing in the next fifteen minutes," the pilot yells over his shoulder.

Captain Rebel doesn't ask if we are ready; he knows we are. "When we get close to the ground, make sure to stay low when you land. Keep your head down and locked and loaded, ready for anything. Drake, you hang with me. We'll be out front. Severs, you divide the rest of the team and split them on our wings. You stay in the back with Barker." I know he wants me with him so I can scout out in front and take out any necessary targets.

"It's going to take us some time to make it to Bari's house on foot. Get your jackets on and make sure to drink plenty of water. I don't need you getting dehydrated on me. I'll protect you, but I'm not carrying your sorry asses across the desert because you tried to be a tough guy," Captain Rebel orders.

"Remember, our mission is to bring Bari in alive unless we can't. None of you are to go in alone. Always have your backup partner."

"Sir, I'm bringing this bird as close as I can to the ground," the pilot says.

One by one, each of us jumps with his gear to the ground. We roll and stay low, making it into the ridge of a mountain. The darkness helps hide us, but we don't know what's waiting for us. Each of us puts on our night goggles and gets our weapons ready.

Eight men strong, we take off in the direction of Bari's house. There are areas we have to crawl on our hands and knees to get under sheets of barbed wire that have been laid out to keep out their enemies. Strands of clothing and flesh hang from the barbs where others have tried to make it through. I blow out a deep breath. We've trained for this, and I won't let fear take hold of me.

When we all make it out, Dutch pulls out his bomb-detecting equipment and starts running it back in forth in the sand. We follow one step at a time in his path. He finds several buried and changes our direction. We have to move due east before we can start moving north.

"This is a designed path to keep people out. Keep your eyes open for Bari's men." I pull my weapon closer to my body.

I drop to the ground, aiming my rifle in front of me. All the men follow suit and drop to the ground. Captain Rebel crawls up next to me. "What do you see?"

"There, in the hole in the side of the mountain, there are two men on lookout."

"Can you take them both out?"

"Does a monkey eat bananas?" I laugh quietly. Reaching inside my pocket, I pull out my silencer and place it on the end of my rifle. Then I take aim, dropping one and then the other right behind him.

Without a word, we get up, and Dutch continues his search for bombs until we make it to where our path is all hard rock.

"Shit," Byrd says under his breath. "There are wooden spikes stuck between the crevices of the rocks." He's holding pressure to his thigh.

"How bad is it?" Captain asks him.

"It ripped through my skin pretty good."

Darcy, being our medic, removes his goggles and pulls out a small flashlight from his pack and examines it. "He could really use some stitches."

"Clean it up and slap some Steri-Strips on it," Byrd says.

Darcy takes out his first aid kit and rinses out the wound, then pulls the skin together and applies the strips to hold it together. "Done."

"We need to keep moving, keep away from the spikes, and look for other booby traps. Drake, you scout out ahead of us. Stop when you get to the ridge," Captain orders.

"Yes, sir." I take off up the side of the mountain. Spikes are ripping through my pants, but I keep moving, not letting it slow me down. I make it to the top to see faint lights from a compound. Men are guarding the front. I scan the area with my goggles, and there is a troop of armed men not far from where the Gunners should round the mountain. I adjust my position to head off and warn my team.

I wait silently until I see them in the gap of the

mountain. Then I take my flashlight from my bag and flash it on and off in Morse code. I know Barker will get the message, it's his specialty.

I make it down to them in no time. "Sir, once you cross the next section, there is a camp full of armed men sitting between us and Bari's house. There are too many of them for us to take out." I'm out of breath from hustling down the side of the mountain.

"Then we'll go to plan B." Captain pulls out a map of the area from his bag.

"I don't remember there being a plan B." Dutch takes off his helmet and scratches his head.

"There is always a plan B with Rebel." Severs laughs.

"We'll set up camp here for a few hours. Just before dawn, we are going to change our route and come in on the other side of them." He points to a path on the map.

"But, sir, his house is built inside that mountain. If we go around it, we won't be able to get inside," I add.

"Then we better hope that Bari has an escape exit out the back of this mountain. In my experience, there is never just one way in and one way out."

"So why don't we keep moving. The plan was to take him in the dark," Bryd questions.

"Because there's a good chance we won't find the other entrance in the dark. I'm sure it's very well camouflaged." He looks at his watch. "You have two hours to get some shut-eye. I'll keep watch here, and Drake can keep an eye out from his perch on the mountain."

"Yes, sir." I take off into the dark.

I make it back up and lay out all the gear I'm going to need to make sure no one makes a move toward the Gunners. I set my alarm for two hours later.

CHAPTER 6

LIVING HELL

I show up right on time to hear Captain Rebel already barking orders. "Listen up. We're going to follow Drake up this mountain and over the other side. Then we're going to make our way behind Bari's mountain. He may have more of his men guarding the backside too. I want dead silence as we move. Keep your eyes open at every angle. Don't shoot your weapons unless it's necessary. Drake, that doesn't include you. You keep your silencer on and if you have a clear shot, take it. Now let's move."

Most of our climb is vertical. I don't know how I did this in the dark and didn't tumble down the side of the mountain.

"Climb up a few feet and tie some rope off.

We'll have to go up a section at a time. How in the hell did you make it up here not once but twice in the dark?"

"I'm like a cat, sir. I can climb anything." I skate up like it's nothing while the rest of the men pull their weight up with the rope, one by one. Then, we move to the next section, repeating the process of tying off the rope until we've made it to the top. Orange and pink are slathered across the sky tucked in between dark gray rain clouds.

"Great, that's all we need in this shit," Captain snarls.

"I fucking hate getting rained on," Barker grumbles and pulls his helmet lower. "I'm getting way too old for this shit. I'm thinking retirement on some island that never gets rain."

"You'd miss the action too much," Captain says as we start making our way back down the other side of the mountain. He stops on the ledge and looks out. "There are smooth areas over there. I bet we could sit on our asses and slide down. Tie all our gear together, and we'll pull it down behind us." He points.

We start looping together our gear. Once we reach the softer area, the first man down takes the rope with him. The next one sits and grabs one of the bags to help it move down. One by one, we each make our way to the bottom and gear back up.

I'm the first man down, and I'm on lookout with my binoculars.

"Any sight of Bari's men?" Captain asks.

"No, but if there is a back way in, I'm sure they are out there."

"Keep moving. Scout out the area before we get there and keep your head low."

I nod and take off in a trot.

"We need to make it across this open area as fast and as quietly as we can. Keep your eyes peeled for traps but keep moving," I hear him say before I put distance between us.

Once I'm hidden from the enemy and have a view of the team, I see the men following close behind the captain. They all have their rifles out and ready. When they make it halfway across, I wave for them to run. They make it in time to hide behind some rocks as a caravan drives through the pass. They're moving slowly and are filled with armed men in the back, leading away from Bari's house.

"Do you think they spotted us?" Barker ducks his head lower.

"No, but they're looking for something. Other-wise, they'd be moving quicker," Captain responds.

A few of the trucks stop, and several men pile out, keeping their weapons drawn. "We've got to get the fuck out of here. If they see our footprints, we're done for. Get your bags and crawl to the other side," he orders us.

As soon as we start to move, the rain lets down, making some of the rocks we're crawling over slick.

A weapon dislodges in the air from the pass, signaling that they've found something. We crawl faster until we make it to the back of the mountain that Bari's house is in.

"I'm betting that's a way in, sir." I point to where two men are standing guard. "I can take them both out."

"You need to do it in a hurry, son. Those men behind us will catch up with us soon." He turns toward his team. "Severs, you and the rest of the team stay behind and hold them off as long as possible. Drake and I are going into Bari's house. If we capture him, we'll have leverage to stop his men."

"And if you don't?" Severs asks, already knowing the answer.

"Then we're all dead because someone tipped them off that we're here."

I take out both men guarding the back, and we take off in a full run to where they're dead on the ground. One is shot directly between the eyes, the other in the temple. "Good shot. Neither one of them knew what hit them."

"Help me push this rock out of the way." Severs is grunting trying to move it with all his might.

Gunshots ring out from behind us. Captain leans into the rock, and we push it far enough out of the way to get inside. We can see light coming from the other end of the tunnel and voices shouting out. We both move close to the slick walls and make our way toward it. As someone goes out the front door and leaves Bari alone, we both rush into the room, aiming our weapons at him.

"Don't move and don't utter a sound or I'll kill you." Captain aims at his head.

He raises his hands in the air. "Move to the tunnel." He cocks his head in the direction without lowering his gun.

His white clothes glow in the tunnel as he moves slowly toward where we came in.

"How did you get inside my house?" he asks in broken English.

"Shut up and keep moving." I nudge him with the tip of my rifle.

He stumbles but catches himself on the rock wall. "My men will kill you."

"Not if we use you as a shield, and if they kill you, then our job is done here," Captain says from behind me.

"This place is surrounded by my men. You'll never make it out of here alive."

"Never underestimate us. We made it this far." Captain grits his teeth.

When we make it back to the rock, there's smoke coming from the area we left the team. Shots are still being fired, but we can't tell who's firing them.

"I had the other team that was sent here tortured. You, my brother, are going to have the same fate," Bari taunts us.

Captain Rebel loses his cool and decks him. "I'm not your fucking brother. If I had my way, I'd kill you with my bare hands." His fingers are wrapped around his throat.

I don't stay to see if he kills him. I take off running, picking off men as I move.

When we make it to them, I see Bryd laying in the sand with vacant eyes and blood pooling on the earth around him. Barker has a bullet in the thigh and Severs is popping up from behind a rock, still taking out Bari's men.

Dutch, Darcy, and Smyth are partially hidden behind a layer of smoke. Smyth is screaming out in agony. A hot round of mortar struck him, and his foot is lying on the ground next to him. Darcy is removing his belt and tying off Smyth's leg.

"Help him up!" Captain Rebel yells at Dutch. "We have to get moving," Smyth screams out as he hoists him up. We back out of the area and head due east. I stay out in front.

We are within a mile of our pickup point when a loud noise has all of us covering our ears. The last thing I remember is light flashing.

CHAPTER 7

HE SAVES MY LIFE

I hear a faint dripping sound, but I'm not sure where it is coming from. Blinking my eyes, I see Captain Rebel tied to a chair, and his right eye is swollen shut. It's the blood from his face dripping down that I hear.

His head is yanked up from behind by Bari. He has one of our military guns in his hand. I go to move my right arm to get up, only to realize it's gone. The smell of burnt skin mixed with blood and pain has me nearly unconscious, but I fight it.

"I see you're still with us, Captain Derrick Rebel." Bari spits in his face. "So unfortunate for you and your friend." He glares in my direction.

Captain Rebel fights at his binds. "Let him go." His voice cracks. "Where are the rest of my men?"

"You're in no position to be asking me questions, but this one, I will enjoy answering. They're all dead, just like the other team that was sent here. When will you Americans learn that you can't stop me? The more you try to fight me, the more innocent people in your country will die."

"You're a sick little fuck!" the captain yells. I see the moment he frees his hands.

Bari has the laugh of a young boy. "You have no idea how powerful I am."

"Even the powerful fall. We took your father out, and you'll be next."

I can see Bari's anger running through his body. He balls his fist up to strike him but stops. "You're a dead man, but because of your words, I will make it slow and painful." He motions for one of his men to come over. He's yielding a blood-stained sword and has grenades on either side of this thick black belt.

"I made it this far, I deserve to know who tipped you off that we were coming." Captain spits blood out at Bari's feet.

Bari rubs his boot in it and then squats down in front of him. "You do deserve to know because it will cause you much pain."

"Wait, how did you know my name was Derrick?"

Someone with a black mask covering the lower part of their face comes up from behind him and then moves to face him.

"Ekko." I hear the pain in his voice.

She reaches up and pulls down the mask. "I tried to convince you not to come on this mission, but you're one stubborn SEAL."

"You're responsible for the death of my men? They trusted you. I fucking trusted you! Why would you do this?" Blood spews from his mouth as he yells at her.

"They were the highest bidder. Bari realizes my worth. He knows my knowledge will make him more powerful and richer than any other person on this earth."

"Money! This is all about money for you!"

"It's always been about money."

Anguish takes over his face. "Let Drake go. Kill me but let him go."

She kneels down in front of him. "I'd rather you watch him die than kill you." She runs her hand down the left side of his cheek. "I cared enough about you to try to get you out of this mission. Why couldn't you have obeyed orders? I'm going to miss fucking you. Better yet"—she stands—"maybe I'll keep you around and fuck you anytime I want."

I see his ropes fall to the ground. He reaches up and grabs the grenade off Bari's belt. He pulls the pin and topples in his chair. He lands on me hard, covering my body from the blast I know is about to come. I hear the grenade roll across the floor, feet scattering, and voices yelling to run.

The loud explosion echoes through the room. I feel him tuck in his head as debris flies through the room and I feel the hit as something lands on us, and the pain knocks me out.

"Drake, are you alive?" I faintly hear him say and feel for a pulse. He moves off me, and through the slits in my eyes, I see Bari's body. He's got a gaping wound in his neck where all his blood has drained out of him.

I'm in and out of consciousness as I'm bounced on the captain's shoulder. Pain sears my side with every step he takes, and I can't help but let out a groan. He lays me down on the ground and starts looking for the medical kit. He finds Darcy's bag and digs out dressings and applies them to where my arm used to be.

"You're going to be okay. I'm going to get you out of here," he keeps telling me. He holds my head up and gives me sips of water."

"Are they..." I swallow. "Are they all dead?"

He hangs head and tears flood out. "Yes," he sobs.

I get enough strength to raise my left hand and place it on his shoulder before I pass out again.

The next thing I remember is him placing me on the ground. I see a Blackhawk not far from us. Captain waves his arms in the air. As men run toward us, Captain Rebel falls face down in the desert sand next to me.

They pick us both up and drag us to the Blackhawk. I hear Captain Rebel tell them, "They need to be brought home," then I'm out again.

CHAPTER 8

WAKING UP IN THE HOSPITAL

When I woke up in the hospital, I was confused and in a lot of pain. I ripped out my lines and alarms went off. Nurses rushed in to hold me down until they could get me a sedative. It took me a while to remember what happened and how I got here.

I've been in and out of consciousness for several days. Today is the first day I've been awake enough to try to eat. A middle-aged nurse, who's been by my side almost daily, is trying to get me to eat something. I glance through the window in the hall, and I see the reflection of Captain Rebel. At that moment, it all hits me and tears pool down my cheeks.

I see the anguish on his face the moment he clears the door. "I'm so sorry, Theo."

I suck in my tears and raise my head off the pillow. "I'm alive because of you."

He pulls up a padded wooden chair and sits next to my bed. "You lost your arm because of me."

"How do you think any of this was your fault?"

Leaning forward, he rests his elbows on his knees and his head on his fists. "Nina." Her name gets caught in his throat.

"You're not responsible for the actions of our handler. She's the one that killed our team. She set us all up."

He doesn't say anything, but I can tell a lot is being said in his head.

"Please tell me that they caught her?" My sobs escape.

"No, they did not." Commander Lukas says from the doorway. "I was hoping that there was something the two of you could tell us that might give us a clue as to where she went. As of right now, she's a ghost."

"She didn't tell me anything while she was trying to kill me, sir. I do know that we got Bari and that's who she was working for, so she's probably on the run trying to find a new place of employment," Captain Rebel seethes.

"You're confirming that Bari is dead."

"A grenade took him out. Nina was in the same

room when it went off, but there was no sign of her when the dust cleared the room."

"She has made it to the top of our most wanted list for war crimes. It's imperative that you tell us everything that happened."

He nods. "What's going to happen to Theo?"

"He'll be shipped back to the States and fitted for a state-of-the-art prosthetic."

"Will I be able to get back on a SEAL team, sir?"

"I'm afraid not, son. Your war days are over."

I rest my head back, and my broken body starts to shake. Captain Rebel wraps his arm around me and cries with me.

"I swear to you, I'll find her, and when I do...I'll have no problem killing her." He whispers the last part next to my ear.

The nurse gives me a sedative to help calm my body. Captain Rebel stays by me until I finally relax, and I drift off to sleep.

A WEEK LATER, after reliving day after day what happened in my head, I'm released from the hospital in time to go to the ceremony for the men in my team.

The caskets of the men have a flag draped over each of them. Their families have gathered around. I know them by the pictures that the men used to share. I stood back and watched as Captain Rebel shook each of their hands. I don't broach him until he sits with his family.

"Hey, Cap." I take a seat behind him. "I know what you're thinking. I feel it too."

He turns to look at me. "Where's your family?"

"My mom just got remarried and is on her honeymoon."

He stands, grabs a chair from my row and sets it beside him and points to it. "Today you're my brother by all sense of the term." He moves his brother over and takes the seat between us. We sit shoulder to shoulder, listening to the service until it's his turn to speak.

He looks down at the small podium and blinks back his tears.

"I had the honor of serving with these men. They were some of the bravest men in the military. They were my brothers, my best friends." His voice cracks, "I loved each and every one of them and would've given my life for them. They followed me into the most hellacious bowels of the earth without question.

And...I was responsible for them, yet they lost their lives...and here I stand."

I get out of my seat and stand in front of him. "They followed you because you were a good leader and they knew you had their backs." I stand and move next to him. "I know this because I felt the same way. We knew the risk. They knew the risk." I sweep my hand out toward the caskets. "We fought anyway. Each of us had our own reasons as to why we chose to fight. The best thing that happened was when the eight of us got paired together with you in charge. I remember the first day we all met. On the outside, I was a cocky young kid. On the inside, I was terrified. The experience all of you had over me made me look like I should still be in diapers. But you gave me a fair chance. You had read my records and told me not to doubt that I belonged in the team. I watched you grow every one of these men's skills, and you equally learned from them. That's a leader. You're not responsible for these men not making it back alive. It was a choice they made with every mission they took. You're not responsible for me losing my arm. If not for you, I'd be in one of those draped coffins today. You protected me with your life and almost lost yours bringing me home." I pat him on the shoulder and then return to my seat by his brother.

He's quiet for a moment, trying to regain his composure. He clears his throat and continues. "I'm sorry for the loss of these brave soldiers. They sacrificed so that our world could be a safer place for our families. I'm honored to have been part of that with them."

After the ceremonies are over, I stay by his brother's side. He's convinced me to come stay with him while I recover and go to physical therapy. A few hours later, his parents catch a flight back home, and Sean stays behind.

"I think we could all use a drink," Sean says, slapping his hand on the back of his brother's shoulder.

"That's the best thing I've heard all day."

One drink led to another and then another. Sean and I end up carrying Rebel back to his room. "Get some sleep, man." His brother tucks him in.

Sean and I stayed up the rest of the night. I shared stories with him about our mission. He asked lots of questions about Ekko. I didn't have answers for him other than the little I knew about her and how much Rebel loved her.

CHAPTER 9
STARTING OVER

T*wo years later...*

"Hey. Derrick. Check out my arm." I raise and lower it and move my robotic fingers. "This is so cool." I can't believe how far I've come. It's been trial and error over the past two years, getting the right fit. Lots of pain and physical therapy and fighting several infections. I've finally got the right state-of-the-art prosthetic. It almost feels natural.

"Yeah, cool." He downs another beer.

"Commander Lukas signed the recommendation that I could be put back on active duty teaching young new cadets on the firing range."

"Good for you, man. Far stretch from being a

SEAL." He reaches over the bar and gets another bottle of beer.

"He asked about you."

"Who?"

"Commander Lukas."

"Ah, and what did you tell him?"

"I told him you're still being a dick." I laugh.

"Let me guess." He turns on his barstool to face me. "He wanted to know if I'd skipped out on any of my therapy lessons?"

"Skipped out would be stretching it. You actually have to go to one to skip out on one." I use finger quotes with my new hand. "See, isn't that cool."

"Tell him to reinstate me, and I'll go to all the therapy sessions he wants me to."

"That's not how it works, and you know it. Why are you being so damn stubborn?"

He slams his empty beer bottle on the bar. "It's a fucking waste of my time. She's long gone by now. Like he said two years ago, a ghost."

"When are you going to move on? None of us saw through her."

"Move on. Six of my men are dead because I was blind to a woman and she just disappears!"

"All I'm saying is, if you'd go to the classes and quit

wallowing in your own self-pity, you might get your job back. Instead, you enjoy not sleeping, walking around the city at night, drinking your days away. As far as I can tell"—I get up—"you're not the man I would follow into battle. You've let that bottle take all your good senses. As far as I can tell, you've completely given up."

The barstool slams to the floor as he moves toward me. Sean comes out of nowhere and grabs him from behind.

"You ungrateful little shit!"

"Derrick, that's enough." Sean is holding him back.

I laugh. "Ungrateful would've been me sulking for the past two years because I lost my arm. Instead, I've done the work, and I sleep at night. That's more than I can say for you."

He lunges toward me again.

"Theo, I think you need to leave," Sean tells me. "Not that I don't agree with you one hundred percent, but I don't need a bar fight in here tearing this place up."

Derrick shrugs out of his hold. "Get the fuck out of here!"

I raise my mechanical hand and show how well my middle finger works. "You think you're the only person that's ever been betrayed or shit happens to? I picked up my first gun at sixteen years old and started practice shooting every day." I pause as my lip starts to quiver. "My old man used to beat the shit out of my mom routinely. I'd come home to find her laying in a pool of blood more times than I could remember. So, I practiced and practiced my shooting skills, and that's how I'm as good a sniper as I am today."

"Where is your father now?" he asks.

"Six feet under, and my mom is remarried and happy." I turn on my boot heel and head upstairs.

A few minutes later, Sean is beating on my door. "Theo, you in there?"

Opening the door, I let him in, and he takes a seat on my gray couch. "Ignore him, man. I'm glad you're getting your life back. I'm proud of you, and so is he. He just can't get his head out of his ass to see it."

I take a seat on the couch with him. "He used to be somebody I respected and now he doesn't even resemble the man that lead our team."

"He'll get there eventually, but don't let him drag you down. Besides, I'm betting you're not the same man that followed him into battle either. You're a leader now. I don't know too many men that would've kept the good attitude you have after losing your arm. I don't think I've ever heard you complain about it once."

"It's an arm. I'm grateful to be alive." I open and close my hand, making a fist.

"That thing really is lifelike." He chuckles.

"I went to the shooting range the other day and shot a pistol with it."

"How'd you do on aim."

"Completely missed the target, but I'll get there. I've gotten pretty damn good with my left hand."

"How are you going to teach if you can't hit a target?"

"I'll teach the mechanics of it, and I'll keep practicing until I'm the best shot out there."

"I'm sure you will." He slaps me on the shoulder and stands.

"Do you want to arm wrestle?" I flex my mechanical arm back and forth.

"Not so I can be embarrassed by you kicking my ass with that thing." He laughs and heads out the door.

I prop my feet up on the couch and rest my left hand behind my head. Stretching out my mechanical arm, I stare at the components of it. As good as it is, I can't feel with it. If I let myself, in the quiet moments, I try to envision being with a woman and what it would feel like. Would it be repulsive to someone? I've never been with a woman and maybe because of this thing, I never will.

Both Sean and I have tried for a couple days now to get ahold of Derrick, but he doesn't answer the phone. I've been by his place several times, but it's locked down tight. I may be pissed at him, but he's my friend, and I'd like to find a way to help him.

As I'm coming down the stairs to head to the bar, I hear someone talking to Sean.

"Hey, Sean."

I hit the landing and realize it's Derrick. I should give him and Sean the space to talk things out.

"Theo, Sean, can we talk?" he asks as I turn around.

"Not if you're going to be a dick again," I snarl.

"Or tell me to go fuck myself," Sean crosses his arms over his chest.

"Quite the opposite." He pulls out a barstool for me to sit. "I'm sorry, to both of you. I wanted you to know that I've been going to therapy, and I haven't had a drink in over a month. I know it's not much, but it's a start."

My defensives fall. "That's great, man. I'm glad to hear it." I put my hand on his shoulder.

"Does that mean you're going to be my badass brother again?" Sean chuckles.

"Given time, maybe. I hope to be that man you can be proud of again."

"I'll toast to that." Sean fills three glasses with water. "This will have to do." He hands one to his brother and one to me. We clink our glasses together. "Here's to getting my brother back," Sean cheers.

"Me too," I say and man-hug Derrick with one arm. "I've missed you, man."

"I've got a long way to go, but I know I can count on the two of you giving me grief if I go off track."

I release him and clink his glass with mine. "You know it, brother."

"Theo, I'm sorry for not knowing your story. It was my job as your leader to know my men, and I had no idea about your family."

"It's all right. Don't beat yourself up. I hadn't been under your command as long as the other men, and it was about the time you started seeing Ekko."

"So, you're saying he was too preoccupied with a woman to get to know your story," Sean adds.

"Thanks for clarifying that." He glares at Sean.

"All I can say is that I'm sorry and I'll never let a woman cloud my brain again."

"I don't think that's what she was clouding," Sean says and they both laugh.

The bar door opens, and my gaze is glued to who walks inside. The clicking of heels comes toward us in a rush.

"Please I need help," a frantic, out-of-breath woman's voice says, and I turn around. "Someone is following me."

I know this woman.

REBEL'S RETRIBUTION

FATED LIVES SERIES

Book Four

CHAPTER 1

FALLON

"Hazel, what are you doing here?"

I blink twice at the familiar face of a boy, now a man. "Theo?"

"You're trembling," he says as he walks me over to a wooden barstool that butts up against a brass footrail at a high counter. A good-looking man with a scar on the side of his face is staring at me. The other man behind the bar with his white sleeves rolled up, I recognize from hanging the neon sign. The only other person is a businessman hunched over at the end of the bar, grunting for a refill. The sports bar seems out of place for a man with a carefully knotted silk tie; it screams he doesn't belong here. With as many empty bottles that are sitting in front of him,

I'd say he's a man on a mission: to dull the pain as quickly as possible.

The scuff of a bar stool on the floor gets my attention back on why I ran in here. "Someone is following me." I point to the large pane window with the flashing sign.

Theo walks up to it and looks out. "I don't see anyone," he says, craning his neck around.

"I'm Derrick, this is my brother Sean," the man sitting on the barstool says.

"Fallon."

"I thought he called you Hazel?" He motions toward Theo.

"It's a nickname I gave her. Look at those beautiful eyes." He's standing in front of me again. It's not until then I notice his mechanical hand sticking out from his long sleeve.

"How do you two know each other?" Sean asks while he clears the amber beer bottles from in front of his only customer.

"I met Hazel on the plane, right before I joined the Gunners. She was on her way to Europe, and I was the lucky passenger that shared her row."

"That's right, and you were on your way to your first assignment."

He rubs his hand down his arm like it aches.

"Yeah, Derrick was the leader of the SEAL team I joined."

"Are you home on leave?" My curiosity has my fear settling down.

"We've both retired," Derrick says and gulps down his drink and thuds the empty glass on the counter.

"You looked frightened when you walked in the door. What's going on?" Theo sits beside me.

"I think there was someone in my house and in my office. A man with a mask started following me on my way home."

"You live around here?" Theo's brows furrow.

"Yeah, a few blocks over."

"I live here too, above the bar. Funny I haven't seen you around."

Derrick is up and on his feet. The front door to the bar squeaks open on its hinges as he slings it open to look outside. "You said he had a mask on?"

"Yeah, black mask, with only his eyes showing."

"Why would someone be following you?" Sean asks as he throws a bar towel over his shoulder and fills the clear plastic containers on the bar with limes.

"I have no idea." A wave of fear hits me again. "May I have a glass of water?" I ask Sean.

"Sure." He takes a glass from the rack above his

head and sprays water from a nozzle into it. He then slides a cardboard beer coaster in front of me and places the glass on it.

"What type of business are you in?" Derrick asks, sitting back on the barstool. Sean turns down the volume of the TV affixed on the wall behind him.

"I'm an online personal trainer."

He strokes his hand over his scruffy chin. "That doesn't sound like the type of business that would make you any enemies."

"I don't have any enemies that I know of."

A few more patrons come into the bar and take a seat in a booth. Their voices are loud as they laugh about something that happened at work. Sean moves from behind the bar to take their order.

"There's no one out there now. Are you sure you didn't imagine it?" Derrick fills his glass with water and tops mine off.

"Why would I imagine someone in a black mask." My irritation rises with the need to get back to my sister. I jump off the barstool and tug my top down. "May I borrow the phone to call for a cab?"

"We can walk you back to your apartment." Theo elbows Derrick in the side and his water sloshes on the counter.

"No, it's okay, but thanks for the offer."

Derrick wipes the counter with a thin napkin. "I wouldn't suggest you going home alone if you think there was someone really following you." His stool scrapes the floor again.

I get the feeling he's irked at me as his jaw flexes several times. "It's all right. I can manage on my own."

"You're not going by yourself." Theo glares a disapproving look at Derrick. "Don't move a muscle, I'll be right back. Don't let her leave." He points to Derrick and takes the stairs two at a time.

"Tell Theo I couldn't wait." I start toward the door, and Derrick's large hand reaches out and snags my elbow.

"I can't let you leave. Theo would kick my ass."

I scan his body. He's at least a foot taller than Theo and muscles protrude from underneath his clothes. Theo is firm and leaner but has nothing on this man. "I highly doubt that." I laugh.

"Don't underestimate him. He's strong as an ox and scrappy." His gaze holds mine as he searches my body up and down. He looks at me like I'm familiar to him, but someone he doesn't care for and has a bad taste in his mouth.

I'm not sure why this man hates me so much, but

I don't want to be near him. I shrug out of his grasp. "I'll take my chances." I open the door and Theo bounds down the stairs, tucking something into the back of his pants.

He exchanges a look with Derrick, and they follow me outside. The moon is covered by a dark cloud, and a fine mist of rain is starting to fall. Typical for this time of year in Portland.

My limbs feel shaky as I move onto the sidewalk. My eyes are wide looking around. A dull streetlamp flickers overhead, casting shadows on the sidewalk. Cars are starting to line up, parking against the curbs. A tail pipe backfiring has me grabbing onto Theo's arm.

"It's okay. I've got you," he says, placing his hand on mine.

We walk past a mom-and-pop restaurant with a chalk welcome sign on its doorstep. The smell of Italian food fills the air along with soft music coming from inside. I startle again when two kids whiz by on skateboards. The wheels make a thumping sound rolling over the bumpy sidewalk.

Derrick keeps his eyes peeled. "I'm going to hang back and see if anyone follows you," he says, stepping into an alleyway. I look back to see him lean his large muscular frame against a brick wall.

"He doesn't like me much," I whisper to Theo.

"I don't think he likes anyone much." He laughs.

"What happened to your arm, Theo?"

"It got blown off on my last mission. That cranky bastard saved my sorry ass." He motions with his thumb over his shoulder to Derrick.

"I'm so sorry."

"Don't be. I'm better than ever."

CHAPTER 2
REBEL

I cross my arms over my chest and hang closer to the old building to stay out of the rain. "Damn woman reminds me of Nina." Her hair is the same mocha color, and her body is just as lean and muscular in all the right places. Her features are even the same, except the gap in her front teeth. It's kind of sexy, but I want nothing to do with her.

The minute she walked through the door of the bar, my heart nearly stopped beating. It was filled with hatred and something else I can't put my finger on. I know I was a bit of an asshole to her. I should feel bad because she genuinely seemed shaken.

I watch as a man slams his car door and rushes out of the rain. A man on the other side of the street gets my attention. He's dressed in a black coat with his collar pulled up around his neck. He's talking on the cell phone and is watching Theo and Fallon walk down the sidewalk. He skips between a couple of parked cars and falls in a block behind them. He stuffs his phone in his pocket, and something falls out.

I step out of the dark alley to get a closer look. He bends down to pick it up and shoves it back in his pocket. It looked like a ski mask, and my hair stands on end. I pick up my pace and catch up with him.

"Good evening," I say when I'm beside him.

He nods, and I keep walking fast until I catch up with Theo and Fallon. "Keep moving and don't look back," I say to them. "You were right, someone is following you. Tell me your address."

"255 Park Avenue, apartment 3C."

"Don't stop. I'll meet you there." I open the door to a diner that's open twenty-four hours. I walk directly over to the jukebox and pretend to pick a song. I keep my head down but glance up to watch for the moment he walks by.

I grab the bell at the top of the door to silence it as I walk back out onto the sidewalk, but I don't see the can I kick into the street. He turns to the noise and then looks at me. He takes off in a jog across the street, running in front of a car. The horn blows, but he doesn't stop. I chase after him, skimming my way between cars and into the shadows. He ducks between two buildings and climbs on a dumpster and jumps the wall. By the time I top the wall, he's nowhere to be seen.

"Shit!" I dig my cell phone out of my back pocket. "Theo, did you make it to her apartment?"

"Yes, and I've already checked every inch of this place."

"I'll be there in five. Don't leave her alone."

"I have no intention of leaving her. Maybe never." He whispers the last part.

I make sure I'm not followed and head straight to her place. It looks like a newly remodeled small apartment building that's been made to look like a brownstone. Five steps up lead to a dimly light hallway. The stairs zigzag to the top floor. A man at the end of the hall cracks his door open to look out and then shuts it again. Probably a harmless noisy neighbor that heard me coming up the stairs.

I knock on 3C and can hear when Theo lifts the little lever on the peephole to look out. "Did you see anything?" he asks from behind the closed door.

"Let me in," I growl, and he opens the door.

"Throw some things together. You aren't staying here." I point to Fallon.

"I'm not leaving my apartment." She crosses her arms in defiance.

"This place is not secure. There is one lamp post lighting the entrance and very dim lighting inside. I could break in this door with one kick, and you've already said you thought someone had been in here."

"He's right, Hazel. You're not safe here." Theo rubs his hand down her arms.

"I don't have any other place to go, other than my office."

"You'll come with me back to the bar," Theo says.

"No." I step up beside Theo.

"What? Why not?"

"Because the bar isn't secure. People are constantly coming in and out, and there are too many ways to get inside the building. She'll come home with me."

"I'd rather take my chances here," Fallon shoots back.

"He's right. His place is secure," Theo assures her.

"Are you coming too?" She tries to whisper, but she's not very good at it.

"He needs to stay at the bar. Whoever was following you saw you duck in there and us leave. He's likely to show his face there, and Theo can keep watch from there."

"I've no idea who he is," Theo retorts.

"You know when someone looks suspicious or out of place."

"He's right. We might have a better chance of getting a handle on who is following you," Theo concedes.

"More importantly is to find out why, but we'll explore that once we have you safe. Grab your bag and let's go."

"I need to check on my sister first." She disappears into another room.

"Could you try to be a little...less you and be nice." Theo grabs me by the elbow and pulls me out of earshot.

"I'm not here to play nice. If you want my help, we're going to play by my rules."

"I'm thinking with your attitude, she doesn't want your help. She'd rather face whoever is following her."

I blow out a long, hard breath. "Okay, I'll work on my charm."

"We could call the police."

"And them do what? She doesn't even have a clue as to who is following her. It's not like they can put out a restraining order on someone, and even if they could, that never works."

"She could file a report, and maybe they could get some fingerprints from her office."

"If that will make you shut up, then she can do it tomorrow. Right now, we're wasting time."

He waves a finger at me. "You like this shit, don't you?"

"What are you talking about?"

"It makes you feel like a SEAL again to protect someone."

"Look, I didn't ask for any of this. I can easily walk out the door." I don't want to admit it, but he's right. For the first time in a long time, I feel like I have a purpose.

He lifts his hands in surrender. "Okay, Captain, whatever you say."

While I impatiently wait, I check her apartment for bugs, looking under every lampshade, between the blinds, under the cabinets and furniture. I pop open the air vents to make sure there are no hidden mics or cameras. "This place is clean." Fallon comes back in the room carrying a bag as I'm getting off the floor.

"What's he doing?" she asks Theo.

"Looking for bugs."

Her gaze sweeps around the room. "Did you find any?"

"No. Are you ready to go?"

"Not really, but I don't feel like I have any other choice."

Theo cocks a brow at me.

"I apologize if I came off a little too strong." I reach for her bag, and she tugs it close to her body and wraps an arm around Theo's.

"I promise he's a good guy." Theo laughs. "I'd trust him with my life."

She looks me up and down, but finally nods acceptance.

I step out into the hallway first to make sure it's safe. "Theo, you lag behind. Fallon, follow close in the middle." I lead the way and make sure she's only a step or two behind me. I watch closely but don't see anything or anyone out of the ordinary. We don't stop until we make it back to the bar, which is now busy.

"Theo, keep her close. I'm going to update Sean and call a cab to take her to my place." He walks her to the end of the bar where he can keep an eye on her and the entrance.

I step behind the counter with Sean, who's elbow-deep in making drinks. "She was right. Someone was following her. I'm going to take her back to my place for the night to keep her safe."

"Why doesn't she stay here with Theo?"

"This place is too busy. She'll be safer with me."

"Are you sure you want to get involved?" His gaze turns to me.

"She's a friend of Theo's, and she doesn't appear to have anyone else. I'll call you in the morning." I slap him on the shoulder and head over to Theo.

"Are you sure you can't come with us?" Fallon is asking him.

"Come over in the morning, and we'll brainstorm." I don't give him time to answer. "The cab should be pulling up any moment." I take her bag off her shoulder.

"It's okay. You'll be safe." He leans in and kisses her on the cheek.

She looks back at him several times before we make it outside the door.

CHAPTER 3

FALLON

D errick opens the door of the cab, and I climb into the well-worn spongy seats. Dirty floor mats are filled with candy wrappers and bits of trash. There's an air freshener hanging from the rearview mirror along with a pen on a string. The cab driver has his license prominently displayed on the dash next to a digital meter, which he turns on the minute Derrick gets in next to me and shuts the squeaky door.

Derrick barks out the address. "Are you sure that's right? That's an abandoned area." The cab driver peers at him in the rearview mirror.

I glance at him, and he simply nods. I have a pit in my stomach. The only thing that makes me not terrified, is the fact that Theo trusts this man.

The driver tosses out his cigarette butt through his half-opened window and pulls out into traffic. He honks his horn when a car swerves in front of him.

The sound of my seat belt clinking vibrates in my ear. Derrick has reached across me and buckled me in. The car bounces as the driver runs over a pothole, and I see Derrick's jaw flex.

The driver quickly pulls over out of traffic, and the seat belt catches me as it springs me forward.

"What the hell, man? This isn't our stop."

"I'm picking up another fare." He points to a man waving down a cab on the sidewalk.

"Like hell you are." Derrick's large hand grasps the back of the driver's seat. "No one else is getting in this cab." His voice is menacing and the look he gives the driver should've killed him.

The driver doesn't utter a word as he pulls back into traffic.

We head away from downtown, and the road gets darker and darker. I'm terrified when we pull up to an old abandoned building. Derrick unbuckles and hands the driver some cash.

"This can't be the right place." I grab Derrick's arm.

"This is it, doll." He gets out and has the driver pop the trunk. I unlatch my seat belt and slowly walk out and take in the sight of the building. Its exterior is brick, and almost all the windows are broken out, except for the top floor. There's an eight-foot wooden fence surrounding the outside. A bright yellow condemned sign is stapled to the gate.

I stand stock-still and watch the cab driver leave. Derrick takes my hand and leads me to the back of the building. He pulls a key from his pocket and unlocks the chain on the gate. The back wall is filled with colorful graffiti. I'm surprised to see a patch of green grass that isn't littered with beer cans and trash. There's a thick metal door that he unlocks. It opens up into the abandoned apartment building. He reaches down and picks up something. I hear a clicking sound, and a beam of light shines out into a hallway. The first thing I see is a door hanging from its broken hinges and wiring spilling out of a wall like an old corpse's innards. Crusty paint peels and rippled wallpaper line the hallway.

I nearly jump out of my skin when wind whistles through one of the broken windows, causing the pane to rattle. "Nice place you have here," I say as I step over a doorknob that's laying on the floor. I fully expect rats to run out of their holes and nibble at my toes.

He laughs but doesn't say anything. We come to

the staircase, and I think we're going to go up, but he walks by them to the end of the hall.

"Do you live on the bottom floor?" I ask.

"Nope." He swings open a cage door and says, "After you."

I walk over to him to see an old elevator. "I think I'd rather take the stairs."

"Trust me, you'd fall right through them."

I step inside, and he gets in and closes us into the cage. He pushes a button, and the gears make an awful noise as it slowly raises us up. I hold my breath thinking I'm going to be stuck in here with no way out.

"You can breathe now," he says when it jerks to a stop. I walk out onto a tile floor that looks like wood. Another metal door stands by itself in a hallway. He unlocks it, and we walk inside. "Alexa, turn on the lights."

It's like walking into a completely different building. There's expensive-looking leather furniture and artwork adorns the walls. A large television is mounted and a motorcycle sets in the far corner close to a half wall.

"I don't understand."

He hangs his keys on a rack by the door. "I like to be left alone." He punches a few buttons on a keypad, and low-security lights come on, followed by a chirp.

"I can see why you think this place is safe."

"May I fix you a drink? Are you hungry?" He tugs off his jacket.

"I could use something to drink."

"Make yourself comfortable." He waves toward the couch.

"Where will I be sleeping?" I watch him as he walks to the open kitchen.

"In my bed," he says as he reaches into a cabinet and takes down two glasses.

"Excuse me?" I stammer.

"Don't worry. I'll take the couch." He looks over his shoulder.

"I don't mind sleeping on the couch." I yank my jacket snug to my body, feeling a little intimidated by him.

"I won't be sleeping, so one of us might as well get some shut-eye."

He joins me on the far end of the couch. "Tell me about your sister?"

"How do you know I have a sister?"

"You mentioned needing to check on her when we were at your apartment." He sips a glass of ice water.

"Oh, yeah. She's in the hospital."

He rests back and crosses an ankle over his knee. "How sick is she?"

"She's not going to make it if she doesn't get a kidney transplant soon."

"I'm sorry to hear that." He takes another drink.

"Did you get that scar the same time Theo lost his arm?" I don't know why I asked him that. Maybe I need to know something personal about the man that I'm camping out with tonight.

"How did you lose your hearing?"

I touch my ear. The hearing aid I wear is so minute that no one ever notices it.

He chuckles as he sets his glass on the coffee table. "I'm a SEAL, remember? I notice every detail."

"My sister and I were attacked one night on our way home. The guy shot off a gun right beside my ear." Sometimes in my sleep, I can still hear it.

"Yes," he says.

"Yes, what?" I've lost track of our conversation.

"The scar. A bomb went off, and fragments hit me. I was the lucky one. Several of my men lost their lives and Theo..."

"Lost his arm," I finish his sentence.

He stands and rubs his eyes with the palms of his hands. His hands stop their motion, and he pushes them deep into his pockets. "It was all my fault."

"Did you set off the bomb?" My eyes bulge with fear.

"No, but I led them to it."

It's the first sign of vulnerability I've seen in him, and it's my instinct to reach out and comfort him, but I don't. "I'm sure Theo doesn't blame you."

"Theo was an innocent kid and would've done anything I told him."

I get up. "That was part of his job that he willingly took on."

"How long did you say you two hung out together? On a plane ride?" He snatches up his glass and walks back into the kitchen, taking down a bottle from a high cabinet. He takes off the lid and sniffs the bottle. He inhales deeply then places the cap back on it.

"It wasn't long." I join him in the kitchen. "But I very distinctly remember a young man that wanted to be part of a team." I take the bottle from him and pour myself a drink of the amber liquid.

"The kid didn't know any better."

"He doesn't look and act like a kid anymore from what I saw tonight." I take a sip, and it burns my throat. I cough, and he takes the glass from me and pours it out. Then he puts the bottle back on the shelf.

"How can you say that? You were a SEAL too. You must've wanted to belong to something?"

He glares at me with cold eyes for a long moment. "It's late. Why don't you get some sleep and we can try to figure out who's following you tomorrow."

Just like that, his hardness is back, and all vulnerability gone. I'm scared out of my mind, but in the still of all this mess, I want to know what makes this man tick. He's built a wall around him, shutting everyone out. Someone has hurt him deeply enough to live like a hermit. A woman, perhaps? Or, is it guilt for something he's not responsible for? A different time and place, I'd dig deeper to find out.

"I assume. that's the bedroom." I point to the half wall.

He nods, and I walk toward it.

"Good night and thank you for letting me stay here."

I feel him watch me as I walk to the far side of the apartment. I quickly change into a long T-shirt and crawl underneath the covers. I'm so exhausted, I forget about where I am and fall sound asleep.

CHAPTER 4

REBEL

D amn woman. I should've never volunteered to help out. I stuff the couch pillow under my head. I don't need anyone in my business and I've never brought a woman here before. Now her scent will be all over my bed.

Images of Nina flash through my head. There are times I ache for her, but my hate takes over, and I shove all emotions out. My therapist keeps encouraging me to date and give someone else a try. I can't. I don't trust anyone, except maybe Dr. Ruth. I trust her enough that I've told her of my plan to open a security business of sorts. I want to form a team of men that not only set up security systems but a team that goes out on rescue missions. Whether it be from natural disasters, kidnappings or anything in between. Commander Lukas has put me in touch with a private division of the Central Intelligence Agency. Everything is in place; I've been the hold up, trying to handpick my team. I've even gone so far as to name it the Gunners after my SEAL team.

I haven't mentioned it to anyone but now seems like a good time. I want Theo and Sean as members. I want to hire Dr. Ruth to be the shrink. It's a requirement of any form of government agency that deals with security. I think taking on Fallon's case could be our first mission.

I pick up my cell phone and call Sean.

"What's up?" he yells into the phone over the music blaring in the background.

"I need you and Theo to come to my place in the morning."

"My idea of morning is noon." He laughs.

"Okay, then meet me here at noon."

I hang up and sit on the edge of the couch and flip up my computer system that's hidden in my coffee table. I check the perimeter cameras and set the outside alarms. Even though I'm sure she's safe, I don't plan on sleeping, so I make a pot of coffee and check every place I know that I've stashed weapons around the apartment, including in my bedroom. I approach the half wall quietly, and I hear a soft snore and know she's sleeping. I take off my shoes and pad quietly around the room in my socks. A lock of her hair has fallen over her face, and I want to sweep it out of her way, but I stop myself.

I slowly pull open the drawer to the bedside table to see my gun safely stowed away. Then I move to the dresser, where there are two more stashed. I glance back at her one more time before I go settle in with a cup of coffee. She's beautiful, and it makes my heart—that I didn't think I had anymore—hurt.

"Goddamn you, Nina," I growl to myself.

My soul feels the color of this coffee I've been drinking all night.

"Good morning."

I look up to see Fallon coming out of the bedroom. Her hair is a mess, and she has on a long T-shirt that shows off her firm legs.

I glance up at her and back down. I don't want her to think she has any effect on me. "Coffee's made." I blow on the mug that I have a death grip on to stave off my horniness.

She looks down and stops in her tracks and turns

a nice shade of pink. "Sorry," she says and skates back to the bedroom. She comes out a few minutes later with her hair in a ponytail, a pair of skinny blue jeans, and a long white lightweight sweater. She saunters by me and heads straight for the coffee.

It didn't change one bit how pretty she is, which she seems clueless about. "Did you sleep well?"

"Surprisingly, yes," she says as she joins me on the couch. "Did you sleep at all?"

"No." A knock on the door keeps me from saying anything more. I already know it's Theo because I saw him on the camera. She jumps at the sound.

"It's okay. It's Theo." I show her on my computer screen.

"Wow, you have cameras everywhere in this building." She studies the screen.

"Is someone going to let me in!" Theo beats on the door.

Fallon gets up and unlocks the door, letting him inside.

"I brought breakfast." He opens the lid to a white box that is full of Danishes. Fallon swipes one like she's starved.

Theo offers me the box. "No, thanks. I'm full up on coffee. Did you see anything suspicious at the bar last night?"

"Nothing out of the ordinary. Anything happen here?" He looks between the two of us.

"Nothing popped up on the security screen. Now that you're here, let's put our heads together and try to figure this thing out."

"Do you want to wait for Sean?" he asks.

I glance at my watch. "He's just now getting some shut-eye. He said he'd be here around noon."

"I want to call and check on Josie before we get too engrossed in trying to find out who's following me." Fallon marches off to the bedroom.

"Did she give you any clues?" Theo sits beside me.

"Nothing, but we didn't get into any deep conversation."

"Ah, she tried to ask you personal questions, didn't she?" He rests back and laughs.

"Look, she's not here to get to know me, and I don't want to know her. I'm here to do a job," I bark.

"I didn't realize you had a job."

"That's something I've been working on, and I want to talk to you about it when Sean gets here."

Fallon comes flying out of the bedroom with her bag over her shoulder. "I don't want to be your job!" She heads straight for the front door.

"He didn't mean it like that." Theo cuts her off in her path.

"I'd like to get out of here." Her jaw clenches together along with her fists at her side.

I stand and rub my hands down my jeans. "I'm sorry. I really do want to help you."

"You've a funny way of showing it." She drops her bag to the ground. Theo walks her over to the couch.

I decide to cut to the chase. "I need to know anything new or different in your life."

She sits in the chair, not on the couch. "I have new clients, but they're a sweet old couple, and that wouldn't make any sense."

"Tell me more about what's going on with your sister."

"She's on life support, waiting for a kidney. She has to make it a few more weeks, and she'll get one."

"I take it that she's in the national database."

"Yes, but they don't have a match for her."

"I'm confused." I square off my shoulders to focus on her.

"A company called geNetics.com has located her a kidney."

"Is this a private organization?" I switch my

computer from surveillance mode to Google the company.

"Yes. They do DNA testing among other things, like locating organ donations."

I scroll through the website, and it looks completely legit. It was organized two years ago in Germany and has some pretty big pharmaceutical backers. There's a picture of the CEO and a bio of her. She's an older blonde woman with dark-rimmed glasses. Under her picture, it says, N.P. Parrot.

"That's who sent me the letter stating they found a kidney for my sister." She points to the computer.

I make a mental note of the other members listed on the board. There are several lists of reviews from people that received organ donations from them.

"That's a dead end. Maybe you have someone that's stalking you because they like you," Theo says.

"Wearing a ski mask?" Her eyes grow wide.

"I didn't say it wasn't some sick fuck, but nothing else seems to make sense."

"I need a list of all your clients."

"I don't know, maybe I imagined all of it." She rubs her fingers on her temples.

"I saw him and chased him over a fence last night. I'm pretty sure you didn't imagine him."

"There was this one guy....no, it can't be him."
She flops back in her chair.

"Tell me." I push her to talk.

"Brent Dagwood." I type the name as she starts
to tell her story. "My sister and I went to the movies
one night, and he was in the theater. I knew him
from high school. He was in the military at one point.
He was acting really weird and left the movie." I
watch her hand trace her ear, and I know it's the man
who shot the gun, causing her hearing damage. "We
were walking home, and he thought we were his
enemies. He had a gun. I talked him into letting my
sister go, and he and I struggled with the gun."

"Where is he now?" Theo is up on his feet and
fuming.

"Last I heard, was rehab."

"It wasn't him following you," I add.

"How do you know that?" Theo is yelling.

"It says here, he hung himself over a month ago."
I swivel the computer screen where they can see it.
She gasps and covers her mouth.

"Oh, my God. I had no idea."

Theo starts pacing and doesn't stop as we
continue to brainstorm. Sean finally arrives and
joins in.

I tell them about the Gunners, and they're both

all for it. Sean's bar will be home base, and I'll set up all the equipment we're going to need in one of the upstairs apartments.

"I don't have time to sit here anymore. I really need to go see my sister." Fallon stands.

"I'll take her," Theo volunteers. "Count me in on the Gunners, sir." He salutes me like old times, except now he has a mechanical arm.

"I'll need the names of your clients when you're done visiting your sister." I stand. "Sean and I will run them through a database and compile files on all of them."

"What are you two going to do in the mean-time?" Theo is halfway out the door with Fallon.

"We're going to go set up shop at Sean's."

CHAPTER 5

FALLON

"Has he always been such an ass?" I ask as the caged elevator makes its slow descent.

"He changed after he lost all of his team. He needs more time to move on. Believe it or not, he's better than he was." Theo's brows draw together.

"I tried to ask him questions, and he shot me down cold."

"He doesn't like to talk about it."

"Was there by chance a woman involved? Is that why he seems to hate women?"

He raises the gate as we make it the bottom and make our way outside. "She was our handler. She should've been someone we could trust with our lives, but she betrayed us all."

"So, she's the reason the men died?"

"Yes, and she broke his heart. He was in love with her and wanted to marry her, but she kept putting him off."

"Damn. Now I feel really bad for him. No wonder he's so uptight."

"He'll eventually warm up to you and get the stick out of his ass."

"Is this our ride?" There is a sleek black motorcycle parked in the back.

"Yep, isn't she gorgeous?" He chuckles.

"How do you manage that with your hand?"

"This thing?" He holds it in the air. "It works better than my other hand." He opens and closes his fingers. "It's got a grip so strong I could crush a Coke bottle."

"Okay, Crusher, let's go." I hike my leg over the front of the bike.

"You driving?" He laughs and hops on behind me, handing me a helmet.

"I haven't ridden in years. My dad used to own one, and he taught my sister and I to ride."

Traffic is terrible as usual, so I decide to cut across town through the tunnel, weaving in and out of traffic. Theo grips my waist as I take a turn a little too quickly.

"Whoa there, Sparky. Slow it down a little," he says in my ear.

"My daddy always said, 'ride it like you stole it!'" I yell over the wind and traffic noise.

He chuckles, and I speed up.

The parking garage at the hospital is full, so I wedge the bike between two cars on the third floor.

"Damn, remind me never to race you on a bike." Theo gets off and shakes his pants legs down.

"That felt so good. Thank you for letting me ride it." I pull the helmet off and run my hand through my hair.

"Anytime, Hazel."

I've been so absorbed in myself that it's the first time I've noticed him smile. He's very handsome, with his boyish looks and sandy-colored hair. He's different than when we met before. Not just more mature, but strong, and yet at the same time, he still has that happy spirit about him. His injury hasn't stopped or even slowed him down. He seems to take everything in stride and has such a good attitude.

We take the elevator up to the fourth floor and sign in at the ICU desk.

"Ms. Davis, the doctor has asked to be notified when you got here. I'll get ahold of him. Please don't leave before he sees you," the nurse says and picks up the phone.

"He's never done that before." I look at Theo, and I'm sure I have concern written all over my face.

He takes my hand in his, and we walk to her room. She looks worse than she did yesterday. Her skin is so pale, and her hands and feet are swollen. There's even some swelling around her eyes today that wasn't there yesterday. All kinds of tubes are in her body and monitors are flashing.

"She's beautiful," Theo says, staring down at her.

"You should see her when she's not sick." I run my fingers through her curly hair.

"Ms. Davis." Josie's doctor comes into her room and sticks out his hand.

"Hi, Doc, this is my friend Theo." He shakes his hand.

"I'm afraid the news is not good. Josie has taken a turn for the worse. We've upped her dialysis to daily, but her body isn't tolerating it very well. I've spoken with the company who says they have a kidney for her, but they can't give me a confirmation on when it will be available."

"Can you check the national database again?" I sob.

"We've been on it all morning and can't find a match for her."

"There has to be something else we can do." My legs feel weak, and I stumble back as Theo catches me.

"Whoa," he says and grabs a chair, placing it behind me. I sit, and he puts his hands on my shoulders.

"We're doing everything we can, but the situation is very grave."

"I'm going to call Rebel and have him make some phone calls." Theo squeezes my shoulders.

"Rebel?"

"Derrick, sorry. I'm in military mode, and that's what we called him." He pulls his phone from his pocket and walks over to the window.

"I'm sorry for the bad news, but I wanted you to be prepared." Sadness shows in his eyes.

"Thank you," I say and stand. "But I'm not giving up on her yet."

"That doesn't surprise me." He chuckles. "She's been my patient for a lot of years. She's very strong, and I know the two of you are fierce."

"Thank you for all that you've done for her."

He nods and leaves her room.

"Rebel is going to make some calls to some of his

government contacts. I'm going to run down and get us some coffee so you can visit with your sister." He kisses my forehead.

"Thanks, Theo." I drag the chair to her bedside and sit next to her so I can hold her hand.

"I know you can hear me. You need to fight for a little while longer. You can do this." Out of my periphery, I see a man dressed in all black walk slowly by Josie's room. Fear rushes through me thinking they might be after Josie and not me.

"I'm not going to let anyone hurt you." He walks by again a few seconds later in the other direction. I pull my phone from my purse and text Theo.

There's a man dressed in black that keeps walking by Josie's room.

He responds: *I'm headed back up, don't leave her side.*

THE SOUND of running echoes down the hallway. Theo is out of breath when he hits the doorway. "Where is he?"

"I don't know. He hasn't walked by again."

He leans over and places his hands on his knees to suck in some air.

"Did you run up the stairs?"

"Yes," he pants, "the elevators took too long. He stands up straight. "Which direction did he go in last?"

I point to the left.

"Stay right here. I'll be back." He takes off in a run again.

The thought runs through my mind again, are they after me or Josie? I can't leave her here alone. I don't know why she would have any enemies either. None of it makes any sense at all.

"Whoever it was is gone." Theo comes back into the room still sucking in air.

"What if they're after Josie and not me?" My heart races as I'm in full-blown panic mode.

He responds by taking out his phone. "Rebel, we need someone stationed at Josie's bedside. Fallon saw a man scoping out her room. For now, I'll contact security here at the hospital and let them know what's going on."

"I'm not leaving her side," I interrupt.

He raises his hand in the air. "She won't be left alone until someone is watching her twenty-four seven."

My heart rate starts to slow a bit, knowing there will be someone protecting her at all times.

"Don't worry. Rebel will have someone outside

her door within an hour." He rests his hand on my shoulder.

"Thank you, Theo." I squeeze my sister's hand, hoping for any kind of responses so I can let her know that she's safe.

I ramble over the next hour, sharing happier times with my sister. I want her to hear my voice and know that she's loved. Theo has stood outside the door talking with hospital security, giving me some privacy.

As promised, a man in a black suit arrives, and Theo fills him in on the need to protect my sister.

"We need to get you out of here so you can get the files that Rebel wants," he says quietly at my side.

"I really don't want to leave her."

"I know, but the sooner we figure out who is hunting one of you, the sooner both of you will be safe."

He's right; this isn't going to stop until we get some answers. "Okay." I lean over Josie and kiss her forehead. "Hang in there as long as you can."

Theo tucks my hand tight to his elbow and leads me to the stairs. He looks up and down before we take our first step in the stairwell. We take each step carefully, listening for any sounds that anyone might be following us.

"Do you think someone is really after Josie and I led them to her?"

"Does she have any enemies?"

"Not that I know of, and I can't imagine what anyone would want from her. She really doesn't have anything or anyone but me."

"Stay here and let me make sure the coast is clear," he says, pulling open the door that goes into the garage-level parking.

The silence in the stairwell is broken by the sound of a woman's heels on the steps. A door creaks above me, and then the sound is gone. I chew on my nails waiting for what seems like a really long time before the door opens again.

"Is everything..."

I'm cut off when a man reaches in and jerks me out by the arm. Theo is lying facedown on the concrete floor by his motorcycle. A man is standing over him pointing a gun at his head.

I watch for any movement from Theo to tell if he's dead or alive. My captor drags me toward him and speaks German to the other man with the gun.

"What do you want from me?" I cry out.

Neither one of them acknowledges that I've said anything. He jerks my arm harder toward a van that is all blacked out. I stumble, and his grip loosens enough for me to twist free of him, but he catches me by the hair, yanking me backward.

"Ahh! Let go of me!"

He wraps his hand around my throat from behind me. The other man steps away from Theo and opens the back door to the van. He shoves me inside, and I flip over and plant my foot in his chest, sending him to the ground. The other man comes into view, and I see Theo jump him from behind. I scramble out of the back and reach for the gun that left the man's grasp when Theo hit him.

I dive for it, and my captor has moved in the direction of the gun too. We struggle, and he comes up off the ground with it. I kick out again and connect with his hand. The gun flies through the air, and Theo snags it. Both of the men race to get in the van and squeal out of the garage.

Theo tucks the gun in the back of his jeans. "Get on," he yells and throws me a helmet. I climb on behind him, and the engine roars to life, and black smoke flows from the pipe as he takes off. It forces me back, and I grab onto his waist so I don't fly off the back.

He leans the bike low around the curves, and I hold on tighter. By the time we make it to the exit, there is no sign of the van.

"Damn it!" Theo yells. He turns right and looks down every crossroad. Traffic is thick, and there's nothing but brake lights in front of us. "How the hell did we lose them?" He rests his booted foot on the asphalt, stopping behind a car.

"I don't know. Unless they already had an escape route."

The bike starts rolling forward, and he inches his way between cars until he gets to an exit. He races down the interstate until we make it to my downtown office exit.

As soon as I'm off the bike, he's on my heels. "Listen, we are going to go in your office, grab what we need and get out of here. Don't make one step without me." He cranes his neck to one side and rubs the back of his head, and he winces.

"Did they hit you?" I walk behind him and run my hand lightly through his hair and find a goose egg-sized knot. "We should probably head back to the hospital to have you examined."

He pulls my hand from his head and starts walking. "I'm fine. I'm sure I've had a lot worse knocks to the head."

"I didn't know if you were dead or alive when I saw you lying on the ground."

He stops and looks at me. "You can kick some ass, by the way," he says, half laughing.

"I've taken plenty of self-defense classes."

"Remind me never to fight with you." He leads me toward the front door. We skate up the stairs, and I unlock my office door. He checks every nook and cranny before he locks the door behind us. "Hurry up and get what you need, and I'm going to call Rebel."

I take a jump drive from my desk drawer and copy everything I need from the main drive. My entire business life is on this system, including financials. I snatch the picture of me and my sister off the corner of the desk and shove it into a bag.

"Are you done?" Theo asks, disconnecting his call.

I nod.

"Good, let's go. Rebel wants us back as soon as possible."

CHAPTER 6

THEO

My head is throbbing, and I know Rebel is furious at me for letting those men slip through my hands. I heard the van door open next to the motorcycle, and before I could turn around, one of them hit me in the head. I did get a good look at them when I woke up so we can run their faces through a database.

I can't believe I didn't protect Hazel better, but now that I've seen her in action, she can at least defend herself.

I hear Rebel's cameras buzzing with our movement as I park the motorcycle around back. Both of us get off and go through the gate to the metal door that's unlocked. The sound of the elevator being sent down to us rattles the first floor of the apartment building.

When we make our way up, at the top, I can see Rebel standing tall with his arms crossed over his chest. A stance I've seen many times before.

He glances at me, then over to Hazel. "Are you okay?" He reaches out and holds her chin up, looking at the red mark on the side of her face.

She cuts her eyes to me. "He's the one with a lump on his head."

"He'll live." He laughs. "It's one of many he's had."

"We both got a good look at the two men that jumped us."

"They were speaking German," Hazel adds.

Rebel holds out his hand. "Let's look at your database first. Once it's loaded, we'll pull up the CIA's files and see if the men who attacked you are on there."

She hands it to him, and then we follow him inside. "I'm sorry they got away," I whisper to him as he locks the door.

"We'll catch them."

The three of us gather around the table. "Where's Sean?" I ask.

"He's back at the bar, waiting for equipment to

be delivered. In the meantime, we're going to use what we have to access the files." His fingers are moving across the keyboard.

"I'd appreciate it if you didn't go through my financials." Hazel's fingertips tap on the table.

"I don't care about your financials." He pauses then looks up at her. "Unless you've not paid some bills, and this is their way of collecting." He raises his eyebrows.

"I don't owe anyone any money." She juts her chin out.

"What about you, sister?" he keeps typing.

"She owes tons of medical bills, but if someone was trying to kill her for them, they'd never get paid."

His fingers stop moving as he scans the screen.

"I don't think they're after Hazel's sister or they wouldn't have attacked us in the garage." I get up and stand over his shoulder.

"Nothing," Rebel snarls. "Everything looks in order. I'll run your client's names through the CIA systems too, to see if anything pops up on any of them."

"Is that really necessary? I feel like it's an invasion of their privacy." Hazel sits back and crosses her arms over her chest.

"No, it's not necessary if you can tell me who's after you?" He mimics her body language.

"If I knew that, I wouldn't need you." She rises. "Actually, I don't need you. I'm sorry I ever stepped foot in the bar."

"Well, if you hadn't, you might be dead right now," he huffs.

She snatches the jump drive out of his computer and stuffs it in her bag.

"Okay, you two!" I point between them. "That's enough. You aren't going anywhere unprotected." I turn to Rebel. "And you could be a little nicer and quit pissing her off."

He gets up and shoves his hands in his pockets. "He's right. I'm sorry, I'll watch my tone."

She doesn't say anything but sits back in the chair.

"Let me see if I can get into the CIA database from here or if I'll have to wait until we get our new system installed."

I move the computer from in front of him. "Here, let me try." A few seconds later he answers, "I'm in."

Rebel turns it back toward him. "Where did you learn how to hack into systems?"

"I have plenty of skills you know nothing about." I wink at Hazel, and she smiles.

He clicks on the keyboard. "Here are the files of men who speak German on their list." He takes it and turns it toward Hazel, and I move a chair to sit beside her. Rebel gets up and starts pacing the floor.

Hazel and I flip through pages of pictures as Rebel starts asking questions. "The only thing new in your life is the geNetics.com. You filled out a profile..." He stops. "Wait, wasn't that company based out of Germany?"

Hazel drags the computer close to her and changes screens, typing in geNetics in her Google search. "Yes, Bremen, Germany."

"It can't be a coincidence." I'm up on my feet.

"What would they be after?" Fear covers her face. "Then they really are after my sister."

Her chair scrapes across the floor as I turn it toward me. I squat down and take her hands in mine. "Josie is safe where she is. It's you I'm worried about."

"But if it's really this company, it has very little to do with me and more to do with Josie."

"Not necessarily." Rebel grabs his keys off the hook.

"Where are you going?" I stand.

"To see if our new computer system has been

delivered yet so I can dig deeper into this DNA testing company."

Hazel's phone rings, and as she digs it out of her bag, her face grows pale. "It's the hospital."

She answers, and I watch as tears fill her eyes. Her hand covers her mouth as her lips begin to quiver. Her phone crashes to the wood floor. "No!" she cries.

I pick up the phone to hear whoever is on the other end, telling her how sorry he is that he couldn't save her sister. I disconnect the line just in time to catch her in my arms before she crumples to the ground.

My own eyes fill with tears at her gut-wrenching cries. I've never been in this situation and have no idea how to make it better. Rebel gets his phone and steps out of the room.

"I'm so sorry, Hazel."

"She can't be dead," she sobs on my shoulder.

I kiss the top of her head and cradle her in my arms, rocking her back and forth like a broken child. "I'm so sorry," I say again.

I don't know how long I held her before Rebel says he needs to let someone in. When he comes back, he's with a striking woman in a navy skirt and white blouse. Her hair is in a bun and glasses sit high on her cheekbones.

Rebel walks over and takes Hazel out of my arms and carries her to the bedroom, followed by his friend. When he comes back out, he's alone.

"Who's that?"

"Dr. Ruth. She's a psychiatrist and a friend of mine. She'll give her something to help her sleep.

My fingers tug at my hair as my hands run through it. "I can't believe she died. Do you think the men who were after her will disappear now or that they somehow got to her and killed her?" I whisper the last part, not wanting Hazel to hear me from the next room.

"No." He pulls me to the other side of the apartment and lowers his voice. "I have my suspicions that they were hired to bring Fallon to Germany."

"Why?" I'm not following his line of thinking.

"I'm betting they had a high-paying client who needed a kidney and Fallon is a match."

"No, no way. That only happens in the movies."

"Come on, you're not that naive. You and I've both seen things that we know shouldn't be real but are."

"You seriously think that's what's going on here?

Wait, do you think they killed Josie?" I whisper, again.

"No. I called our man that was guarding her. He said he had not left her side. The alarms in her room start buzzing, and as soon as one of the nurses got to the room, they started chest compressions. He said they never got her back."

"You can't tell her any of your suspicions until you know for a fact. She's going to need time to take care of things and our protection."

"I agree. You watch over her while Sean and I do some research."

"I've never wished you were wrong about something, but this...this I hope you are way off base." I don't want to admit that I trust his gut, and if he's right, I don't know that we can keep Hazel safe.

CHAPTER 7

FALLON

There's a mist of rain hanging in the cool morning air. The dreariness matches my emotions, which I've found very hard to control the past several days. I've gone from sadness to denial, to anger, and then repeat. I can't believe she's gone.

The casket in front of me says something entirely different. I want nothing more than to trade places with her, but I know Josie would hate me for feeling this way. My eyes grow wet as I think about how utterly alone I am now.

The tightness in my chest increases as the casket is lowered to the ground. Theo, who's been my rock, untangles my hands that I've been wringing together and twines his fingers with mine.

I kept the ceremony small. No church eulogy, only Rebel, Theo, Sean, and myself. Josie has lost touch with the few friends she had, being sick the last few years. There was no other family to invite. Both of our parents were only children, so no aunts, uncles, cousins...nothing. Even the rare moments my eyes have been dry, I keep crying on the inside, thinking her life had to matter. I know it mattered to me, but there has to be something more. It may be for purely selfish reasons...but I have to find something to hold on to.

The massive wall of Rebel and Sean have stood behind my chair in high alert. Both are wearing black suits and dark sunglasses, even though it's not bright out. To add to the gloominess of the day, a thick fog is rolling in from the west, and the mist is turning into sprinkles.

Theo raises an umbrella over me to keep me dry. Not that I care, but it's very sweet of him. I break my stare from the black dirt filling in the hole and glance over at Theo. He looks so handsome in his dark suit and tie. His mop of hair that's usually unruly is combed back, exposing his forehead. His sandy-colored eyes are dark and watching my every move. He's barely left my side since I got the news, and he's lain next to me every night while I've cried myself to sleep.

Dr. Ruth gave me something the first night, but it made me so groggy I couldn't function for an entire day. I like her, and I especially like the way she handles Rebel. She softens him a bit, and I don't think he realizes it.

"It's time to go, Hazel." Theo places a bent finger under my chin and raises it.

"I don't want to leave her," I hear my own voice shake.

"I know you don't, but it's over. They've thrown the last bit of dirt, and the rain is starting to pour down.

He's blinking back the raindrops. I turn to look over at the gravesite, and the men are leaving with their shovels. I slowly stand, and Theo gets up. "No, let me do this alone." He tries to hand me the umbrella, but I push it away.

I walk over to where the dirt meets the grass and stare down. "I'm so sorry, Josie. I love you." I raise my head and let the rain soak into my body. I don't know how long I stood there before Rebel came up beside me.

"We need to get you home," he says softly.

I nod and turn around with him, wrapping my

arm in the crook of his elbow. He takes me back to the vehicle we all came in, and I slide in the backseat and scoot to the middle. Theo joins me and lays his hand on my thigh. I stare at it like it's a foreign object. He sits quietly next to me, but Sean and Rebel talk among themselves on the ride back to Rebel's place. I'm so lost in my grief, I couldn't tell you anything they've said. It's words muffled together in my head.

I haven't gone back to my apartment yet. Theo went over and grabbed some clothes out of my closet so that I'd have something to wear to the funeral.

Sharon has contacted my clients and let them know it would be a while before I would return, but each of them has plans laid out to follow, and Sharon has picked up the slack answering their questions. Right now, I don't care if I ever get back to it.

I blindly follow everyone out of the car and up to Rebel's apartment. Theo has my hand, and he leads me to the shower. I stand still as he brushes the hair out of my face and then starts unbuttoning my blouse. Once he has it undone, he reaches past me and turns on the showerhead, and I can already feel the heat of the water filling the air.

He pushes my blouse off my shoulder, and it falls to the ground. "Turn around," he says.

I do, and he unzips my skirt, letting it meet on the floor with my top. Then I feel his finger behind my heel as he pushes the strap down. "Step out."

One at a time, my shoes come off. "I might need a little help with these." He puts his finger at the band of my pantyhose. I pull them off without a second thought that all I have left on is my bra. I'm going through the motions without feeling anything.

Turning around to face him, his gaze sweeps down my body and then back up to my eyes. He covers his eyes with one hand and reaches behind me to unclasp my bra. I shimmy out of it and let it fall. Then I reach up and remove his hand. His eyes are closed at first, but he slowly peeks through them. I don't know what possesses me, but I need him to see me.

I stand on my tiptoes and place a soft kiss on his lips. "Thank you, Theo," I whisper against them. I feel him swallow hard.

I step back and then into the shower. The hot water consumes me, and I dip my head back, letting it rain into my hair. When I raise back up, Theo is still standing there staring at me.

I hold my hand in his direction. "Are you going to join me or stand there gawking at me?" I need someone to touch me so that I know I'm still alive.

His feet kick off his shoes as his hands work to yank off his jacket and tie. He's stripped bare in a matter of seconds, and he steps in with me. Our wet skin slides together as he wraps his arms around me.

"Just hold me," I say and tuck my head under his chin.

"I can do that," he whispers. "But, I am a man, and I'm sorry for my body's reaction to your beautiful...womanhood being pressed against mine."

For the first time in days, I laugh, and he joins me.

We take our time and wash each other. I get a chance to explore his body without it being a sexual thing. He's gorgeous, even with his mechanical arm. For the first time since I met him, I no longer think of him as a little brother; he's all man standing in front of me. Every inch of him is sculpted into something beautiful. I don't know exactly what my feelings are for him right now, but I know I need him, and I like the feel of his hands on my skin.

As he turns to rinse off, I kiss him again, but this time I slip my tongue in with his. He's so gentle, but I can feel the eagerness behind his kiss.

"Theo, make love to me."

He stops kissing me and places his forehead against mine. "Any other time, I would have gladly jumped all over you, but...I think you need time. You're lonely and need someone to hold you. I don't want to be just someone to you, Hazel. You're too important to me to take advantage of whatever you're feeling right now."

A soft laugh escapes my lips. "Why do you have to be such a gentleman?"

"Because it's who I am and what you need right now." I look down, and he raises my chin. "I'd love nothing more than to bury myself inside you, and when I know it's me you really want and not just comfort, trust me, it'll happen. In the meantime, I'll bathe you, admire you, and watch you sleep, but I will not touch you until you want me as much as I want you." He releases my chin and kisses the top of my wet hair.

"Thank you, Theo." I curl into him, and my warm tears run down his chest until I'm all cried out and the water is cold.

He wraps my hair in a towel and dries me off. Then he scoops me in his arms, carries me to bed and covers me up. I curl up and fall sound asleep for the first time in days.

I wake up to the clock flashing five. I've slept almost the entire day away. The towel has fallen off my head, but my hair is still damp. Escaping from under the covers, I dig into my bag and pull on a gray T-shirt and a pair of loose-fitting sweatpants.

I can hear Rebel's voice in the open living room.

"Here is a computerized sketch of the two men you described. I ran them through a system, and they both have criminal backgrounds and are linked to an underground organization that's involved with child pornography, trafficking woman and children, obtaining non-FDA approved expensive drugs, and stealing organs and selling them to the highest bidder."

Theo snatches the file from his hand and rummages through it. "So, you were right."

"I'm afraid so."

"Who do they work for? That's who we need to take down." Theo throws the file on the coffee table and has both his hands running through his hair.

"I don't know, yet. Evidently, his men are loyal. If not, they're dead."

"Shit! How are we going to keep her safe?"

"We're going to put her in a safe house guarded with military security, and then we're going to hunt them down." He throws another file on the table. "Open it and look at the pictures of the people they've stolen organs from. And, when you're done with that"—another file goes on the table—"here are pictures of their sick pornography ring, and a list of women and children missing that they are believed to have sold."

"If you have all this information, why has no one stopped them?" Sean flips through a file.

"They can't find them."

"So, how the hell are we supposed to find them?" Theo is on his feet.

"We're going to set a trap for them, using Fallon as bait before we send her to the safe house."

"No fucking way!" Theo yells.

"I'll do it." I walk toward them. "But you're not sending me to a safe house. I'm going where ever you go." I point to Rebel.

"Hazel, you have no idea what you're saying. These are some sick bastards, and they aren't playing games. If we let you walk into their hands, you won't make it out alive."

"She'll be bugged, and we'll know where she is at all times."

"That doesn't mean we can get to her quick enough."

"We can if we have a man on the inside."

"We don't have any such person." Theo's voice is getting louder.

Rebel turns to his brother. "They don't know who you are."

"Me? Oh, no. I've never had any kind of training. Besides, I have the bar to run."

"I'll train you, and you can hire someone to work the bar."

"I don't think that's such a good idea," I interject.

"I'll do it. I'll be the inside man." Theo steps up.

"They've seen your face," Rebel says.

"The only two that have seen my face are the two goons that are after Hazel. Once we take them out, they'll have no idea who I am. I can wear a disguise."

"What he said." Sean points to Theo. "I'll run surveillance from the bar."

"Why don't we just call the police," I ask.

"And tell them what? If the CIA hasn't been able to locate them, then what makes you think the local police will be able to help you?"

I sit beside Rebel on the couch. "Well, what makes you think you can infiltrate them if the CIA hasn't?"

"I'm a SEAL, and I've done things and seen things they never have."

"He's right," Theo adds. "I'm going to find out as

much as I can about their organization. I want to know every little detail before I go deep inside."

"I'll study the system and have the kid here teach me how to hack it," Sean says.

"What are you going to do?" I ask Rebel.

"The first thing I'm going to do is put a tracker in you."

"In me?" I rub the back of my neck.

"It can go under your armpit or your hip and be undetectable."

"We have equipment like that?" Theo questions.

"We will. I've been granted full access to whatever I need."

"What can I do?" I ask

"Not leave my side for one minute until we're all set up."

CHAPTER 8

I t's been two weeks since we put our plan in motion. I've been researching almost day and night. When I'm not on the computer, I've been in the gym working out. We've all been holed up in Rebel's apartment under each other's feet. I think it's starting to wear thin on all of us. Sean has been the only one who's been able to get out and act like normal.

Rebel's been doing push-ups, pull-ups, sit-ups, and whatever other ups he can do. I swear he's nothing but muscle. He had all our equipment shipped over to his place rather than the bar. The only thing left over there is what Sean will need to track us and monitor our every move. He will be our motherboard.

I've had to take up running to keep my horniness at bay. Fallon looks damn sexy in everything she wears, and it's getting to me. It was all I could do that day in the shower to resist her; sometimes I'd like to smack myself in the head for it. I've tried to give her some distance, but it's hard when we're in the same space. There's still sadness behind her eyes, but she's driven to help take geNetics down.

I'm going back to my place above the bar tonight. I don't think I can take one more night of watching her run around in her long pajama pants and long sleeve shirt. I've seen what's under there, and it doesn't matter how much she hides it, I still want to touch her. My balls can't take any more.

The bar is full at ten o'clock when I finally leave the gym. I wave at Sean behind the bar as I hit the stairs to my apartment. I take a quick shower, change clothes and head back down for a cold beer. There's one spot left at the bar top, so I make a beeline for it. I rap my knuckles on the bar to get Sean's attention.

He throws a towel over his shoulder and heads over.

"I'll take whatever you have on tap that's ice-cold."

He fills a tall glass and hands it to me. "Are you

ready." He doesn't say the rest because I know what he's talking about. I leave tomorrow for Germany.

"As ready as I'll ever be." I take a swig of my beer.

"Does she know you're leaving tomorrow?"

And by she, he means Hazel. "I'm going to let Rebel tell her."

"Tell me what?" Her voice comes up from behind me.

I turn on the stool to see her. "What are you doing here?" She steps between my legs.

"She needed a night out. Don't worry, we weren't followed." Rebel walks up beside us.

"What is it that you want Rebel to tell me?"

Shit, she's not going to let it go. "Our mission is ready. I leave for Germany tomorrow."

"What? No. We haven't set the trap yet."

"We'll set the trap when I'm ready," Rebel says and takes a drink of water from the glass Sean hands him.

I run my hand down her arm. "Are you afraid?"

"No, I'm ready to get this over with. These men had some part in killing my sister and apparently control the lives of many others. It's time they're punished."

"You sound really badass," I joke with her.

"She is badass. I've been teaching her some fighting skills, and she took me to the ground." Rebel rubs his hip.

"Is that what the two of you've been doing when I'm at the gym?" I chuckle.

"That, and we've been to the shooting range a few times." She looks over at him, and he smiles.

They seem to have finally bonded, but I hope not too much. I'd hate to be in competition with Rebel. "Well, at least he's smiling at you now and not baring his teeth."

"Is that what you call that," she teases and slaps him in the chest.

"You have a mean streak in you, woman." He takes his water and stations himself by the door.

"Were you really going to leave without saying goodbye?" Her hazel eyes are boring into mine.

"I'm not good at goodbyes, remember?"

"Ah, that's right. You like to leave notes." She holds out her hand.

"I haven't written it yet." I laugh.

"I really need to talk to you." She takes my hand, and I get off the stool. She heads for the stairs, and Rebel watches her every move. She hesitates at the bottom and then winks at him. He smiles or shows his teeth at her, I'm not sure which, but he nods, and she pulls me up the stairs.

"Which one is yours?"

I walk in front of her and dig the keys from my pocket. I rigged the lights to come on with motion, and the room lights up.

"Um, nice place you have here." She looks around the room.

"It's small, but all I need."

"Can we sit down?" She motions toward the couch.

I lay the keys on the table and follow her. She sits and draws one leg up close to her.

"I don't like the idea of you going to Germany alone, with no one to watch your back."

"I think you're worried about me." I sit next to her and wrap my arm around her shoulder. "Does that mean you're over the age gap between us?" I laugh.

"About that. I'm sorry for leading you on after the funeral. I needed to be near someone."

"Oh, I was close by." I undrape my arm and lean forward on my knees.

"No. I'm glad it was you. I wasn't in a good place, and I appreciate you being a gentleman."

"I didn't want to be." I turn to face her. "Why

can't you see me as a man? I know I'm young, but I'm old for my age."

She lays her hand on my thigh. "I do see you, Theo. You're a young, hot, gorgeous, sweet man. But, now is not the time. We both need to be focused on what we're doing and not on each other."

I sweep a piece of her mocha hair out of her face. "Why do you have to be so damn tempting? From the day I sat next to you on the plane, you made me feel something." I place my hand over my heart. "I know I was just a teenage boy at the time, but I swear you took my breath away."

She stands. "I can't, Theo. Please don't be hurt or angry with me."

I tug her hand, and she sits back down. "I'm not angry with you. I know your sister dying and someone stalking you has to be overwhelming. I want to protect you."

"I know you do, and I'm so grateful for you taking care of me. I need to get through this and get back on my own two feet." She wipes at a stray tear.

"We'll find who's after you, so you can have your life back."

"My life." She half laughs. "I don't know what that looks like without my sister in it."

I pull her into my arms and kiss the top of her

head. "I'm so sorry, but if it's the last thing I do, I'll make sure you have a life."

"Thanks, Theo. Do you think I could stay here with you tonight? Rebel smiling at me scares me."

I can't help the laugh that comes out. "He can be kind of scary. I'll sleep on the couch."

"You've seen me naked. I think we could curl up together...unless"—she points to my crotch—"you think that's too much to ask."

"It will be hard, no pun intended, but I'll keep the boy at bay." I chuckle.

"Can I ask you a question?" She tilts her head up at me.

"Yes, it's big. Really big," I tease, and she turns bright red.

"Oh, my God, that is so not what I was going to ask you!" She's laughing, and it's good to see it on her.

"I thought all girls wanted to know about a man's package."

She giggles harder. "Stop."

"What's your question then, since you don't want to hear about my most prized possession?" I love making her laugh.

"Have you ever..." She's redder than before.

"Have I ever?"

"Have you ever had sex?"

"Sure I have."

She sits in the corner of the couch, faces me, and crosses her arms over her chest. "With who?"

"That's not important." I clear my throat.

"Theo." Her voice pitches up.

I tuck my hands in my jeans and pull them out some and look down.

"What are you doing?"

"I'm looking for the balls you just crushed."

She swats me in the arm. "Seriously."

"No, I haven't. Are you happy now?" I stand, and she pulls me back down. "I've been a little busy. I'm not into guys, and that's who I spent all my time with in the Gunners. Then, I come back with no arm, and well, women don't exactly fall all over a man with one arm."

"When I look at you, all I see is you. A real woman wouldn't care about any of that. That's not what makes you Theo. This is." She places her hand over my heart.

I have to fight the urge to kiss her. Her words that she spoke to me in Europe come ringing in my ear. *"You're like a brother to me."* Maybe she'll never see me as anything more than that. I'm not that kid on the plane ride; I've lived a million lives since then. But I care about her enough to give her what she needs. In the meantime, maybe she will come to see me as the man I am now.

"I'll have to take your word on that." I remove her hand from my chest. "It's getting late. Do you want to go downstairs and get a nightcap? I'm sure Rebel has somethings he needs to fill me in on."

"As long as things between us are okay."

I stand and drag her with me. "As long as you don't expect me to see you naked again and control myself." I laugh.

"I promise to keep my clothes on." She makes a crossing motion over her heart.

"That's one promise you can feel free to break."

CHAPTER 9

REBEL

The bar closed hours ago, and I've stayed up all night keeping watch and researching every detail of geNetics. What I find odd is that there are no pictures of the president of the company and/or anyone else but the CEO. The middle-aged lady is not the face of someone with a list of crimes behind them. She looks more like the grandmotherly type. I'm thinking it's a fake. It says their financial backers have asked to remain anonymous. The CEO is someone named N.P. Parrot, which is the person that Josie received her letter from. I tried several times to call the number listed for their company, but a recording is as far as I got. There's an email listing for the CEO, so I drafted a correspondence requesting information about the company stating that I'm interested in tracking my ethnicity. I've created a fake identity with a detailed background. This is my plan B if they don't take the bait with Fallon.

I need time to let Theo infiltrate their company. In the meantime, I need to work more with Fallon on self-defense. She's physically strong, but I'm not sure emotionally she can handle anything right now.

I turn on the barstool when I hear footsteps coming down the stairs. Theo has a tan backpack thrown over his shoulder. "You look like shit. Did you get any sleep?"

A smile broadens over his face. "Who needs sleep? I can get some rest on the long plane ride."

"I wish my equipment was here to put a tracker in you before you head out."

"I wouldn't want it anyway. If they found it, they'd kill me."

"I want you to pick up a burner phone when you get there. Don't use it unless you're in trouble." I reach over to the stack of papers by my laptop. "Here is the information that you need. Study it and all the names on here, then ditch it. I have an apartment already set up for you. Here is the address." I point on the paper. "I'm sure you won't be there long before you're deep undercover. If you need to leave me a clue, hide it here. I'll find it." I reach in my bag on the floor and grab an envelope. "Here's enough cash to get you whatever you need while you're there."

"Shit, man. What did you do, rob a bank?" He takes it from me and shoves it in his backpack.

"Our government funding came through."

"You work fast when you really want something."

"It helps when you have the right connections and have some high-ranking military friends."

He throws his bag over his shoulder again and looks toward the stairs. "Keep her safe."

"I will. You need to focus on the mission, not the girl."

"I'm going to get out of here before she wakes up and I miss my flight."

Holding out my hand, I stand. "Be safe and watch your back. You have a month to make this work before I bring my sorry ass in your direction."

He shakes my hand with his mechanical hand. "I'll get in and get what we need to bring them down. It's the only way Fallon will be able to have her life back."

Theo is walking out as Sean walks in the front door holding a brown carrier with four cups of coffee. Theo takes one out of it. "You headed out?" Sean asks him.

"Yeah. I'll get set up with a laptop when I get there so you can send me what information you find other than what Rebel's given me. I need you to hack the private files of geNetics. He has a complete list of names, look specifically at the backers behind the scenes. There's not much to go on, so you'll have to dig deep."

"I will, and you be careful," Sean tells him.

"Were you up all night?" Sean lays the carrier on the bar and takes a seat next to me.

"Yeah, I'll sleep later, but thanks for this." I take a cup.

"Do you really think we're equipped to pull this off? This isn't a military mission." He sips his coffee.

"I'm broaching it like any other mission I've been on. I do my homework, check out every detail possible, and lay out a plan. It's always worked for me before."

Sean gets up and goes behind the bar. "Except when it didn't."

I bite my tongue so my anger doesn't slip out. "Those were different circumstances. We were all betrayed by someone we trusted."

"You're right, I'm sorry. I shouldn't have said that." He lays his hands flat on the counter.

"No. I get your concern. It's just the three of us working together, and there is no one else in this world I trust like you guys."

"Are you ever going to let another woman in your life?"

"I..."

"Did Theo leave?" Fallon's voice comes up behind me.

"Yes." I turn in her direction. "He's got work to do, just like we do."

She sits in the barstool next to me. "Tell me what I need to do."

"You and I are going to see an old buddy of mine who owns a boxing ring."

"You're taking her to see Lawson?" Sean starts wiping down the counter.

"Yeah, I called him yesterday and reserved us some time."

"Why are we going to a boxing ring?"

"I want to teach you some defensive moves."

"Didn't we already do that at your apartment?"

I place my hands on either side of her barstool, and it makes a scraping noise on the floor as I drag her close to me. "We've barely scratched the surface.

I need to know you can fight for your life, because if you insist on coming with us, that may be just what you have to do to survive, and we've only got weeks to make it happen."

"I really think the safe house is a better option," Sean chimes in.

"No, I'm not going to run scared." She squares her shoulders.

"It's not running scared, sweetheart. It's playing it safe until this is all over with," I tell her.

"And how long is that going to take. How long am I supposed to not live my life? Years?"

"That's not the plan."

"You don't know how long, and in the meantime, I'd rather help, not be locked away like a scared child."

"You could take her kicking and screaming," Sean interjects.

"Whose side are you on?" She squints at him.

"I'm on the side that keeps you alive."

"What if it were one of you? Would you hide or fight?"

Neither one of us answers her.

"Exactly. Just because I'm a woman, doesn't mean I can't do the same." She juts out her jaw in defiance.

"Fine," I grit out.

Sean throws a heavy glass in the sink, and it shatters. "She should be locked away safely. We're into something that none of us have experience with. I know you were a SEAL, but this different, and her life is at stake!"

"I'm not giving him a choice. One way or another, I'm going with you." She hops off the barstool. "Are you coming or not, or are you afraid I may kick your ass in that ring?" Her long hair sways behind her as she makes her way to the front door. Damn woman's toughness is getting under my skin.

"I know what I'm doing, you have to trust me on this. Theo is good at blending into his surroundings, and you have the computer skills we need to help us access the system. Let me worry about the rest." I smack my palm on the counter and follow Fallon out the door. "Hey smart-ass, slow down." I rush to catch up with her. "Don't ever go outside without me."

"It's broad daylight. I think all the scary men have crawled back in their holes."

"I wouldn't be so sure of that. People are taken during the day all the time. It's when they least expect it." I scan the area, but for now, the streets are quiet.

"I've lived here all my life, and I don't remember

seeing a boxing ring." She stops on the corner of the street waiting for the walk signal.

"That's because it's an underground ring."

"So, it's illegal?"

"Let's just say it's frowned upon." The light changes, and I take her by the elbow to walk to the other side.

"Have you ever participated in these 'frowned upon' activities?" She makes finger quotes.

"Yes. Lawson and I grew up together and have beaten the crap out of each other a lot."

"Wait, you fight your friend?"

"That's how we both learned to fight. He loved it so much, he bought the business. I, on the other hand, needed to take my fighting to another level. I wanted to take what I learned and defend our country."

"Wow. There are many layers to you." She stops in her tracks. "Do you ever let anyone peel them back?"

"Leave my layers alone and keep walking." She falls in step with me.

"I bet under all that bravado, there's a nice guy under there."

I swing open the door to the building that leads to the ring. "You'd lose that bet."

CHAPTER 10

FALLON

The front of the old brick building houses a men's clothing store. Rebel waves at the man behind the glass counter, but never stops moving. We walk through the door that's labeled, employees only. Once we walk in, there's another door in the back with a scanner on it. He places his middle finger over it, and the door slides open. It leads to a set of stairs that go downward at a steep slope. He turns around and grabs onto the rail.

"This is this the easiest way to go down. Watch your step," he says as he descends.

I turn around and mimic his movements. Once we get to the bottom, there's another scanner. This time he places his pointer finger on it, and another door opens into a brightly lit large room. There's a ring with red ropes linked together sitting in the middle of the room. Two shirtless men are beating on a punching bag off to the side of the ring.

"Hey, Rebel." A man about Rebel's height, with long brown hair, slaps him on the back.

"Lawson, good to see you brother." They bump fists. "When you going to get this shit cut off?" He points to his hair.

"When you can kick my ass." He laughs. He's Rebel's height but built like solid steel. Rebel is muscular, but this man's muscles are massive. He turns toward me. "Who is this pretty lady?" He holds his hand out, and I place mine in his. He kisses the back of my hand, and Rebel swats him away.

"This is Fallon and keep your hands to yourself."

"A little competition between brothers never hurt."

I can tell he's teasing Rebel by the mischief in his eyes.

"She's a job, not a girlfriend."

I don't know why, but his words sting.

"Even better for me," he continues to razz him.

"Do you have any women's clothes," Rebel ignores him.

"You cross-dressing now?" Lawson snorts.

"Not for me, asshole." Rebel punches him in the shoulder.

"We don't get too many women down here, but I think there are clothes in the last locker on the right."

Rebel takes my hand again. "It was nice to meet you," I say over my shoulder.

"I'm not going anywhere. I plan on watching you kick his ass," he yells between his hands.

I follow Rebel to the locker room. Evidently, there isn't one for women, because when I walk inside, there is a man completely naked walking around and one getting out of the shower. I look down at my feet and then back up. It doesn't seem to faze them that a woman is in their space. I follow Rebel to the very last locker, and he opens it up.

"Here, put these on." He throws me a wife beater tank top and a black pair of shorts. He steps down to a locker that has his name on a piece of tape covering the front of it. He flings it open and starts to strip.

I stand straight in front of my locker and try not to cut my gaze at him. I can't help it. I want to look. Maybe Theo was right; we want to know about the package.

"Are you going to change or stare at me," he says pulling the hem of his shirt over his head.

Bastard. Two can play his game. I take my top off and slip out of my jeans. Right now, I'm very thankful I chose a sports bra and boyfriend underwear. I look down and run my hand over my flat, firm abs. I don't dare look at him, but I hear him gulp down a swallow. I smile to myself and pull on the clothes.

I jump when he slams his locker door. "Hurry your ass up." He heads out the door.

Why is he so damn cranky? Does he treat all women like this or am I the only one? I thought he was warming up to me, but I guess I was wrong. I gently shut the locker and head out to the ring. Rebel is climbing in through the ropes and then hits his red boxing gloves together.

"Grab a pair before you climb in." He motions to a wooden box outside the ring.

Lawson bends down and grabs me a pair. "This should be fun." He grins and hands them to me.

"Getting my ass kicked is not my idea of fun." I pull one on.

He takes the other one from me, and I hold out my hand. "Rebel hates to be pinched. Not big pinches, just small ones, like with the tips of your fingers," he whispers.

"Thanks for the tip." I smile, and he lifts the rope for me.

"You two girls done with your chitchatting." Rebel is bouncing around the ring.

My jaw nearly drops watching him. His leg muscles are well defined. He's stripped off his shirt, and he has that sexy V at his waistline with a small trail of hair dipping beneath his shorts. He is one fine-looking man. Too bad he's an ass.

He walks over to the ropes. "Get her a helmet, would you?" he yells to his buddy. He tosses him a black helmet that is open other than a bar that sticks out to protect the face. He grasps it between his gloves and shoves it on my head.

"Where is yours?" I say as I adjust it.

"I don't need one." He chuckles.

I hit my gloves together to see how it feels. I've worn gloves for kickboxing, but never this kind. They're bulkier and heavier.

"I'm going to teach you the basics." He stands in front of me and holds my hands out.

"Why are we doing this? I don't think the men that are after me are going to be boxing." I drop one gloved hand and place it on my hip.

"It's all about the moves and strength." He takes my hand off my hip and repositions it where he wants it. "You learn to be quick and place a hit in a vital spot."

"You mean hit them in the crotch." I smile thinking about knocking him to his knees.

"No. I'm talking about breaking his nose or hitting him so hard he can't see. Taking him off guard." He pushes his foot out and nudges my legs until I'm in the stance he wants. "I've already taught you that if you're grabbed from behind, you stomp his foot then rear your head back into his nose. But what if he doesn't get you from behind. He comes straight on. What would you do?"

"Run."

"He's faster."

"Scream."

"No one's around to hear you."

"Kick him in the balls."

"He catches your foot and breaks your leg."

I drop my hands. "I don't know, Rebel. Why don't you tell me?"

He grabs my hands again. "You protect your face. When he swings at you, you block him. Like this." He raises his fist toward me and shifts my arm upward so that my forearm would take the blow. "Got it?"

I nod, and he takes a step back. "Now let's practice." He swings in slow motion a few times for me to get a feel for it, then he speeds up, punching a little harder.

I block every blow.

"When he swings, and you block him, it's your chance to get a swing in. He's off-balance from the blow, moving forward. You're on your toes and ready to move. You swing with the opposite arm. Make straight-on contact." He steps back again. "Try it."

We practice each motion slowly.

"Now try it for real," he says.

"You want me to really hit you?"

"You're not going to hurt me." He raises his gloves. He swings, I block, then throw a punch, but he grabs my arm and twists it so I turn, and my back is to his front.

I hear Lawson laugh.

"That's not how we practiced it." I look over my shoulder at him.

"You have to be ready for anything." He lets me go. "Don't worry. I'll walk you through all of it over the next couple of weeks."

I'M LYING on my back in the middle of the ring, covered in sweat and trying to catch my breath. We've practiced and practiced. I only thought I was in good shape. I already feel every ache of every muscle in my body. I'm not going to be able to move, but it felt good not thinking about my sister for a couple of hours. My mind needed the break. Rebel stands at my feet.

"Are you camping down there or what?" His legs are wide apart, and his muscles gleen with sweat. Why is it women look terrible all sweaty, and men look like gods? It's really not fair that he looks so good.

"Could you throw me a pillow?" I roll to my side and curl up into a ball.

He leans down and wraps his arms around me, pulling me up.

"No, I don't want to play anymore." My body goes limp.

He stops me from falling to the ground and turns me around. Next thing I know, I'm upside down over his shoulder. I want to fight, but I'm exhausted. At least it's a free ride to the locker room.

Lawson spreads the ropes apart for him to climb down. "Is that how you get women? Throw them over your shoulder like a caveman." He chuckles.

"This is how I carry my prey once I've defeated them."

"That must've been a hard catch. What is she, a hundred and twenty pounds soaking wet?" He continues to egg him on.

"Don't you have someone else you can harass?" My body bounces on his shoulder.

"Yeah, but it wouldn't be nearly as fun." Lawson laughs.

Rebel opens the locker room door and kicks it shut with his foot, then sets me on my feet. "Go shower, you stink." He places his hands on my shoulder and turns me toward a room with a shower curtain hiding it. Thank god; I was thinking I was going to have to shower in front of him. God knows he'd boldly watch me and get a kick out of embarrassing me.

It's all I can do to take my own clothes off and get under the spray of the water. I let it soak my hair and run over my body. It takes me forever to wash myself because my arms feel like lead.

"Are you alive in there?" Rebel's voice is on the other side of the shower curtain.

"Just give me another minute."

I see the outline of his body through the white shower curtain. He has a towel wrapped low on his waist. He stands there for a moment like he's going to say something, then I see his hand sweep through his hair and the shadow of his bicep. My tired body stirs with something I've never felt before. I stave it off by tilting my head back into the stream of the water and shutting my eyes. I can't feel anything for anyone right now. I don't deserve any happiness with my sister fresh in the ground.

CHAPTER 11

FALLON

"Why haven't we heard from him?" I've worn a path in the wood floor pacing back and forth over the past month.

"He's undercover. We're not going to hear from him."

"Then how are we supposed to know that he's okay?"

Rebel throws the pencil down on the map he's been studying and leans back on the couch, locking his hands behind his head. "Theo can take care of himself."

"I'm not sure any of this was a good idea. We haven't seen anyone following me since my sister died. We could be way off base about them even being after me." I plop down on the couch next to him.

"We've been holed up at my place and haven't left. Nobody knows where I live so they can't find you." He grabs his computer off the end of the table and turns it in my direction and punches a few keys. "Look."

I stare at the screen, and it's the inside of my apartment. "You bugged my place?"

"I had cameras installed to prove that someone is after you. It's part of the protocol for the government to be able to send men out."

"Did you see anyone?"

He scrolls through the video. " This was two days ago, and there are more like it before this date."

Two men dressed in all black wearing masks come through my front door. The time on the computer says two in the morning. I can't help the gasp that escapes my mouth. I could've been there sleeping, and there's no telling what they would've done to me. I can't watch anymore, so I get back up. "They're going to find me sooner or later."

"They will," he says flatly, "but not until we want them to."

"When? This needs to be over with so I can go on with my life." An ache in the pit of my stomach starts. I have a life, my sister doesn't, and I'm talking about going on. Tears well up in my eyes.

"Hey, your sister would want you to go on." Rebel slips his hand on mine, and I find it strangely comforting coming from him.

"I know. I just need more time."

I stare at him when he reaches up and wipes a tear that has fallen down my cheek. He's very handsome despite the scar on his face. I follow suit and run my finger down the side of his face, tracing his scar. "I'm sorry she hurt you," I whisper and watch him close his eyes. I crawl off the couch and kneel down in the small space in front of him. Placing my hands on either side of his face, he opens his eyes, and I softly place my lips on his. He doesn't blink, and he doesn't return the kiss. I draw back only slightly, enough to look into his eyes.

In my periphery, I see his hand raise, and he puts it on the nape of my neck and draws me into him. His kiss isn't soft like mine; it's rough and full of passion...maybe anger. It's like I lit something inside him, and his punishing kiss consumes me. It's raw with tons of emotion behind it, but I don't think the emotion is directed at me.

He stops abruptly, leaving me wanting so much

more. "I'm sorry," he says softly and lays his forehead against mine.

"Don't be. You need to move on too, you know." I lick my lips and taste him still on me. My lips throb with a need for him to do it again.

"We can't." He gets up, moving me out of the way.

"We can't? Or you don't want to?" I take his hand.

"Theo," he breathes out his name.

"What does you kissing me have to do with him?"

"Aren't the two of you a couple?" He squints his dark eyes at me.

"No. Theo is like my brother. I care for him deeply, but not like you think."

"Have you told him that?"

"Yes, I have." I stand.

"Still, I think he really likes you."

"I think he's infatuated with me. He's too young, and I've told him as much."

I move past him into the kitchen and grab a bottle of water from the fridge. "You're too much in that head of yours. Theo told me about Nina. Her betrayal, according to Theo, changed you. And, I can understand you not trusting very easily, but don't push away what's right in front of you because you're scared."

His feet carry him in my direction. "I'm not afraid of anything," he growls at me.

"Really, then why did I see nothing but fear when you opened your eyes and saw that it was me that you were kissing?"

His jaw juts out as he runs a hand through his thick hair. "Because you're a job, nothing more, and I can't lose my focus."

"Excuse me for thinking we had a moment between us," I huff and try to move past him, but he snags my arm.

"I was trying to comfort you. It won't happen again."

I snatch my arm from him and walk into the bedroom, wanting to slam a nonexistent door. Instead, I slip on my shoes and head for the front door.

"Where do you think you're going?" His voice is loud as it bounces off the walls.

"I need some fresh air and to get away from you." I yank open the door, and he's right behind me. His large hand lands on the metal door and slams it shut. His body presses mine against the door, and I can feel his breath on my ear.

"Is this what you want?" His hips push into me, and I can feel that he's hard. "You don't think I want you? I was hard the entire time we were in the boxing ring, and when I saw you standing in your undies."

My breath hitches.

He turns me around, and his mouth is on me again. He pins my hands on the door above my head.

"Stop," I force myself to say. "I'm not her, Rebel."

He lets go of my hands. "I know you're not Nina. You're far too innocent in so many ways."

"She really did screw with your head, didn't she?" I lay the palm of my hand on his chest. "I'm so, so sorry that she hurt you, but I would never do that to another person, not even my worst enemy." I drop my hand, and he stares at me for a moment.

"I can't give you my heart if that's what you want," he whispers.

"You don't have to promise your heart, Derrick, but you have to let someone in and why not me? I won't hurt you."

He leans his forehead against mine. "Because I don't want to hurt you either. You're sweet and innocent, and I'm tainted."

"You're not tainted. I've gotten to know you over the last couple weeks. You're gruff on the outside, but on the inside is a strong man of character who cares deeply about people whether you want to or not. Why can't you let that heart of yours beat for someone else? Someone who sees you and could love you."

His mouth covers mine hard and fast, making my head spin. He sweeps me off my feet and carries me to his bed. "I can't promise you anymore than right now."

"Then I'll take it." I raise my arms for him to remove my shirt. He kisses every inch of me down to my waist. My body feels like it's on fire and it can't be put out by anyone but him. I've never been bold, but I find my hands unbuckling his belt and working my fingers inside his jeans. He hisses when I touch him and backs up, ripping off his pants. He presses his body into mine until I'm lying flat on my back and he's hovering over me, taking me in.

"You're so damn beautiful."

I raise up and capture his mouth as I grip his hair. Never in my life have I ever wanted someone so badly. I no longer have any confusion about the difference in what I feel for Theo and what I feel for this man right now. I can't control it, nor do I want to.

He stands and pulls my pants from my hips, taking my panties with him. I reach behind me and remove my bra. I want him to see me as I take him in. I can't hide how my body reacts to the sight of him. My nipples are painfully hard, and my core is wet and throbs with a need to feel him inside me.

"Shit." He leans back.

"What is it?"

"I don't think I have a condom."

"You don't think, or you don't?"

He shakes his head.

"How does a good-looking man like you not have a need for a condom?" I run my hand through his hair.

He turns and sits on the side of the bed. "I haven't been with a woman since her."

I'm stunned by his admission and sit on the bed next to him. "Really?"

"Yeah. I haven't trusted anyone enough."

I run my hands down his leg. "There are other things we could do." I get on my knees between his legs. There's a drop of dew already formed on the tip of his hard cock. I keep my gaze on him as I lick the tip.

He groans and throws his head back. I cup his balls and lower my lips and suck in his cock. His hips lift off the bed, and he hisses. "Damn."

I continue with my torture of him, and I feel him

grow even harder in my mouth. I pull up, and his hands go under my arms. He lifts me up and throws me on the bed. Before I can adjust, he's in between my legs. His tongue is lapping me, and his fingers are scissoring inside me. His other hand is squeezing my nipple. I'm all sensation. He doesn't stop until he has an orgasm screaming from my body. He wickedly lulls it out of me and makes it last for so long.

"Please," I beg him, but I'm not sure what for.

He leans over me and his cock is in his hand, stroking himself. I want my hands where his arm is, so I wrap my hand over his and he slides his out. I grasp him hard and stroke like he was.

"That's it, baby," he says between clenched teeth. Two more strokes and he releases with a roar. I watch it spurt from him and onto my skin. It's sexy as hell thinking he let go enough with me to find his release. Even if there is never anything more between us, I'm glad I could give him this, even if he wasn't buried inside me.

He gets up and goes to the bathroom, and I hear the water running. He comes back out with a towel and wipes me clean. "Sorry I didn't have a condom."

"I'm not. I like that you haven't slept with anyone else."

He sits beside me. "That wasn't sleeping, doll." He laughs, but I see sadness in his eyes.

"Are you okay?" I sit up and place a kiss on his shoulder.

"I will be, and for the first time in a long time, I really believe that. Thank you." He gets up and pulls his jeans on. "You need to go get dressed and pack your gun like I showed you."

"You're kicking me out?"

"No. I'm setting you up. We need our plan in motion, and I want you to practice totting that gun. You've given me my life back in more ways than one, and you deserve to have yours back too."

I reluctantly get out of his bed because I'm afraid it will never happen again. I get dressed and grab my bag and take the gun out. He's taught me how to handle it, and now it's time I carry it. He doesn't speak, but he shows me different ways to carry it on my body. I can't help but notice the way he looks at me has changed. His look is softer, and even if he doesn't want to admit it, I think he cares about me.

He puts the gun back in my bag and takes my hand. "Come on."

I follow him out the door and into the caged elevator. "Where are we going?"

"Sean's Place first to tag you." His gaze scans my

body. "I'm sorry I was such an ass earlier. I worked with Nina every day and didn't see it coming. I won't be blindsided again by anyone."

"I won't hurt you, Derrick." It's sad because I think hidden inside him is a loving man. I see shadows of it every now and then by the way he smiles or touches me. It comes out without him thinking about it, and when it does, he suppresses anything he might feel and puts that damn wall back up. A wall that I broke through only moments ago.

He runs a knuckle along my cheek. "I don't think you'd hurt me, but it's not a chance I'm willing to take when I'm trying to save your life. This, that just happened, can't happen again."

"Then let's get this over with, shall we?" Straightening my spine, I march out of the elevator to his car. I told him I'd take what he could give me, and I meant it. I'll cherish our moment together, but I'm not going to be angry that he's not capable of more. We don't speak again until we're at the bar with Sean in what Rebel now calls headquarters.

Sean is keying in codes to the computer and talking a mile a minute. "This is the coolest system. I can zoom in almost anywhere." A screen on the wall lights up. "I saw Theo go into his apartment two days ago, but I haven't seen him since."

"You saw him? Was he okay?" I stand to the side and look at the empty apartment on the screen.

"He appeared to be in a rush, but he looked fine."

"I'll go to his apartment as soon as we get there. I'm sure he left a clue. Pull up the tracking software on Fallon. I want to make sure it's working before I place a tracker under her skin." Rebel opens a metal box he pulls down from a shelf.

"Where are you going to put it?" I ask as he holds up what looks like something that would go into a breaker.

"It normally goes in the back of your neck or under your armpit, but these guys will know to look for it there. Pull down your jeans," he orders.

"Uh...I don't think so. You're not putting it in my..."

"I'm putting in in your hip, Fallon." He smirks at me.

"I was beginning to wonder too." Sean chuckles, and his gaze tracks between us. "Is there something going on between the two of you?"

"No!" we both answer in unison.

"Okay, my bad. You don't have to take my head off." He raises his hands in surrender.

Rebel loads the tracker into a small tube with a button on the end. "Turn around."

I lower my jeans just below my hip. His large hand grasps my side, and I feel the cold end of the tube press into me. "On the count of three."

I nod.

"One, two..." I hear the click and jump. "Three," he adds.

I glare at him over my shoulder. "Your counting sucks."

Sean laughs.

"Trust me when I tell you that it's better when you don't expect it." His hand is rubbing the insertion spot.

I move away from his touch and pull up my jeans. "Trust you...huh, I'm not the one with trust issues." I open the door.

"Where the hell are you going now?"

"To pee, if that's okay with you. I'm sure your brother can track me to the bathroom."

I hear Sean laugh as I slam the door.

Damn frustrating man. I wish Josie was here to talk to her about him. Maybe she would set me straight and tell me to keep my heart away from him. I need to toughen up in more ways than one.

When I walk back into headquarters, Sean is opening a small box. "This arrived early this morning." He hands something so tiny to Rebel that I can't see it.

"This will be virtually invisible. Have you programmed it yet?"

"I'm finishing the final upload for it. We should be live any minute." Rebel hands it back to his brother.

"When you're done, put it on her, and we'll test it out."

"Put what on me?" I walk up behind Sean to see what he has in the palm of his hand, but I don't see anything. "Where did it go?"

He takes his finger and flips whatever it is over in his hand. It's the same color as his flesh. "What is it?"

"It's a microphone. We'll be able to talk to each other through this system. It's like real spyware." Sean is smiling like a little kid on Christmas morning.

"When you two are finished, you can try it out," Rebel grumbles and steps out of the room.

"Who peed on his Cheerios?" Sean hikes a thumb over his shoulder at Rebel.

I don't dare tell him about what happened between us. "From my short experience with him, I'm thinking that's his general mood." I slide a chair up next to him. "Do you think any of this is going to work?"

"My brother may be an ass, but he's good at what he does."

"He was a SEAL team leader, not a secret agent or whatever he's calling himself now."

"He's smart, and I trust him. So does Theo or he wouldn't be in Germany." He stands behind me. "Pull your hair away from your ear."

I do as he says and lean my head to the side. He presses the skin-colored chip onto the back of my ear.

"Go out into the bar, and I'll test it."

I walk out in the empty bar, and Rebel is sitting in a booth talking to someone on the phone. He ends his conversation as soon as he sees me. "Gotta go."

I slide in the seat across from him and hear Sean in my ear.

"Testing, testing. Fallon, can you hear me?"

"Loud and clear."

CHAPTER 12

REBEL

The past two days I've avoided any additional conversation with Fallon. It's hard, because every time I look at her, I want to touch her and so much more, but I have to keep my wits about me.

We've gone over and over our plan a million times, and we've trained at the ring daily. She and Lawson have become friends, and it irritates the hell out of me. Why does she have to be so damn likable? Everything she does gets under my skin. She lounges around in those soft blue pajama bottoms and a black tank top without a bra on, and I have to excuse myself every time I see her in the morning so she doesn't see my hard-on. I no sooner get it tamed, and she's in the living room with her head tipped downward brushing her long hair. I can see straight through the neck of her shirt. I suppose if I were a nice guy, I'd tell her, but I'm a dick, and I like watching her.

"Today is the day," I say from behind the couch so she can't see my crotch.

She flips her hair back. "Good, because I'm ready to get this over with. Has Sean seen any more of Theo?"

"No. Go get dressed. I'm going to call Sean and make sure he's ready and has his ears on. He's hired someone to watch the bar while we get things moving. That way he doesn't have to leave head-quarters."

She bites her lip nervously. "Do you think I'm ready?"

"Yes," I try to say with confidence like I would with my men on the Gunner team.

I talk to Sean, and he assures me all systems are go. Within a few minutes, Fallon is back, dressed in a pair of skinny jeans, a navy top and a white pair of Keds. She has her purse tucked close to her body.

"I'm ready."

"Talk to Sean."

"Can you hear me, Sean?"

"Yes."

She smiles. "This is really cool."

I grab my black leather jacket and escort her to the door. The sun is starting to set, and this will be the first time in weeks that Fallon has been out at night or has left my side.

When we make it to my car, there's an eerie feel to the air. I shake it off and stay focused on our task at hand. Which is to flush out the two men who'd been following her and get the name of whoever is giving them orders. With Theo being deep into their organization, it should make them easier to find and infiltrate their entire illegal system. These two characters are only the tip of the iceberg. I'm sure they're only pawns in a bigger scheme of things, but it will get Fallon out of harm's way and access to the leader.

I park the car in the dark alley behind Sean's bar. Street parking is full, and the bar is buzzing with people. I take a seat in the back corner, and Fallon starts to mingle in the crowd.

She's so fucking beautiful that men start to notice her right away. One young guy is eyeing her up and down, and I don't like it.

"I think you like her," I hear Sean in my ear.

"I don't know what you're talking about." I put my hand over my mouth so people don't think I'm talking to myself.

"I see you watching her from the cameras."

"I'm supposed to be watching her, you idiot."

"Yeah, but you're jealous. It shows all over your face every time a guy flirts with her."

"I'm not jealous." I lean back in the booth and casually drape an arm over the back.

"You push people away long enough, they won't come back," he says.

"You sound like my goddamn therapist."

"Ah, so she's smart then and sees right through your bullshit." He laughs in my ear.

"Quit badgering me and keep your eyes open," I grumble at him and watch as a man dressed in all black cuts into the crowd of people and makes a beeline toward Fallon. "Do you see him? Tell her to quit flirting and pay attention to the man headed toward her."

"I'll switch back over to the two-way so you can talk to her too."

I see her facial expression change, and I know that she's hearing him now. She casually turns around and flips her long hair over one shoulder. I watch as she places the bottle of beer to her lips and I want to groan, but don't make a sound.

He comes up beside her and tries to get the

bartender's attention. "Busy night here." I faintly hear his conversation with her through her mic.

She nods.

"Make conversation with him, Fallon," I say quietly.

She turns toward him and starts talking about the bar. He orders her a drink and stirs it for her.

Within seconds, he asks her to go to another bar with him.

"Go with him. I'll be right behind you, and Sean has eyes and ears on you."

She hugs her bag and smiles at him, then follows him outside. I stand to make my way out, and a large man comes out of nowhere and bumps into me with his beer, splashing it all over me.

"Shit!" I try to shove by him, but it's like trying to move a brick wall.

"You need to get outside, man. He's dragging her into an alley." Sean sounds a little frantic.

I bump my shoulder into the man, and he grabs me by the forearm, then takes a swing at me. I duck just in time, and his fist goes into the wall behind me. I snag his wrist and twist it behind him, and he grimaces in pain.

"Who the fuck are you working for?" I'm at his ear.

He rears his head back at me, and I shove it into the wall, knocking him out cold. I lower him into a booth then push my way through the crowd.

"Shit, man. He hit her hard," Sean is yelling.

"Stay put. I'll get to her. Don't lose her. Fallon, I'm coming, where are you?" Dead silence. "Fallon!" I run out the door and to the back alley. I look both ways but don't see her. The only sign of her is her purse laying on the asphalt.

"Shit, Sean! Where is she?"

"They took off in a black van, headed due east." I pick up her purse, and something crunches beneath my shoe. I bend down and pick up the small pieces of her micro hearing aid.

"What ear did you put her mic in?" I growl at Sean.

"What difference does it make?"

"What ear!" I yell again.

"I don't know...um...left, yeah, her left ear."

"Goddamn it! She can't hear out of that ear without her hearing aid in, which I have pieces of in my hand."

"It must have fallen out when they struck her."

I start my car before my door is even shut, and I screech out into the road, causing several cars to slam on their brakes and honk their horns. I shift into gear and race toward the highway, but the traffic is terrible.

"Do you see them?"

"They're headed toward the airport." I can hear Sean tapping his finger on something.

I make a quick turn to try to find a shortcut, but there's road work slowing the traffic even more. I shift out of my lane and into oncoming traffic. Cars swerve out of the way as I speed straight for them.

"Derrick, they went through the tunnel and didn't come out the other side." Sean's voice is distraught.

"That's not possible." I lay on the gas and race to the tunnel.

"I've lost them!"

"Fallon, I don't know if you can still hear me or not but hang on. Fight them off as long as you can. I promise I'll find you."

I make it into the tunnel, but there are no cars on the side, and traffic is moving slowly. There's no sign of them. "Check your feed again. They're not in here," I all but yell at Sean.

"I've checked it twice. They went in, but never came out."

"See if they came out the other direction."

"Okay, let me back it up." I hear his equipment

running. "They did! They headed back the other way. Let me see if I can locate them."

"Zoom out and look for them." I do a U-turn in the tunnel in front of a limo.

"I don't see them."

"Keep looking. I'm headed back your way."

I don't stop until I'm back where I started. I rush in the back door of the bar and into headquarters. "Did you find them?" I lean on the desk.

"No." He shakes his head.

"Go back to where they entered." I point to the screen.

He does, but because there was too much time before he figured it out, they've disappeared with Fallon.

"Fuck!" I slam my fists on the table, then I remember the large man I knocked out in the bar. I run out there to find him getting out of the booth. I hoist him up and jab my gun into his back. "You're coming with me." I drag him upstairs to Theo's apartment and unlock the door. "Sean, get to Theo's room, now!"

A few seconds later, I can hear him running up the stairs, and he rushes into the room.

He looks at me holding a gun to the man's head. "Take my keys and go get the rope that's in my trunk." I fish out my keys with one hand and toss it to him.

"Don't fucking move!" I keep my gun aimed at him as I drag a dining room table chair over to him. "Sit and keep your hands in the air!"

He does, and Sean comes back with a rope looped over his shoulder.

"Tie him up."

Sean walks wide to go behind him.

"Put your hands behind you." I wave the gun at him.

"Make sure it's tight," I tell Sean.

Once he's secured, I tuck the gun in the back of my pants. "Where did they take her?"

"I don't know," he says.

I take my gun out again and press it to his temple. "Tell me what you do know."

"We were paid to deliver her, nothing more."

"Deliver her to whom?"

"I don't know. We've never met them. We get our bids online, and then we hand them the merchandise."

"Does money get wired into your account?"

"Yes."

"What bank?"

"It has a German name. I don't remember, I swear."

"Where was your drop-off point tonight?"

"We were told to swap her car in the tunnel, and they'd handle it from there."

I cock my gun. "This isn't your first rodeo. Where are they taking her?"

"Germany."

"Sean, get me the next flight out and then call the CIA. The agent's card is on file. This bozo is going to tell them where his cohort is, and they're both going to jail."

CHAPTER 13

THEO

I hate this place and everything about it. The stench of fear hangs in the air. When I got here a month ago, I easily inserted myself into the criminal market by using the fake background and name that Sean created for me. It made my stomach turn when I first read it. It insinuated that I hated women and used them for my own sick plea-sures and then sold them to the highest bidder. My new identity is Sam Larkin. I have no idea where he came up with the name, but it's one that I'll hate forever.

It worked. One of the connections I made by Sean mapping him out is a high-ranking employee in the geNetics game. Lance is ranked third in the company, and he brought me into their underground world.

Women who've been stolen or previously sold before are brought in once a week. It's sickening how they line them up like animals being led to the slaughter. Several of their other illegal practices are bartered here too. They're held on different nights. The auctioning of human organs plays out here too. They generate a report of people on a waiting list to receive organs, then they search their database from geNetics testing and find what they need. It's all done under the guise of finding them a donor, but it's all for their black market. The highest bidder gets the organ.

They contact the donor and tell them they've been accepted but need a couple weeks to set it up. What they're really lining up is having them kidnapped and brought here to take what the highest bidder has purchased.

Tonight is the women trafficking auction. Lance has convinced the other members that I'm on the up-and-up so that I can attend tonight. He's told me that to show my loyalty, I must purchase one of the girls before I can start selling them to my connections, which are all made up. If I do this, he'll introduce me to the person who's responsible for the entire operation.

The thought of buying a woman sickens me, not to mention the things they do to these scared women. My beard has grown thick, and I even look like most of the members here. I've changed since I've tried to mold into their ways. I have a hardness about me that I never did before. I'm trying to hold on to the man I was versus the coldness I feel brewing inside me.

I follow Lance to the door of the black building with no windows that sets out on a piece of land in the middle of nowhere. Barbed wire fencing surrounds the property along with armed guards. Someone uninvited would never gain access.

Lance flashes his ID. "Who is he?" A massive man guarding the door grunts in my direction.

"He's the new guy I called in about earlier. Go ahead, check him out."

I dig my fake ID out of my wallet.

"Up against the wall," the baritone voice of the big guy says.

"He doesn't want your ID, man." Lance laughs.

I spread eagle against the wall, and the guard leaves no part of me untouched. I feel very violated.

"He's clean," he barks.

I straighten my clothes and square my shoulders

at the guard, letting him know I'm not intimidated by him. He looms over me with a nasty scowl, and Lance pulls me inside before he pummels me.

"Don't piss off the guard. It won't work in your favor."

The place is dark on the inside; some spots are almost pitch-black. The only lighting I see is on a stage in the middle of the room. We stay on the lower level and take a seat center stage.

"These are the best seats in the house to get a good view of the merchandise."

I want to strangle him for thinking of these women as a commodity. Sick bastard.

"Up there, I know you can't see it, but that's where the owner sits and watches every purchase made."

I look up above the stage, and he's right. You can't see a thing. "How do they see anything?"

"They have cameras pointing at the stage, and they can view them on their computer screens."

So, when the lights from their computers come on, I should be able to see their faces.

A ray of light shines through the back door as young girls are herded through the door. They're bound and gagged and tied together. One man has the front rope and is pulling them through the door.

The bidding starts as soon as they have the first girl on stage. I keep glancing upward to see who comes into the owner's seat. I only see shadows of two people walk in and sit. As their computer screens lite up, I can see their faces are covered with dark masks.

"Have you ever seen them without their masks?" I nudge Lance.

"No, and I don't ever care to. Rumor is, someone did, and they never lived to tell about it." He raises a bidding card in the air for the girl on stage. He's outbid quickly. "Damn, I have the perfect owner for her. Too bad she's already out of his price range."

I envision myself taking him out with a single shot between is eyes.

"What do you think about the next girl up." He elbows me.

She's a young woman, I'd guess around twenty. Her dark red hair is tangled, and she looks thin and scared. She has bruises on her arms, and her yellow dress has been torn. It looks like they dress the girls up to parade them around.

"She's got a nasty reputation of being a fighter." Lance raises his card as soon as she steps on stage.

She spits at the man who shoves her up there, and he backhands her hard. She wobbles but doesn't go to the ground. Instead, she straightens her spine in what I assume is defiance.

"Oh, I might have to keep her for myself." Lance sits up tall and waves his card again when he's outbid.

Someone yells from behind me, "She's going to be too much trouble to train, Lance."

He looks over his shoulder. "I like the taming process." He laughs.

The bidding continues between Lance and one other man. As the auctioneer is calling for the final bid that Lance will win, I raise my card.

The auctioneer points to me, directing Lance's attention at me. "Oh man. Are you sure you want her for yourself? Can you handle that wildcat?"

"I'll have her under my submission in two days," I say with all the seriousness I can muster. I even add a deep-seated scowl and lower my voice. I have to appear to know what I'm doing, even though I've never dominated a woman in my life, nor do I want to.

"She's all yours then, and this I have to see." He lowers his card.

"Sold!" the auctioneer yells.

It's all I can do to sit beside him the next few hours, watching girl after girl be sold to the highest bidder. I keep glancing upward for something from the two watching that would help me identify them later. A repetitive movement or gesture. Something that once they're outside here, I would know without a doubt who they were.

Once the auction is over, we line up to collect our goods. Lance purchased six of the women for his buyers. I pull out the cash and pay for the girl, and I've already been informed that she'll be delivered to my room. I'm handed a file with all the information I need on her.

I left the apartment behind that Rebel had rented me once I found out where all the big players were living—in a renovated posh hotel that had been converted into condominiums. Members-only type club, so no one knows what's really taking place.

I separate from Lance once we make it back. I deadbolt the door behind me and open the file on the counter. Her name is Fiona Petit. She was taken from her home two years ago at the age of eighteen. She's been sold six times since she was kidnapped. No family is listed, and she was reported as a runaway. It says she's been resold multiple times because she was too difficult to manage and untrainable. At the very bottom of the file, there's a picture of her. She's beautiful, with her dark red locks and big green eyes that have flecks of orange in them. She has faint freckles that line the bridge of her nose, and her pale skin looks like it belongs on a porcelain doll. Her petite frame doesn't look like a fighter.

I can't imagine what this young woman has been through the past two years. I don't want to make her life worse, but I have to make them believe that I can handle her to delve deeper into the organization.

A hard knock on the door has me turning around. I draw in a deep breath and ready myself for what I'm about to do. I open the door to two big men manhandling the petite girl. Her hands are bound behind her back, and I have to hold in a laugh when she kicks one of them in the shin.

He punches her between the shoulder blades, causing her to stumble inside my room. He pulls her up by the hair, and I stop him.

"I will take care of her punishment."

"But that little bitch..."

"I said enough. I own her now, and if you lay another hand on my property, I'll kill you." I flex my mechanical fingers back and forth.

He glares at me but backs down. I shut the door behind them and gaze quickly through the peephole to make sure they're really gone. When I turn back around, Fiona has made it to her feet, and the look on her face has me dead where I stand.

"Don't touch me!" she screams.

I raise my palms in the air. "I'm not going to hurt you."

"That's what my last owner said right before he broke my arm in two places!"

Damn. How could anyone hurt someone like that? I swallow my thoughts. I've killed many men in my day being a SEAL, but I could never hurt an innocent woman.

"I swear, I won't hurt you. I'll untie you if you promise not to slit my throat."

"I'll kill you the first chance I get," she seethes.

"Then I won't be untying you anytime soon." I walk over to the thickly cushioned chair. "Will you at least sit down so we can talk."

Her face scrunches together. "You think I'm going to fall for that, 'oh let's talk' thing?"

"Okay, what can I do to convince you that I'm not going to hurt you?"

"Let me go."

"I can't do that, but if you give me a chance, I can explain."

"Explain what, that you're some sick fuck!" She stops talking for a second and looks hard at me.

"Aren't you a little young to be so perverted? All my other masters have been old and ugly."

"I'm not your master."

"You bought me, I see the bill of sale sitting on that file." She tilts her head toward the counter.

"Fair enough. I did purchase you, but not for the reasons you think."

She cautiously steps up close to me. "What makes you any different from my other masters. They all wanted the same thing...to fuck me and then to beat me."

"I don't want either one of those things."

"Why not?"

I don't trust her to tell her that I'm undercover, but I don't know how else to explain my purchase of her. "I'm here to bust up this organization, and I needed to be legit."

"You"—she laughs—"you think you're going to take these people down?"

"Me and a few of my friends. I need you to act like I've tamed you. Like you're submissive to me."

"If anything you're saying is true, untie me." She turns her back to me, showing her hands.

I take a knife out of the kitchen drawer and cut her ropes. She turns toward me and rubs her bleeding wrists. Then as quick as a cat, she runs for the door. I make it to her before she gets it unlocked. My body crushes her to the door, and I pin her there.

"I don't want to hurt you, please don't make me."

"Then let me go."

"I can't. Please sit down." I release one hand from the doorframe and splay it toward the couch.

She reluctantly gives in and sits, but her body remains rigid like a wild animal ready to run.

"My name is Theo Drake. I'm a...was a Navy SEAL ...

She interrupts me. "Was...because of your arm?"

"Yes. But I got involved with someone who was being hunted by this organization, and I plan on ending it."

"Do you have an army of men?" She laughs.

"No, there's only three of us."

"You're naive, aren't you? I've tried I don't know how many times to escape only to be beaten and brought back. The woman that runs these monsters is pure evil."

"Woman? Have you seen her face? Is it one of the masked people that was sitting above the stage?"

"Yes. I got a glimpse of her by accident. She came to visit one of my masters. He locked me up, but I managed to see her through a vent in the wall."

"What did she look like?" I scoot closer to her, and she inches away from me.

"She's tall. Taller than my last master. Dark hair and wears a patch over one eye."

"A patch? Like a pirate?"

She nods.

"Could you tell from her accent where she was from?"

"I don't know, she was speaking German."

"Did you ever hear her name?"

"No, but I can tell you she had him beat me to try and break me." She leans forward and pulls down the shoulder of her torn dress. There is a thick scar that mars her body.

Anger rages through me like never before. I see my father's face for the first time in a long time as I envision him beating my mother. I stand and pace to try to ward off my anger. "I'll find a way to get you out of this and send you back home."

"I...I don't have a home. I was living in an orphanage and finally reached the age where they let me go."

I sit back down. "How did they take you?"

"It was simple. They run shelters for homeless women. I went there my first night to get out of the cold, and they took me in my sleep."

Tears well up in my eyes at the thought of the life she's had. "I'm so sorry for what they've done to you, Fiona. I swear to god, I will make them pay."

Her hand shakes as she reaches out and touches me. "You really mean that, don't you?"

"I do, but I'm afraid I'm going to have to be awful to you to make them let me get further inside their group."

"I can handle it as long as you promise to let me go."

"I promise."

CHAPTER 14

FALLON

The smell of stale bodies and sweat wakes me up to a room that is almost completely dark. I try to scream only to realize my mouth has been gagged and a metallic taste on my tongue almost makes me want to puke. I can faintly hear echoes of voices dancing around me. My head and ear aches from the blow to the side of my face. My hands are tied behind my back, but I manage to get off the bare concrete floor.

I feel the effects of being drugged, and I stumble, falling on a thin mattress pad. I sit on the side for a minute, catching my breath and trying to get my eyes to focus on what's around me.

There are bunks lining the corrugated walls. A single bulb hangs dimly from the ceiling. The buzz of spotty electricity is loud. There's a young girl that looks no older than sixteen staring at me. She's wearing what looks like dirty, tattered pajamas, and her hair is greasy and unkempt.

She stands from the bunk across from me, and her legs wobble as she steps closer. Her shaky hand reaches up to my mouth and removes my gag.

"Where are we?" My throat burns, and my voice comes out raspy.

"I don't know." She sits beside me and starts working on untying my hands.

"Do you know how long I've been here?"

"They brought you here yesterday and dumped you on the floor. I tried to pick you up, but I couldn't."

"How long have you been here?" I try to help free my hands.

"I lost track of time, but I think about a week."

"I'm Fallon. What's your name?"

"Rachel."

"Do you know who took you and why?"

She shakes her head and tears stream down her dirt-smudged face. She gets the last knot out, and I shake my bruised wrist before I hug her trembling body to mine.

"We're going to find a way out of here."

"This room was full yesterday. They left me here and said it wasn't my night."

"Do you know what they meant by that?"

"No."

"Was it only women in here?"

"No, there were three...no, four men. They tried to escape when they opened the hatch, but they shot them with darts, and the men passed out."

"Can you show me the hatch?"

She grabs my hand, and we walk to the end of the room. She points up. There's a ladder ascending upward to a hatch above us. I place my hand on either side of it and start to climb.

"Please don't leave me!" Rachel tugs on my leg.

I step back down to the floor. "I'm not going to leave you, I promise." I place my hand on her cheek, and she nods. I climb back to the hatch, and it's hard to see, but I can feel that it's reinforced and tightly secured.

"I've tried to open it," Rachel cries below me.

I climb back down the ladder and hear a high-pitched hissing noise. "What is that?"

"It's the air conditioning kicking on and circulating through the room."

"Someone doesn't want us dying from the heat. Do they give you food?"

"Yes, once a day they drop it through the hatch in a box." She reaches behind me and turns on a faucet behind me. I hear the gurgle of running water. "There's plenty of water if you're thirsty."

"We're in a bomb shelter." I glance around the dim room. "Were you awake when they brought you here? Do you have any idea where we are?"

She sits on one of the bunks. "The last thing I remember was my dad telling me goodnight. I went upstairs to my room and went to bed. I had a weird dream that someone was trying to suffocate me, the next thing I know, I'm here."

"Where did you say you lived?"

"Alabama."

"Do you remember anyone watching you or following you?"

"No."

"Had you met anyone new?"

"I made a friend online that my dad was pretty upset about."

I sit next to her. "Why?"

"He...he asked me to send some pictures of me in my panties and bra."

"Did you?"

"No. I told my dad, and he took my computer away."

I run my hand through her knotted hair. "Sounds like you have a good dad."

"I miss him, and I want to go home." Her tears fall harder.

"I promise not to leave you behind. Even if they take me away, I'll come back for you."

A pressure sound echoes loudly from the hatch, then bright light fills the small room. Rachel shakes and clings to my arm. I blink my eyes hard to see booted feet stepping down the ladder. The butt of a gun leads the way. A man dressed in baggy khakis and a navy shirt comes down the ladder. His face is covered, all but his dark eyes, with a black bandana. Wisps of short, dark hair pokes out from under a solid navy hat.

His feet hit the ground, and two more men descend downward.

"Get on your knees!" he barks at me and waves the gun. "Hands behind your back."

"No! Please don't take her!" Rachel screams, and he slaps her across the face.

"It's okay, Rachel. Remember what I told you," I whisper to her.

One of the men roughly ties my already aching wrists and hoists me to my feet. "If you try to run, I'll drug you again."

As I climb the ladder without the use of my hands, one of them has me by the collar and is pushing me. Without my hands, I can't fight him like Derrick taught me. Derrick, where the hell is he? I can't hear him in my ear. My hearing aid must have fallen out when I was hit in the head. Even though I can't hear him, I know he's on his way. I still have the tracker in my hip. He'll be able to find me once I'm outside this bomb shelter.

The sunlight is even more blinding when I make it outside the hatch. I look around trying to find anything I could use to mark this area. It opens up into woods not far from a grassy patch of land. There's a large black building with no windows that we're walking toward. Large bays filled with semis surround one side of the building. A perimeter fence encloses the land, and armed guards are out front.

The men that have me start speaking in German to one another. *It can't be. I can't be in Germany.* As we get closer to one of the bays, there's a sign written in German. *This has to do with geNetics. Derrick was right about all of it.*

I'm shoved through a set of doors that lead upstairs to a building with a stage in the middle. We walk past several closed doors and come to an area that has white dividers hanging. It looks like something almost sterile. They push me through them, and there're clear plastic walls set up and a silver table in the middle of the room.

"I'll stay with her," one of the men says, and the other two leave. He tucks his gun in his holster and stands with his hands crossed in front of him, but not before he unties my hands. "Don't get any ideas."

A man with a white jacket and a blue mask walks into the room, holding a file.

"Fallon Davis, I'm a surgeon, and I need to perform a physical on you."

"You're not touching me," I snarl.

The man that brought me here places his hand on his gun. "You will do as you're told."

"What's this all about?"

"I need to make sure your organs are in good working order."

My heart nearly stops. He wants to remove my kidneys and give them to someone else. One was supposed to go to my sister. I can't breathe and fall backward. The guard moves quickly to catch me.

"I think she's going to need time for the drugs to clear her system before we can test her." The doctor steps toward me. When he does, I stomp on my captor's foot and rear my head back and hear the crack of his nose. He lets go, and I reach around to his holster and take his gun. I aim it at the doctor and step away from both of them.

"Where is this place, and who gives you your orders?" I cock the gun back.

"There's no way out of here," the man says, cupping his nose and taking a step toward me.

"Don't make me kill you."

He stops. "You pull that trigger, and you'll have hell rain down on you like you've never seen before."

"I'll take my chances rather than lay down and die. You, tie him up," I tell the doctor.

He ties him, and I pull on the ropes to make sure it's tight. The doctor backs up and stands in the corner with his hands in the air.

"What are you going to do?" he asks.

"I'm going to make sure you can't perform any surgeries." I aim the gun and squeeze the trigger. Blood splatters on the wall behind him, and he screams out in pain, holding his hand.

I take off down the hall, and I hear my captor yelling for backup, but not kill me because I'm worth too much money. I run the way we came in, and there's a man standing at the bottom of the stairs with a gun.

"Where do you think you're going?"

We both aim our guns at one another. "You're not going to kill me," I tell him.

He lays his gun on the concrete floor and motions for me to come to him. I take aim again, but I'm shoved down, and the wind is knocked out of me. I roll over, and one of them is coming directly at me. All Derrick's training kicks around in my head, and I get to my feet. I block his punch and move so the next punch can't hit me. I swing at him like Derrick taught me, and I connect with his jaw. He jolts backward, and the next man pushes by him and knocks me down, landing on top of me. He pins me to the floor, and someone comes up from behind me and jabs a needle in my neck.

When I wake up, I'm back in the bomb shelter.

CHAPTER 15
THEO

Fiona and I've been holed up for two days in my apartment. I can tell by the way she moves around me that she still doesn't trust me. I've fed her, bought her some clothes that actually fit, and let her sleep in my bed by herself. She looks healthier than she did two days ago, and her bruises are starting to fade.

A knock on the door has her jumping out of her skin. "Go to the bedroom," I whisper and watch as the door shuts before I open it to whoever is knocking.

"Hey, man. You got that wildcat under control yet?" Lance walks in and looks around the room.

"I told you in two days' time I'd have her tamed." I shut the door.

"So, where is she?"

"Fiona! Come out here!" I hope like hell she plays along.

The bedroom door slowly opens, and she walks out with her gaze pointing to the ground and stops when she's standing beside me. "Tell Mr. Lance who your master is?" I deepen my voice.

"You're my master, Sir." She keeps her eyes downward as she speaks.

"Wow! I don't know how you did it." He walks up to her and runs his knuckles down her arm. She doesn't even flinch. "Now that she's tame, I'd love to fuck her."

She doesn't look up, but I see the hair on her arms rise. "I don't share the merchandise."

"That's too bad because I'm sure she's a spitfire in bed." He walks behind her, and her gaze cuts to me without lifting her head.

"You would've had to purchase her to find out, and she's not for sale."

He laughs. "Everything is for sale, but for now, I'll let it go. I have another situation I need handled, and since you're only dealing with her at the moment, I need you to handle it for me." He walks back over in my direction.

"What do you need done?" I want to kill him

right now for treating her like a piece of meat, but I rein in anger.

"There's someone else who is very valuable, but she's put us in a bind until we can replace our surgeon. You're aware of our...organ procurement program." He clears his throat and glances over at Fiona who is still focused on the ground.

"Yes, you informed me of it."

"We're getting paid millions of dollars for this person's organs, and we need to make sure she stays put and doesn't harm herself or anyone else. We've kept her subdued, but to be able to perform the surgery to remove her kidneys, we have to let the drugs clear her system or they'll be no good to us. We've hired a surgeon to replace the one she took out, but he'll not be here for a few more days. He's ordered us to stop giving her drugs so she'll be ready when he gets here."

"So my job is to babysit this woman? What about my clients that are expecting me to hand them their merchandise?" I have to play the part, but this woman could connect me with the bigger fish.

"Call them and tell them there has been a delay. I'll offer them a discount."

"You must be making millions off her." I laugh, but inside my anger is rising.

He clasps my shoulder with his hand. "Consider yourself her handler, and this one can stay in my apartment while you tend to her."

I reach over and take Fiona's hand in mine before she can move. "She'll stay with me and no one else."

"I'm not sure you can handle both of these women at the same time." He gets in my face.

"You let me worry about that." I don't back down.

He chuckles. "You'll have to tell me your secret. This one had one more chance before we slit her throat." He points at Fiona.

I could cut his open right now and let him bleed out in front of me, but that wouldn't finish the job. "Where's this woman?"

"Be at the building in an hour, and I'll take you to her."

He slams the door as he leaves, and I lock it behind him.

Fiona lets out the breath she had been holding. "Please let me be the one that kills that bastard."

"I'll take care of him. Get your things together. I need to make a stop before we meet up with him."

"You're taking me with you, right?"

"I don't want to, but if I don't, when they catch

you, they'll kill you or worse. So for now, you're safer with me."

She turns to walk away and then comes back over to me. "Thank you for helping me." She places a tender kiss on my lips.

I want to kiss her back, but I don't dare touch her. I want her to trust me completely, and I know she's been so abused that she would run from me. "You're welcome, but this is far from over."

She rushes to get her things, and I grab what I need including the file on Fiona. I call for a cab, and we head to the apartment that Rebel had rented. I tell the cab driver to wait and take Fiona's hand to follow me.

"What is this place?"

"It's where my partner will show up." I unlock the door, and she follows in behind me. I unscrew the metal vent and place the file inside. Before I close it up, I find pen and paper and jot down a note for Rebel, then place the vent back on.

"Why can't I stay here?"

"Because if they connect the dots, they'll find this place and I can't risk that."

I lock up, and we head back to the cab. "Don't speak unless I tell you to. Do you understand?" She nods. As I stare out the window, I feel Fiona's hand on my thigh. I look down and watch her as she squeezes my leg. Looking up at her, I see a different girl, one that's not scared and fighting all alone anymore. Her color is better, and she has the first smile I've seen on her face. She's beautiful, and she deserves so much more than she's gotten in life.

Slowly, I place my hand on hers, and she laces her fingers with mine. I mouth the words, *I promise to set you free*. I'm surprised when she feels comfortable enough to lay her head on my shoulder. I squeeze her hand in mine and kiss the top of her head. Something in me wants to be near her and never let her go. It's the first time that I realize that Fallon was right. Our relationship is not like this. I love her...but I feel a connection with this girl that's grasped a hold of my heart.

We make it through the gated entrance after I produce my ID. This place looks totally different in the daylight. The property it sits on is lush green surrounded by trees. I didn't notice the semis at the bay the last time I was here. It looks like it used to be some sort of shipping facility. The big trucks must be what they're using to bring in their merchandise, to use their words.

Fiona walks quietly beside me as we go through

the door to the building. Lance is sitting on a bleacher-style seat, plugging away at his laptop.

"Keep your head down," I tell Fiona. When I get beside Lance, I see the name Sam Larkin in his web browser.

"Still running my background?" I try to play it off, but it makes me very uneasy.

"Yeah, I got a call from the second in charge to run it again, but everything checks out like the first time." He shuts it.

"Where is this woman?" I glance around the building. I can see Fiona shaking from the corner of my eye. She has to hate being here. Every time she is, she's sold to a different devil.

"You haven't seen it from this point of view," Lance talks to her.

"No," she whispers and lifts her head.

"Well, now that ole Sam here has made you fall in line, you can stay off that stage. Then again...that wouldn't give me a chance to see what you taste like."

My fists ball up so tight, I can feel my short nails dig into my skin. I'm concentrating so hard on not killing him that I don't see Fiona move in time enough to stop her. She lunges at him and scratches her nails down his face deep enough to draw blood.

He deserves a whole lot more, but I know this is only going to be trouble.

"You bitch!" He's on his feet and grabs her by the wrist. "I knew she couldn't be controlled."

"Let go of her."

"Fat chance in hell. I've been dying to punish her." He starts unbuckling his belt

"I said, let her go. I own her, and I'll take care of it."

A man in an expensive-looking suit comes out into the open area. "Then punish her."

"Who are you?" I turn in his direction. Everything about him screams money from his watch down to his leather shoes.

"I'm his boss." He points to Lance but never gives his name.

That would make him number two in charge. I bet he was sitting above the stage with the owner.

"Lance did not have the right to speak to her. I didn't give him permission." I flex my jaw.

"That's not how this works." He laughs. "Any person employed by me is allowed to do whatever they want with these women." He positions his body in front of me in a stance that says he wants to intimidate me.

"I own her outright. That makes whatever rule you have, null and void." I glare at him.

"Oh man," Lance says and backs up.

He takes a step closer and eyes me up and down. "She is on my property."

I grab her hand. "Then I'll take her back to my apartment." Her hand starts to tremble in mine, and I grasp it tighter to let her know there's no way that they're going to touch her.

"You see...Sam, I know this one very well." He rubs his hand down her arm. "She will run the minute you don't have eyes on her."

I push her behind me and stand between the two of them. "Don't touch her." I know I'm about to blow the entire operation, but these men turn my stomach, and I won't let them hurt her again.

He takes a step back. "You're the kind of man I need in this organization. You don't back down." He shoves his hands deep in his pockets.

"What the hell?" Lance throws his hands in the air.

"Shut the fuck up, Lance." His gaze bores into him, and Lance juts his jaw out but doesn't say another word back to him.

"I understand you'll be the handler for the she-devil we have waiting to make me an even richer man."

I hate the word handler; it reminds me of Ekko. "Yes, so he's told me." I angle my head toward Lance who's tapping his foot on the concrete floor.

"Before our friend here takes you to her, you'll punish this one for her actions." He points to Fiona. "And I have just the thing." He walks backward toward the stage.

"I'll punish her in my own time and my own way."

Lance pulls a gun from his belt. "You'll do it now and prove that you're one of us or I'll blow your fucking head off, capiche?"

I turn toward Fiona, and she lets a tear slip down her cheek. She mouths, *just do it.*

I grit my teeth so hard I can feel one chip. I take her hand and pull her down the stairs and over to the stage.

He comes back out of a storage closet, popping a whip in the air. "Have her bare her back and bend over the stage."

No fucking way. Fiona tugs out of my hand and takes her shirt off and bends over.

Everything in me is frozen. The one thing I hated about my father, I'm about to do and become the same devil. My mom lying in a pool of her own blood flashes before my eyes.

"It's your choice, Sam. Either you do and prove your loyalty to me, or I'll kill you both. It's that simple." He holds out the whip.

Fucking monster. I'm not sure if I'm calling him that or myself. I take the whip and sling it through the air a few times. There's no way of doing this without hurting her. I take a few steps back and inhale deeply, holding my breath. I hate myself for what I'm about to do. I raise my arm with the whip in my hand and contemplate if could I kill them both and get her out of here. The answer is no.

I blow my breath out and swing my arm forward. The whip slices into her skin, and she screams out. I'm horrified at what I've done, but I don't let it show.

"Again," he yells.

Three more times her back slices open at my hand. In this very moment, I'm no longer the same man. I can't even look at her when she puts her shirt back on and walks over to me.

"Take him to the woman," he orders Lance.

Outwardly, I appear calm and collective. Inwardly, my insides shake as I follow him. I need to touch her to make sure she's okay, so I reach behind me and take Fiona's hand. Relief washes over me when she twines her fingers with mine.

We walk out past the grassy area into the woods. Lance kicks some shrubs with his foot and exposes the hatch to a bomb shelter. He turns the metal handle, and it makes a hissing noise.

"She's down there," he says as he lifts the lid. "You first."

I turn around and start climbing down. Fiona's face is inches from mine, and her eyes are bloodshot. "I'm sorry," I whisper. As soon as my head clears the hatch, it slams down over me, and it's dark. I beat on it with my fists. "Fiona!"

"You've been caught, Theo!" Lance yells loud enough for me to hear him. "Someone ratted you out!"

Fiona is the only one that knew my name. I deserve her betrayal after what I did to her.

"Theo?" I hear from the ground below me.

"Oh my god. How did you find me?" I nearly pull Theo down the ladder.

"Hazel? How the hell did you get here?" He crushes me into a hug.

"I was drugged and taken. They want my kidneys," I cry. "Derrick was right. All of this is over my testing for my sister. geNetics sells your organs to the highest bidder, and they still plan on taking mine, but I stopped them temporarily." I'm out of breath by the time I say all that.

He pulls back from me and looks over my shoulder. "Who is this?"

"This is Rachel. She was abducted from her home in Alabama." I pull him out of earshot. "I think they're trying to sell her."

"They are. They steal them by the truckloads and auction them off here along with other illegal activities."

"You look different." His face is hard, and his eyes have a coldness in them that I've never seen before.

He runs his hand through his scruffy beard. "I don't know how anyone comes out of this mess unscathed."

"What've they done to you and why are you down here with me?" I lay my hand on his cheek, and he closes his eyes like he's longed for someone's kind touch.

"I can't even begin to talk about the things I've seen since I've been here or the things I've done." He pushes my hand down like he doesn't deserve it. "They found out who I am and locked me down here."

"How?"

"I was helping a girl, and I told her why I was here but I..." He looks away. "She must've told them." He looks around the bunker. "We have to find a way out of here before they come back."

"There is no way out but through that hatch. Trust me, I've looked."

"Then we'll make a plan for when they come back."

"Wait." I rip the flesh-colored chip off my ear. "I lost my hearing aid, and I can't hear anything. Sean programmed it for this ear. I've tried it on the other, and it won't work."

"It won't work on me if he programmed it for you." He pushes it back toward me, and it surely wouldn't work down here. "Did they find the tracking device?"

I rub my hip. "No, it's still intact."

"Good. Once we get out of here, Sean will be able to locate you."

"We've been down here for two days, and this is the first time the hatch has been opened. I was hoping they were bringing us some food. We've been rationing what we have."

"You look like you've lost weight."

"They were drugging her, and she wasn't able to hold anything down," Rachel adds.

"I'm okay. They must've stopped so they don't kill my kidneys."

Theo turns in a circle then scares the shit out of me when he punches the wall. "Fuck!"

I've never seen him angry and out of control.

"I should've taken them all out the minute I knew what they were doing! I've sat back and watched them sell young girls and ship them off and did nothing!"

"Theo, none of this is your fault. If you would've shown your hand, you'd be dead."

"And, if I can't get us out of here, we're all dead anyway! God knows what they've done to Fiona!" He punches the wall again, and Rachel curls up into a corner.

"Theo. You have to calm down. You're scaring me." I place both my hands on his elbows. "You're a Navy SEAL. You can get us out of this, but you have to keep a cool head. Derrick has told me many times how good you are at the job. This is the job. You can't lose your shit because if you do, I'll lose mine and then neither one of us will be able to get us out of here. Now, get your shit together!"

"You're right." He walks over to Rachel. "I'm sorry I lost my head for a moment. It won't happen again." Then he walks back over to me and hugs me. "I'll get you out of here, and I'll find Fiona."

"Is she the girl that betrayed you?"

"Yes, but I gave her good reason, and I need to make it up to her."

I get the feeling that he really cares about this

girl. We sit on the edge of one of the bunks. "Tell me about her."

"She's feisty. You'd like her." A slight smile crosses his face.

"I think you like her." I nudge his shoulder with mine.

"If I don't get her out of here, I'll never get the chance to know if I do or not. She's complicated and had such a hard life. I'm not sure if she's capable of feeling anything."

"We need a plan."

"You sound like Rebel. How's he been treating you since I've been gone?"

"Like crap." I laugh. "He's been teaching me how to box."

"Really? That, I would've like to have seen. Did you kick his ass?"

"No, but I've definitely learned to defend myself even more." I look away from him.

"What's that?" He chuckles.

"What's what?"

"That look on your face. You've fallen for him, haven't you?"

"No, no I haven't. We've just been getting along, that's all." I stand.

"If you say so." He laughs again. "His cranky ass has a way with women."

"Yeah, he has a way of making them run away from him." I know I'm lying to myself, but I haven't had the time to explore how I really feel about him. I've been in danger since the day I met him, and that's been my focus. We've shared a few moments that in a different place and time, maybe more would've come from it. But he's so jaded from Nina, I don't know that he'd ever really let me in.

"There has to be a vent system in here." He stands and looks around.

"There is, but it's too small for us to escape out of it. I tried."

"You said they bring you food. Do they come inside or drop it?"

"They usually open the hatch and drop a box."

"What about water?"

"We have a faucet." I point to the corner.

"Damn things are built to stay in, not break out." He climbs up the set of ladders to look at the hatch. "They've reversed the locking mechanism on here to the outside." He pushes on it, but it doesn't budge.

"My private plane just landed. Now tell me again where you located her," I talk to Sean as I get my bag from the overhead bin.

"It's been two days since her tracker lit up, not even the slightest blip has registered, but I'm sending you the last coordinates."

My phone vibrates as the information is transferred. "I'm going to Theo's apartment first then I'll head to this area." Once I'm off the plane, and in an open area, I try Fallon again. "Fallon, can you hear me?" Still nothing but dead silence. "Sean, don't take your eyes off that screen. If you hear or see anything, let me know. Call our contact at the CIA and see if they can reprogram our computer system with the satellite that covers Germany."

"Will do." I hear him pushing buttons on the phone.

I pick up my rental car and head for the apartment building which is only a few miles down the road. Taking the stairs one flight up to his flat, I notice the door is ajar. I set my luggage down and take my gun from the holster strapped over my side. Slowly, I open the door and look around the studio apartment. Cushions have been sliced open, and every drawer is pulled from its hinges and thrown on the floor.

"Sean, are you there?"

"Yeah. I'll have access in the next hour."

"Theo's place has been broken into, so I can only assume his cover has been blown."

"Did they find what he hid?"

"I don't know." I kick the broken drawers out of my way. "Could you see on that camera of yours anything?"

"I was so focused on tracking Fallon that I didn't monitor his apartment for the last few days. I'm sorry, Derrick."

"Don't be. You can't have eyes everywhere when we're a small unit." I notice one of the vent's shutter pointed upward; all the others are shut. I run my finger over them, making them move, and I can see something inside. "I think we just got lucky."

"Did you find something?"

"Give me a minute." I reach in my pocket and pull out a knife with a multitude of tools built in it. Unscrewing the vent, I reach in and pull out a note and a file.

"What is it?" Sean's voice is in my ear.

"It's a note from Theo." I read it out loud so Sean can hear me.

If anything happens to me, find this girl and keep her safe.

I open the folder and study the picture of a young girl with the name Fiona Petit written beneath the picture.

"I'm searching her name." I can hear the keystrokes. "Missing girl from Utah is what the head-line reads. This was two years ago."

"If Theo has a file on her, she must've been taken for their trafficking ring. Memorize her face, and if you see anyone that resembles her, let me know. And, as soon as you have visual here, start searching the area where you saw Fallon."

"I'm all over it."

I leave the apartment and head for the area that

Fallon was last tracked. Driving further outside the city, I see a lot of old abandoned warehouses, then it opens up into lush green land for miles.

"I've got eyes on you," Sean who's been quiet for a while, chimes in. "You're not too far from the turn-off."

"Any sign of Fallon?" I say as I pull off the road into a wooded area.

"No. Why are you stopping?"

"I want to go in on foot and scope out the area." I park the SUV far enough back that it can't be seen from the road. Pulling out my duffel bag I threw in the back seat, I change into the camouflage clothes that I haven't worn since I was overseas. After smearing black under my eyes, I check my gun and place some extra clips in the back of my belt. I tuck a knife in my boot and lock up the vehicle.

"I can only see you in black and white, and at a distance, but you look like you're going on a hunt." Sean laughs.

"I am." Checking the directions on my phone, I take off in a trot. I have the advantage of nightfall starting to seep into the horizon. It will help me stay hidden in the trees.

A car turning on its headlights is coming down the dirt road, and a semitrailer is following close behind, moving slow. I duck down low to the ground and watch. There are no markings on the side of the trailer, and I can't see in the dark-tinted windows of the car. I wait until they pull out onto the main road before I move again. "Can you zoom in on their plates?" I find myself whispering to Sean.

"Got 'em. You should know there are more big trucks on the move headed your way. Stay out of sight."

"I PLAN ON IT." I wait and watch as three more trucks roll down the road.

"That's all of them," Sean says.

I take off in a run again until I get to a fence line surrounding a dark metal building with no windows. A man in a dark suit is out front on the phone, and two men with rifles are patrolling the grounds.

"Do you see any more than two guards?" I ask Sean.

"No. It looks like there is a high-security fence in the back and one man in the gated entrance."

I watch for any other movement.

"Shit!" Sean says.

"What?"

"There's a caravan of cars headed your direction."

"How many?"

"At least ten."

I stay low and watch the cars pull up, and four men get out of each car. They're all dressed in dark suits and carrying some sort of bag. Each of them is checked by a guard before they enter the building.

"I have to get in there. Do you see an entry point in the back?"

"There's a door on the east side of the building."

I wait until the last man is inside and the armed guards are headed in the other direction. I cut the links in the fence and take off running at a full pace. I make my way to the back of the building, ducking behind a truck when I hear voices. I can't make out what they're saying because they're speaking in German. Footsteps come closer, and I crawl underneath one of the trucks. A pair of boots and a pair of high heels stop close to me. I can tell they're arguing over something because the woman's voice is raised. He says something back to her, and they part in two different directions.

"That was too close," Sean says, and I cover my ear.

"Could you hear what they were saying?"

"No, I can only hear you, but I nearly shit a brick when I saw them stop in front of where you were hiding."

"Is the coast clear?"

"Yes, to your left."

I crawl back out and move slowly this time, peering beyond the trucks. I make it to the back door, but it's locked. It's then that I hear the hum of a camera, twisting in my direction. I move behind the corner of the building just in time.

"Can you do anything about that camera?" I ask Sean.

"I don't have the technology to do that."

"Remind me to add it to the list of things we need." I wait until I hear the camera move again. I take the tool from my pocket and pick the lock on the door. Moving inside, I quietly close it behind me. This part of the building is dark, but I can see lights on deeper into the building. I step into the shadow of the darkness when I hear footsteps. I see a man open a door a few feet from me, and I hear someone cry out as he shuts the door behind him.

I keep moving further in and see the lights dim, and someone starts talking over a microphone. It's broken English, but he's announcing for bidding to start.

I come to another door and place my ear against it. Someone is crying. I jiggle the knob, and the door but it's locked. I take a run at it leading with my shoulder and it breaks open. There's a faint light on, and a girl curled up on the floor covered in a blanket. Her head pops up when I shut the door behind me.

"Please, no more," she cries.

"I'm not going to hurt you." I raise my hands in the air and squat down next to her.

She uncovers her head, and I recognize her as the face in the picture.

"That's her," Sean says. "Fiona Petit."

"I'm a friend of Theo's," I tell her, and she sits up. "My name is Rebel."

"You have to help him. They found out who he was, and they're going to kill him." Her lip quivers.

"Do you know where he is?"

"There's a bomb shelter on the edge of the property, hidden in the woods. They took him there two days ago, and I haven't seen him since."

I reach out to touch her shoulder, and she winces.

"Did they hurt you?"

Tears stream down her face. "They made Theo hurt me, and when they locked him up, they beat me some more."

"I've never known Theo to hurt a woman."

"He was protecting me so they wouldn't kill me."

"I'm sorry." The microphone screeches louder. "Do you know what they're doing out there?"

"I heard them say it was organ night, but I don't know what that means. I only know what it means when I'm out there."

"Which is what, Fiona?"

"They steal woman and young girls from their families, and they sell them to the highest bidder. They do unspeakable things to us. I've been sold so many times I've lost track."

"I'm going to get you out of here, but I need to find a friend of mine first and Theo. Have you seen any other women here?"

"I only see the ones they throw in the trailers with me or who are being sold the same night. But Mr. Lance wanted Theo to handle some women who messed up things for them. He was taking him to her when they locked him in the shelter."

That has Fallon's name written all over it. "You think she's in the shelter with him?"

"I don't know, maybe." I stand, and she grabs my hand. "Please, take me with you."

I nod. "You have to do everything I tell you and don't make a sound."

She scurries off the floor and becomes like a second skin.

"Sean, I want you to scan the area by the woods and tell me if you see anything?"

"Who are you talking to?" Fiona whispers.

"I have a device in my ear that I can talk to one of my partners. He's watching out for us."

CHAPTER 18

REBEL

"Can you take me to the bomb shelter?"

Fiona nods but doesn't speak.

I open the door to her room and peer out and look side to side. I feel her hand tuck inside the back of my belt as I step into the hallway. She stays only a step behind me. Opening the door that I came in through, I look at the camera to see its direction. It's pointed straight out, so we're able to move against the side of the building to stay from its view.

"Which way?" I whisper.

"It's over there by the trees, but we won't be able to find it in the dark."

"Sean, can you locate the hatch?"

"Yeah, but she's right. You aren't going to able to see anything."

"Let me worry about that. Stay close," I tell her, and she moves again with me.

I hold my hand out for her to stay in place as I walk between the semis to look for the guards. One is leaning against the front of the building, smoking a cigarette. The other one, I don't see.

I turn around to wave her to me, and she's right behind me. "I told you to wait."

"Well, I'm not real good at taking orders, and it's dark out. I can't see you that far ahead of me."

"From where you are, you need to walk straight out into the tree line and then move about a hundred feet west," Sean is in my ear.

"I want you to crawl under this truck and don't come out. I'll be back after I get that hatch open."

She doesn't move.

"If you don't do as I say, I can't protect you."

This time she gets on the ground and rolls her body under the trailer. I look beyond the truck again and still only see the one guard. Staying in the dark shadows, I move slowly and quietly to the trees.

"To your right," Sean directs me.

I sidestep in line where he tells me and stop when my foot hits something hard. I squat down and feel the round circle of the hatch. Placing my gun in my holster, I use both hands to turn the wheel. It moves and pops up. A faint light shines up from the ground. I position my body to block it from getting the guard's attention. Before I stick my head in, I call out quietly.

"Theo. Are you down there? It's me, Rebel."

A noise echoes, and I feel the ladder rattle in my hands. "Rebel?" Theo's face appears in the dim light.

"Please tell me Fallon is with you."

"I'm down here."

I lean in to see her and a young girl clutched to her arm. "Thank god you're all okay."

Theo climbs back down the ladder and helps the girls up. Fallon crushes her body to mine as soon as she's out. "I knew you'd come for me."

I don't know what possesses me other than I'm lost in the moment; I press my lips to hers and slide my tongue in her mouth, and she returns the kiss. I pull away when Theo clears his throat.

"You need to get them out of here. There's someone I need to go back and find."

"Fiona? She's hiding under the trailer of that truck." I point to where I left her.

He takes off in a full run and gunshots fire out. His body slams to the ground, and I shove the girls behind a tree and pull out my weapon. Sliding my hand inside my boot, I take out the knife and place it in Fallon's hand along with the keys.

"Take her and scale over the fence. Run parallel with the property but stay in the woods. There is an SUV hidden before the road. Take it and get on the next plane out of here."

"I'm not leaving you."

"For god's sake, do as you're told and get her out of here."

She takes the young girl's hand and disappears into the darkness.

"Sean, can you see where the shots are coming from?"

"The far end of the building, in the back."

"Theo!" Fiona screams and runs toward him.

"Get down!" I yell, and another shot rings out.

Several men run out of the front of the building, and the guard that was leaning against the building has his rifle up and a light pointed in Theo's direction.

Moving quickly, I take off toward Theo and lie down next to him. "Are you hit?"

"No, and I don't have a weapon."

I dig the pistol out of my other boot and shove it into his hand. "We're sitting ducks out here. We need to move. I'm going to stand up and start shooting. You run for the woods."

"I have to get to Fiona. I'm not leaving her here with these sick bastards."

"I'll cover you, and you haul ass to where she is, but I don't know how long I can hold them off or how to get us out of here."

"Are you two crazy! Get your asses out of there now!" Sean is yelling.

"You might not want to watch this," I tell him, then stand and spray bullets in the direction of the guards who've now joined forces.

Theo gets off the ground and hightails it to the girl. All of a sudden, the perimeter lights come on and shine directly in my face.

I hear Theo yell my name and scream at me to run as he unloads his pistol. I take off as bullets breeze by me and don't stop until I'm hidden by a trailer.

"We have to find a way out of here before they surround us," I tell Theo.

"It's too late for that," a voice says behind me and shines a light in my eyes. The man has a gun pointed at my head.

"Lance." Theo raises his hands in the air.

The guards rush around the corner and slam us

to the ground. One of them plants his knee in the middle of my back to the point of it being painful.

"Tie them up and bring them inside, then you two tell everyone to continue the bidding. I have this under control."

Once we're tied up, they drag us off the ground, and we follow them into one of the bays that are empty. Lance pushes a button, and the metal door slides upward.

"Take them in there." He points the gun at a door. "Not you," he says to Fiona. "You go with him." He cranks his head toward one of the guards. "You know what to do with her."

"No!" Theo yells. Lance crushes the gun to Theo's face, and he falls backward as blood pours from a spot above his eye. The guard drags him into the room, and the other one shoves me through the door.

Lance waves them out of the room and shuts the door behind him. "She knew you'd show up." He points the gun at me.

"I'm afraid you have me at a disadvantage. I have no idea who she is?"

"My boss. She recognized your boy here." He glances at Theo who is getting off the ground.

"It wasn't Fiona who ratted me out." He stumbles, and I grab his arm before he falls back on the floor.

He lays the barrel of the gun to Theo's forehead. I twist my wrists, trying to work my way out of the binds.

"You've created a fine mess for her, not that she wasn't good at that herself." He laughs and takes a step back. "She's going to wish she was dead when we're done with her."

"You fucking coward!" I step in front of Theo before he can lunge at him.

"Why don't you untie me and fight like a man instead of someone who can't defend themselves."

"It's a little more fun toying with someone who's helpless."

"You're a sick fuck, and when I get out of these ropes, I'm going to kill you and enjoy watching the light leave your eyes."

He laughs louder. "You're awful cocky for a man with a gun pointed at him." He moves back and slings up his arm that's holding the gun. The door behind him flings open, and Fallon rushes him from behind, knocking the gun from his hand.

He slams into the floor face first, and she drills her elbow into his back several times. He arches up in pain.

Theo scrambles for the gun, and I break free of the ropes.

Lance flips over, sending Fallon flying into a wall. I tackle him before he's off the floor. His fist flies into my jaw and blood splatters from my mouth. I come back down on him hard and press my forearm into his throat. He tries to fight me off, but I'm much stronger and bigger than him. His face is bloodred, and his eyes start to roll back. I let off pressure, and he gasps for air.

"Tell me who your boss is?"

"Fuck you!" he says and spit sprays from his mouth.

I apply pressure again until he's almost out and then back off again. "Tell me!" I yell in his face.

He starts laughing. "She'll always be an echo in your head."

It takes me a minute to register what he's saying. "Ekko?"

His eyes cut to Theo. "She knew his face even in the dark. She said you'd come to save him. It's in your DNA to be the hero."

"Where is she?"

"You won't find her. She's a ghost, and her right-hand man won't let you anywhere near her. She's made a fortune not only for herself, but for him, and he'll kill anyone that comes after her."

I choke him again.

"Don't kill him until he tells us where he took Fiona." Theo is standing over me.

I let up. "Where did they take her?"

"She deserves to die, and I'm not telling you shit!"

"Theo, take Fallon and get out of here."

"Come on, Theo." Fallon pulls him out of the room.

"I told you I was going to kill you." I apply pressure and don't let up until he passes out. I could kill him but choose not to. I take the ropes that Theo and I were bound with and tie his hands and feet.

"Get the hell out of there, Derrick," Sean says, getting my attention.

"I'm not going anywhere until I find her." I get off the floor and wipe the blood from the corner of my mouth. "It's time to call in the cavalry. Get ahold of the CIA and tell them this location. They can send the local troops out here."

Theo and Fallon are up against the wall when I walk out. "They're leaving," Theo whispers and points toward the main room of the building.

"So are you. Take her and get out of here."

"I can't leave Fiona."

"I'll find her, now go!" He tries to hand me the gun. "You might need it." I push it back at him.

I move past them and make my way to the main room where men in suits are showing their ID's and bank cards to a man handling the sales. Movement up above catches my eye. Two people dressed in black masks are moving from their seats that set above the stage. The man is large. The other, the way she moves, I know it's a woman. I recognize the familiar sway of her hips even after all this time.

"Nina."

"Nina? As in Nina Pax? The woman that betrayed you?" Sean is going on and on in my ear.

"Wait..." I hear him shuffling paper. "N.P. Parrot is who signed the note to Fallon. N.P. Nina Pax."

"Parrot is for Ekko," I mutter.

"She's the one that runs the organization? Damn."

"It appears that way. She always said she'd work for the highest bidder."

"Lance said she knew you would come. You have to get the hell out of there."

"Not going to happen, brother." I reach up and pull the chip from my ear so he can't stop me from what I'm about to do.

"We can't just leave him here to fight by himself." Theo is pulling me out of the building.

"I have no intention of leaving him here alone, but I need to get you to a safe place." He hasn't stopped his pace, and I yank free from his hold.

"I'm not going anywhere without him. You heard that guy. The woman that betrayed him is here."

"And you're afraid of what? That he might kill her? She deserves to die after what she did to the Gunners."

"Do you really think he can kill the woman he was in love with?"

He seems to mull over my words. "Right now, my priority is getting you to safety then I have to find

Fiona. Please, don't fight me on this." He holds out his hand for me to take.

"Hide," I tell him when men start piling out of the building. It looks like their show is over, and they're headed for their cars. None of them aware of anything that has gone on here tonight.

The two guards that took us are escorting them out the building and shut the gates behind them when the last car has left.

"What's that noise?" A whirling sound is in the distance.

"Sounds like a helicopter. I bet that's how Nina and her henchman leave. I can't let them get on it. Listen to me, I want you to get out of here before it's too late. I'm going to go stop the chopper." He takes off in a sprint toward the sound of the blades.

I'm not sure what to do, but I don't want to leave Derrick. I creep back inside the building and check the room that I left him in. Lance is tied up and out cold. I hear a noise coming from the back of the building, so I quietly make my way toward the sound while watching out for the guards I know are still around.

A gun being fired has me rushing through a large door with silver vats that have rusted out, and the sounds of shots are ricocheting off them. The bright lights flick on, and I dash behind one when I see a woman step out aiming a gun around, looking for someone.

"I know you're in here, Derrick." A large man in an expensive suit stalks behind her with his back to her, aiming in the opposite direction. "I can make you a rich man."

"I don't want your dirty money!" His voice rings out on the other side of the room, and she continues to prowl in his direction. As they move, I move to the next vat and stay out of sight.

"I don't have time to try to convince you to leave. You've never listened to me anyway, so you're forcing my hand. I don't want to kill you, but you're leaving me no choice." She stops and says something to the guy behind her, and he veers off to the left of her.

I go to take a step toward her, and a hand covers my mouth, and an arm wraps around my waist. "I told you to get out of here." Theo's hushed voice is in my right ear. "I took the pilot out, so they have no way to leave."

He slides his hand from my mouth. "They're going to kill him," I rasp out. "The guy that was with her went that way." I point in the direction he left.

"Stay here and keep your head down." He stalks off with his gun raised.

"Come on, Derrick. I'm sure we can work this out. You can join forces with me. We were a good team at one point. I've missed us being together." Her voice is so silky.

I can't just sit here and watch. I move closer and around one of the vats to get a look at her. No wonder Rebel hated me in the beginning. We have the same hair color and body structure. She's lean and has well-defined arms. She's more graceful and controlled in her movements than I am. She's like a well-planned-out machine taking controlled steps toward Derrick.

Shots ring out again, and I hear a thud on the concrete floor.

CHAPTER 20

REBEL

Theo steps from behind a vat after he opened fire on Nina's second-hand man. When he reaches for a pulse, the guy swings up and catches Theo square in the jaw, sending him to the ground. I watch it all play out as the guy holds his blood-soaked side and scrambles for Theo. Both of their guns fall out of their reach. One goes under a conveyor belt and the other one, I don't see.

Nina is inching her way in my direction. If I could get my hands on that gun, I could take her out.

Theo lets out a blood-curdling scream, and I see the guy rip Theo's mechanical arm from him and throw it off to the side. Theo grabs the guy's foot as he reaches under the belt to get the gun, but he doesn't stop him soon enough. He slings around, shooting into the air when Theo manages to push his arm down. The guy shoves Theo backward, and he smashes the side of his head into a metal container. He's dazed, but he manages to get back up and fight the guy one-handed until the gun goes off again between them, and the guy falls to the ground. Theo has the gun in his hand and drops it. He wobbles and collapses to the floor.

In that split second, I rush over to the gun and pick it up. When I turn around, Nina is standing over me with her gun pointed directly at me.

She nudges the guy with her foot. "Too bad. I really liked him."

"Like you liked me?"

"That's where you're wrong, Derrick. I loved you. If you remember correctly, I tried to save you." She squats down but keeps a steady aim. "Why do you have to play the hero?"

"Why'd you have to be such a lying bitch? You betrayed my team!" Spit flies from my mouth. "They're all dead because of you."

She ignores my words. "You wanted to marry me at one point. We can still do that, you know. I've never forgotten the way you touched me." She stands. "As a matter of fact, the night that I saw Theo sitting out there bidding on one of my girls, I knew you'd come, and I've thought about nothing else since." She licks her lips. "You can't tell me you don't miss us."

The moment she blinks, I kick my leg out and knock her to the ground. The gun fires as I rip it from her hand. My turn to stand over her.

"I fucking hate you," I yell.

She slowly stands. "There's a fine line between love and hate, Derrick."

"There is no line for us. You killed anything I felt for you the day my men died." I want to pull the fucking trigger, but it's the first time in my life my hand shakes.

"I'm sorry about your men. If I could've had it play out any other way, I would've. I didn't come out of it unscathed. I lost my eye when you threw the grenade."

"Theo lost his arm, and I'm left with a nasty scar down my face. I could give a shit about your eye. Why did you do it? Was it all about money for you?"

"Yes, and the power it gave me."

"And, this?" I wave my hand around.

"Do you know how much money I've made selling organs and trafficking women? I'm just one of many. You may stop me, but you're not going to stop this business. There's too much money to be made."

"How did you get so fucking evil?"

"I've always been this way, you were just too blind to see it. That's what made your team an easy target."

Rage like I've never felt runs through me. I lift the gun to her head. Sweat is pouring off me, and my hand wavers again. "Ahhhhhh!" I yell out, wanting nothing more than to kill her, but I can't do it. I lower my weapon.

"He can't kill you, but I can." Fallon's voice steps up behind Nina. "My sister is dead because of you."

Nina turns toward her. She looks between the two of us. "She looks like me." She laughs. "I guess you're fooling yourself if you think you ever got over me."

"I'm nothing like you! You destroy people's lives for nothing more than greed." Fallon places both of her hands on the gun, and I know she's ready to pull the trigger.

"Don't do it," I say, and her gaze goes to me.

"Why, because you still love her?" A look of confusion covers her face.

"No, because I want her to pay for what she's

done. Rotting away in prison will be worse than death for her."

"She's smart. She'll find a way out."

As she points the gun at her again, the room is flooded with a German swat team. Men in Kevlar vests, helmets, and guns rush in. All three of us are taken to the ground and handcuffed. Once I tell my story, they uncuff us and detain Nina. Fallon runs over to Theo who is unconscious and lays his head in her lap. One of the swat team members calls for an ambulance while the other team members scour the building.

They find a handful of men and women being held in the back of one of semis, but there is no sign of Fiona. Lance somehow freed himself, and he's missing too.

I watch as Theo is loaded into the ambulance, and Fallon kisses his forehead. The young girl that was with Fallon in the bomb shelter gets out of one of the swat team member's cars and runs over into her arms.

"Thank you for saving me," she cries.

I walk over to where they're standing.

"This is Rachel, and I'm taking her home." She says the words without looking at me.

CHAPTER 21

REBEL

It's been a month since we've flown back from Germany. Theo has physically recovered, but mentally I'm not sure he'll ever be the same. He's checked every database to find Fiona, but there's no sign of her anywhere or Lance.

Sean gave me an earful when I got back and swore he'd never be a part of the team. He thought all of us were dead for sure and couldn't go through that again. I've kept myself busy, cleaning up the bottom half of my building, making it into the new headquarters. Things didn't go perfectly, but it felt good to take down a big crime organization like Nina's. She's being held under the highest security the government allows while she awaits trial not only for the crimes she committed under geNetics but for her military crimes as well. She'll never see the light of day again.

As far as Fallon goes, I haven't heard a word from her, and she won't return my calls. I think whatever she felt for me disappeared the moment she came face to face with me and Nina.

I did love Nina very deeply at one time. Hell, I wanted her to be my wife. Part of me has to admit that maybe I couldn't kill her because of some deep-seated feeling I still had for her. At least, that's how Dr. Ruth has explained it. I've hired her as the Gunners team psychologist. We need someone like her on board to deal with the things we've seen. I intend on going full steam ahead with taking on other missions as soon as I get some more men hired. My old buddy Lawson wants to come on board. He can train the men and/or women I hire to fight. He'll be a great asset to the team.

I turn my wipers on as the rain starts to lightly fall. I've been to the cemetery every week hoping to get a glimpse of Fallon. Josie's gravesite always has fresh flowers, but I can't seem to figure out what day Fallon visits. I pull through the wrought iron gates and drive down the narrow dirt road.

I pull over when I see her standing in a trench coat, holding an umbrella beside her headstone. I hold my breath watching her. I don't know exactly how long I've sat here before she turned around and saw me. She walks my direction, and I get out of the car and open the passenger side door for her to get inside. I take the umbrella from her and shake it out before I throw it in the back seat.

I run to the driver's side and get in and sit so I can face her. She stares out the front window, and I see her lip quiver.

"I've called you a million times."

"I know," she says quietly in response.

I reach over and touch her hand. "I've missed you."

She turns to look at me, and tears are streaming down her face. "I've missed you too, but I can't do this."

"You can't do what?"

"You'll always look at me and see her face."

"You're wrong. I see you. You're nothing like her."

"I'm not the same naive girl that ran into the bar that night. A lot has changed."

"I know that. I've changed too, because of you. I was so fucking lost when I came back from Afghanistan and was no longer a SEAL. I was angry and took it out on everyone, including you, and I'm sorry."

She sobs.

"You're beautiful, tough, and sweet at the same time." I pull her into my lap, and she doesn't resist. "I want to try with you. I can't promise I won't have my moments of being an asshole...but I want to be with you."

I hold her until she's all cried out, and she falls asleep in my arms. I take her back to my place and carry her to my room. I remove her wet coat and shoes, then tuck her into my bed where she belongs. I change out of my clothes and curl up next to her, drawing her body flush with mine.

I close my eyes, thinking she's sound asleep, and then I hear the most beautiful words whispered.

"I love you, Derrick."

I roll her flat on her back and hover my body over hers. I've waited so long to taste her again that I devour her sweet lips. Her hands push my T-shirt up, and I know that she wants this as much as I do. As soon as she has my shirt off, I work on hers. She leans her chest up and squirms her hand behind her back, removing her lacy bra. Her nipples are round and perfect. They perk up as soon as my lips find them.

"God, you're beautiful," I say between sucking them into my mouth. She arches into me and groans. I work my way down her firm body, and she shimmies out of her slacks. She leaves her panties for me to remove. I trace the lacy edge where it meets her soft skin. I see her flesh rise with my touch. Taking them off, I dip my tongue down to her core, and this time she lets out a sexy groan that has me rock hard. I lift my gaze to watch her face as I suck and lick. Her eyes are hooded, but what I see in them is what she feels for me. It's a look I've never seen before. I crawl up her body and settle between her legs.

"Please tell me you have a condom this time?" She giggles.

I reach over to my bedside table and pull out a pack of them.

She laughs again. "I think that'll do."

Our eyes lock, and I know exactly what I feel for this woman. "I love you, Fallon." I press into her before she can speak the words back to me. I don't need to hear them again. I don't know that I deserve to be loved, but I'm going to make sure she knows how I feel about her for the rest of our lives. I slowly rock in and out of her, savoring her warmth surrounding me. Nina was right about one thing; I was blind. She never felt this good to me, and now I see the difference.

I kiss her jaw line and down her neck as I continue my slow movements. She rocks her hips into me.

"I'm not fragile, Derrick. You can move harder," she whispers.

I lean up and look into her eyes. "I'm savoring every inch of you on my own terms. I want to touch you places no one has ever reached and for you to remember where I've been, baby."

She reaches between us and places her hands on either side of my face. "I love you, Derrick. Now screw my brains out already."

"WHERE ARE YOU GOING?" She watches me tug on my jeans.

"I'd love nothing more than to stay in bed with you all day, but Lawson is coming on board today, and he's bringing in two more recruits to train.

"How is Theo?" She glides her naked body from under the sheets and wraps her arms around my waist.

"Quiet. He hasn't been the same since we got back."

"I know. I met him for lunch a few weeks ago and..."

"You two met? He never told me that." I turn in her arms.

"I asked him not to. I didn't think there was anything left between us after Germany. You had made it pretty clear that I was a job and that nothing could happen between us again."

"I was being an ass as usual, and I'm sorry." I place my forehead against hers. "Have I made it clear how I feel now?"

"I think about the third time you made me come I got it." She giggles, and I love the sound of her laughter. "Seriously though, I'm worried about Theo. He used to have such a sweet disposition and always so happy even with the hand he was dealt with his dad."

"He feels guilty for letting those girls be sold and not saving Fiona."

"Is he seeing Dr. Ruth?" She escapes my grasp and throws her clothes back on.

"Yeah, but all she can tell me is if he's fit for duty." I wrestle my arms in my sleeves.

"Is he?"

"I haven't gotten the final evaluation on him yet."

"Rebel!" Theo is yelling from outside. "Let me in!"

I press the button to unlock the downstairs door, and in a few minutes, I hear the cage elevator making its way to the top. I meet him at the door before he can knock on it.

"I found him!" He breezes by me.

"Found who?" He hugs Fallon. "Lance. He's working for an organization right here under our noses."

"In Portland?" Fallon asks.

"Seattle."

"Are you sure it's him," I ask.

"Positive, and I'm going after him."

"You're not doing this alone. Give me your intel, and it'll be our next mission."

"I know he has her, and we have to get to her."

"We will, but we'll do it as the Gunners, not one man's revenge." I place my hand on his shoulders.

"Then get your ass in gear and let's get going."
***

Theo failed to keep Fiona safe. Will he find her before it's too late? Click here to start reading Theo's Retaliation now.

THEO'S RETALIATION

Theo's adventure will be featured in the next book.

You'll meet two more characters up close and personal.

Lawson Reid

Fiona Petit

You'll also be introduced to the new SEAL team members.

You can meet them all on my website.

Continue reading for a sneak peek at Theo's Retaliation

CHAPTER 1

Rebel

"Hey, beautiful. Where are you headed so early this morning?" Fallon's hips sway as she saunters into my office. I purposely push back from my desk and swing my chair to the side so I can draw her into my lap.

"I'm headed to my office because my handsome boyfriend left for work too early." She drops her purse from her shoulder as she rounds the corner of my desk, sits in my open lap, and drapes her arm around my neck. "You've been working entirely too hard." She puckers her lips, and I accept the invite, relishing the taste of her.

"You know, boyfriend seems like an outdated term. I'm no boy." My crotch grows hard underneath her.

"Okay, maybe I should've said my sexy lover left for work too early. Is that better?" She giggles. "By the way, this suit looks hot on you." She straightens my tie.

"I like that, but I was thinking of something more serious."

She leans her body back to look at me. "I moved in months ago. I think that's pretty serious."

"I think we should get married."

She hops off my lap. "I don't think either one of us is ready for that."

I snatch her hand before she can get away from me. "I'm ready."

"We've both been through a lot this year, and I think we need to take more time to get to really know one another."

"I know every inch of you."

"That's not what I'm talking about, and you know it."

She's right. Our lives have been turned upside down with everything we went through with her sister and Nina. I never thought I'd ask another woman to marry me after Nina's betrayal, but I love and trust this woman with all my heart. If she needs more time, then that's what I'll give her. "There's nothing else I need to know about you. I love you, but I can wait until you're ready. Unless..."

"Unless what?"

"You have some unresolved feelings for Theo."

She sits back on my lap. "I love you too, but I want to give us more time as a couple before we make that step. Besides, you have a lot on your plate right now trying to finish remodeling this building. And no, my feelings for Theo were worked out before you and I had sex. Theo has worked it out too. He knows that we're friends, and neither one of us want anything more from the other. I think the moment he met Fiona, he knew what was between us was nothing more than friendship." She scoots close to me. "But I like that you're a little jealous."

"I'm not jealous," I protest, but I'm lying. "Speaking of remodeling, you know you can move your office to the end of the hall." I kiss the line of her neck. "That way I could have you anytime I want."

"That's precisely why I'll not be moving my office here. I'd never get any work done." She hops up. "I have to go. I have a client waiting for me to go over his monthly food plan." She picks up her purse and tucks it under her arm. "I'll catch up with you later." Her hand grasps the doorknob. "Oh yeah, good luck today. And keep an eye on Theo. His mood hasn't gotten any better."

"I'm hoping he controls his temper in our meeting today."

She blows me a kiss and heads out the door.

I straighten the blueprints on my desk to finalize the changes for the builder. The entire bottom floor has been remodeled into a training center for the Gunners. Lawson has handpicked everything we need. He started his first training session last week with the three new recruits I'll formally introduce at the meeting today with Commander Lukas. He's succeeded in making the Gunners part of the military again. We'll be handling the US division and crimes that affect the safety of our citizens. We're considered a US SEAL team. The requirements for recruitment are strict, but I managed to convince them to let me keep Lawson on board. He's our only civilian employee. Our direction and cases will be under Commander Lukas.

The second floor is our main headquarters with several offices, including mine, and a large conference room which we'll be meeting in today. The third floor is apartments for our team. They should be finished by the end of the month. The fourth floor contains Dr. Ruth's office, a large open kitchen and an area for the men to relax or play pool, watch television, play video games, and ping-pong. I felt her office needed to be on the second floor with the rest, but she insisted on being close to where everyone would hang out. I happen to think there's a method to her psychological thinking. I have great respect for her, but I don't like that she knows what's in my head.

After I've signed off on the changes, I glance at my watch. It's time to head to the conference room and set up. I roll up the blueprints and put a rubber band around them. Commander Lukas has assigned someone to handle all the office details. A secretary of sorts. The person will be with him today to get started.

Grabbing the folders off the credenza from behind my desk, I walk down the hallway to the wall of glass that encloses the conference room. Adjusting the A/C before I walk inside, I place a blue folder and a pen in front of each cushioned chair surrounding the oblong table.

The walls are a pale army green with the

Gunners emblem painted on the long wall where a window would normally be. I had the windows removed for focus and privacy. There's a large television screen on the far end for virtual meetings, and laptops available for each team member. The glass wall serves as a brainstorming area and is equipped with colored markers.

"I see you have everything ready for us," Commander Lukas says, coming through the door with a woman dressed in a khaki uniform, and her hair pulled into a tight bun.

"The men should be here anytime." I reach out and shake his hand.

"This is your new assistant, Seaman Apprentice Honor Sanchez."

"Sir." Her spine straightens as she salutes me.

"They'll be none of that here, Sanchez." I chuckle. "Relax."

She drops her hand to her side.

"Any new leads on Fiona Petit?" Commander Lukas gets right to the point and sits in one of the comfortable chairs.

"Maybe, but I don't want to mention it to Theo until I have something firm. The last one that failed sent him into a spiral."

"That was six months ago. Has he been seeing Dr. Ruth?"

"Yes, as ordered. She's cleared him for duty. The man is a beast. He's been working out with Lawson, and he's nothing but muscle. Lawson says he can't keep him out of the gym. I think it's his way of dealing with the waiting."

"As long as it's a healthy outlet." He swivels in his chair.

I know he's referring to me. My drinking was out of control after the loss of my men. Now, I don't have anything but the occasional beer at Sean's Place. I sit on the edge of the table. "He's not drinking, sir, and neither am I."

"Good. How's your brother?"

"He's great."

"He still refusing to join us?" He laughs.

"Yeah, he had his fill with Fallon's mission. Besides, the bar is keeping him busy."

The door swings open wide, and the men start filing inside. Each one stops to address Commander Lukas. I take a seat at the opposite end of the table from the commander.

"I want to make introductions before we get started. This is Seaman Apprentice Sanchez. She'll be handling all paperwork and anything else that needs to go through me. Consider her my right-hand man...or woman."

Theo is already thumping his mechanical hand on the table. I clear my throat and aim my gaze at him. He stops and leans back in his chair.

"You've all met Lawson." I motion to Lawson who is sitting to my right. "He's in charge of your physical training. And don't think for one minute you can take him on and kick his ass. You can't." They all laugh.

"This is Petty Officer First Class, Theo Drake. He's the last of this namesake of our SEAL team, like myself. He was the lead sniper for the Gunners, and damn good at it."

Theo nods.

"Each of you should know Dr. Lauryn Ruth. She's our team psychiatrist. You wouldn't be here if you weren't cleared by her."

She smiles.

"We have three new recruits." I get up and walk behind the first one. "This is Seaman Thorn Beckham. He's been a Navy SEAL for five years. He'll be in the field, working undercover. You'll see his credentials listed in the file in front of each of you."

I move down one seat to the next recruit. "This is

Petty Officer Harley Tate. Her background is medical science and forensics. She served on a recovery SEAL team. She'll be handling findings in the field along with undercover work."

"And this man, you'll want to make your best friend. This is Chief Ronan Maddox, better known as Mad Dog. He'll be in charge of weaponry. If you need it, he's the man to get it for you."

I walk back over to my chair and push the remote control to the television to start our meeting. It's paired with my laptop so that I can give visuals. "If you'll open your files and flip to the third page, we can get started."

Chief Maddox's chair whooshes as its height is adjusted to his size. Files open and papers rustle as they turn through the pages.

"Our main focus is a new group that popped up on our radar. They're trafficking young women and children across this country."

"Are they related to geNetics?" Theo asks, and I already know where his head is going.

"We haven't been able to link them, but there are some similarities in the way they operate."

Theo starts to comment, but I hold up my hand to stop him. "Our other mission is a collaboration of men and women that have formed in Utah. They hate our government and want to overthrow it. Some of its members have proved to have violent tendencies, and we want to stop it before it gets out of hand. This will not be our typical undercover mission. We want them to know who we are and that we'll stop them in their tracks."

"I've set up a team from the Army out of one of our bases in Texas to invade their property with a member led by this team," Commander Lukas fills in the blanks.

"Why isn't our main focus geNetics?" Theo questions. His voice is full of agitation.

"When our intel proves solid, it will be. Until then, we'll go after the ones right in front of us. You'll be going undercover again." I click on a picture on the screen. "Comeback Productions is the name they're using. They lure young girls who've tried numerous times to get in the entertainment business, promising to make them famous. They have mock reviews set up on their websites. They get each applicant to give them all their personal information, and they weed through the ones they want. Eight young girls have now gone missing, and they've all been backtracked to this company." I show the picture of the faces of the girls ranging from twelve years old to twenty.

"Their building was raided and shut down, but their operations continue. No one that has been arrested has any information on who the head honcho is. They had no idea what was really going on." I change the picture on the screen. "We believe that this man is behind all of it." There is a blurry photo of a man parked behind their building on his cell phone. "One of the cameras on their building picked up part of his conversation arguing with whoever was trying to give him orders. I suspect he's talking to the mastermind. The only thing we know is that his last name is Starr and he's operating from Seattle..."

"Seattle? That's were the last lead on Fiona came from," Theo interjects. "Maybe that's the connection you're looking for."

"Don't jump the gun, but it's a possibility." I should've left out the part about Seattle. He's going to get his hopes up.

"I'm taking this mission." He stands and heads toward the door.

"Where are you going? We're not done here," I bark.

"If I know you, every detail I need is in this file. I'm wasting time sitting here."

"I want you to take Petty Officer Tate with you."

"I don't need her involved in this mission."

"Theo. Sit down. You'll either go on this mission as ordered, or you'll sit this one out." I point to his chair.

Buy Theo's Retaliation now.

ALSO BY KELLY MOORE

Next August

This August

Seeing Sam

The Hitman Series- Previously Taking Down
Brooklyn/The DC Seres

Stand By Me - On Audible as Deadly Cures

Stay With Me On Audible as Dangerous Captive

Hold Onto Me

Epic Love Stories Series can be read in any order

Say You Won't Let Go. Audiobook version

Fading Into Nothing Audiobook version

Life Goes On. Audiobook version

Gypsy Audiobook version

Jameson Wilde Audiobook version

Rescue Missions Series can be read in any order

Imperfect. On Audible

Blind Revenge

Fated Lives Series

Rebel's Retribution Books 1-4. Audible

Theo's Retaliation Books 5-7. Audible

Thorn's Redemption Audible

Fallon's Revenge Book 11 Audible

The Crazy Rich Davenports Season One in order of reading

The Davenports On Audible

Lucy

Yaya

Ford

Gemma

Daisy

The Wedding

Halloween Party

Bang Bang

Coffee Tea or Me

ABOUT THE AUTHOR

"This author has the magical ability to take an already strong and interesting plot and add so many unexpected twists and turns that it turns her books into a complete addiction for the reader." Dandelion Inspired Blog

Armed with books in the crook of my elbow, I can go anywhere. That's my philosophy! Better yet, I'll write the books that will take me on an adventure.

My heroes are a bit broken but will make you swoon. My heroines are their own kick-ass characters armed with humor and a plethora of sarcasm.

If I'm not tucked away in my writing den, with coffee firmly gripped in hand, you can find me with a book propped on my pillow, a pit bull lying across my legs, a Lab on the floor next to me, and two kittens running amuck.

My current adventure has me living in Idaho with my own gray-bearded hero, who's put up with my shenanigans for over thirty years, and he doesn't mind all my book boyfriends.

If you love romance, suspense, military men, lots of action and adventure infused with emotion, tear-worthy moments, and laugh-out-loud humor, dive into my books and let the world fall away at your feet.

434488

Made in United States
Orlando, FL
13 April 2023

32038918R00241